RETURN OF THE EAGLES

RETURN OF THE EAGLES

James Follett

Severn House Large Print
London & New York

This first large print edition published in Great Britain 2005 by
SEVERN HOUSE LARGE PRINT BOOKS LTD of
9-15 High Street, Sutton, Surrey, SM1 1DF.
First world regular print edition published 2004 by
Severn House Publishers, London and New York.
This first large print edition published in the USA 2005 by
SEVERN HOUSE PUBLISHERS INC., of
595 Madison Avenue, New York, NY 10022.

British Library Cataloguing in Publication Data

Follett, James, 1939 -
Return of the eagles - Large print ed.
1. World War, 1939 – 1945 - Prisoners and prisons, British - Fiction
2. Prisoners-of-war escapes - Great Britain - Fiction
3. Germany - Armed forces - Officers - Fiction
4. War stories
5. Large type books
I. Title
823.9'14 [F]

ISBN-10: 0-7278-7467-5

Except where actual historical events and characters are being described for the storyline of this novel, all situations in this publication are fictitious and any resemblance to living persons is purely coincidental.

Printed and bound in Great Britain by
MPG Books Ltd, Bodmin, Cornwall.

In fond memory of
Sir Harold Ridley, MD, FRCS (1906–2001),
whose pioneering work in artificial lens implants
has given sight to millions

'If the Americans ask me and my colleagues for the moon, we will be the ones to give it to them.'

General Walter Dornberger,
Head of the German Wehrmacht's
V2 rocket development programme

1

There was no charge, no trial, no conviction, but there was an execution. A brutal and bloody execution.

From his hiding place in the bombed and abandoned farm cottage, Dr Eric Hoffmann peered fearfully through a shell hole and watched the two Waffen-SS officers order the young soldier to kneel. The sound of shouting carried across the bomb-cratered field. The kneeling soldier was waving his arms in terror, pleading and, to Eric's horror, pointing in his direction at the shattered farm-house. The taller of the two SS men shouted something about deserter scum. He pulled his Mauser from its holster and, without a moment's hesitation, shot the officer in the head.

Despite having had little to eat for two days, Eric was physically sick. It was if the departing soul of the murdered man had wrenched everything from him, turning him inside-out. His mind reeled with the enormity of what had happened. A living person, who had been brought into the world, fed, clothed, cherished and cared for, packed off to school, and doubtless the centre of the world for many people and maybe now with a wife and children awaiting the return of a beloved husband and father from this terrible war, brutally snuffed out by the casual pulling of a trigger.

The SS officers' driver ran halfway across the field from the entrance from where he had parked a quarter-track reconnaissance car. He was yelling frantically and pointing to the west. The two officers abandoned their search of the murdered man's pockets and raced to their vehicle. All three piled in and the vehicle took off, heading east, accelerating hard, its tracks grating harshly on asphalt. A few minutes later the heavy roar of powerful engines heralded the arrival of three tanks. Eric's heart sank when he saw them. Before his carefully planned flight, he had acquired an army identification book of Allied fighting vehicles and spent what little spare time he had had learning to recognize silhouettes. These were either British Army Cromwell heavy tanks or the later Comet derivative.

'Whatever you do, don't give yourself up to the Tommies – they'll hang you,' his chief had advised his department heads at a meeting to discuss their flight west to escape the advancing Soviet army. 'You must find the Americans.'

The unexpected appearance of the three British tanks, advancing line abreast to avoid presenting a target in a column that could be picked off, meant that Eric had miscalculated and gone too far west. He hadn't heard heavy gunfire recently so he assumed that the armoured unit was a probe – an incursion to test German defences along this section of the front before the final great push to the Rhine and Germany's inevitable defeat. Eric's guess was that Field Marshal Model had decided to concentrate his Army 'B' group's armour further east along the eastern flank of the Wilder valley where his units would be difficult to dislodge. Eric had been obliged to take a long detour on his bicycle the previous day to avoid them.

The centre tank moved along the road with its companions churning the fields on either side to keep pace. A soldier on the tank that passed near Eric's hiding place accorded the murdered officer a passing glance. A dead German soldier lying in a field was an inconsequential brushstroke on the great canvas that was being painted across Europe.

2

At nightfall Eric ventured from his hiding place. He examined the corpse. The pale moonlight spared him the colours and details of the gaping exit hole in the man's skull. He rolled him on to his back and was surprised to see the gleam of a Feldgendarmerie gorget on the man's chest. The military-police metal plate was secured by a chain around the man's neck. Until an SS takeover, the Wehrmacht Feldgendarmerie had been responsible for guarding Eric's research establishment, so he knew something about them. The gorget's lettering was picked out in luminous paint, which meant that the dead man was an officer. He was about Eric's build and, as far as he could discern in the moonlight, the way that the man had fallen when he had been shot meant that he had bled into the ground – the uniform looked unmarked.

With the beginnings of an idea about concealing his real identity, Eric lifted the man on to his shoulders and staggered back to the derelict farmhouse. He kicked fallen debris clear in the centre of what had been the living room and set the body down on a table. With only the aid of meagre moonlight shining through the roofless building, Eric set to work to get the officer out of his uniform. It would be easier to wait until morning but there was the chance that rigor mortis would start to set in, making the job doubly difficult, and besides, the lack of light was a blessing as he carried out his macabre task. It took nearly an hour for Eric to swap clothes. The uniform and the helmet were a reasonable fit, the boots were a little loose, but better that than have them too tight if, as he supposed, he would have a long trek south before heading west to find the Americans. The bicycle he had bought from a chargehand had an annoying slow puncture and wouldn't last much longer.

His poor diet for the last week and his exertions conspired to tire him. He considered risking lighting his candle stub to examine the contents of the officer's wallet and pockets but decided that that unpleasant task could wait until morning. He found a ripped mattress, made himself as comfortable as he could, and told himself to wake up at first light. The moon swam into view through the gaping roof.

The moon!

Eric never tired of looking at it. It had dominated his dreams since he was boy. He fell into a restless sleep with its ethereal light illuminating his troubled face.

3

Hunger and bright sunlight woke Eric just after nine o'clock. Ignoring the dead man, he resumed his search of the ruined farmhouse for food – a search that had been interrupted the previous day by the two SS men. He dragged aside a fallen dresser in what had been the farmer's kitchen and discovered a full Kilner jar and a dust-coated ham. The preserved fruit was a mixture of pears and peaches in a sweet but welcome syrup. The ham was the remnants of a knuckle, but there was enough meat left on it to provide the best meal Eric had had for a week. Surprisingly, the kitchen tap, hanging out of the wall on its pipe, still worked, so he built a small fire and made chicory coffee. The ersatz drink gave him the fortitude to go through the dead man's possessions, such as they were, starting with his wallet.

He was Leutnant Dieter Muller. The same age as Eric – 38, born in the same month and even in the same city – Düsseldorf. Same colour eyes, too. Eric considered these matching characteristics with the man whose identity he was about steal were a good omen. There were no family photographs, and the only family documents were two gossipy letters from his sister, and an unmailed reply. Eric didn't open it but decided to post it at the first opportunity. Perhaps it was another good omen that like him, the murdered officer was unmarried.

The service warrant card bore a slightly yellowing photograph of a heavy-jowled young man whereas Eric's features were finer, more aristocratic. That could be a problem. He removed the card from its holder and studied it closely. The yellowing was uneven yet the embossed date stamp showed that the photograph was only six months old. It wasn't age that was causing the picture's deterioration; it hadn't been fixed and dried properly to neutralize the silver nitrate in the paper. Eric placed the photograph in full sunlight and set about preparations for continuing his quest for the American lines.

He found another intact Kilner jar containing preserved fruit and stuffed it in his bicycle's large saddle bag. Also amid the ruins was an empty Kilner jar, its sealing gasket and lid intact. Into this went all the accoutrements of his real identity: among the various documents was the works pass that listed all the areas he was entitled to enter. That alone was evidence of his qualifications as a senior research scientist and development engineer. The bulky envelope that he had crammed with his qualifications and references – all intended to impress the Americans – had to be rolled slightly to fit into the jar. One of the most important items was a diary in which he made detailed notes of important meetings, who was present, and decisions taken. Another was a typed copy of the minutes of a meeting in which the bullying thug SS-General Kammler had announced his obscene plans. When the end of the war seemed inevitable, his toadies had gone through the establishment, rounding up and burning such incriminating documents, but Eric had hidden his copy, pleading that it had been lost or misfiled when the bully boys demanded it.

Once every paper that identified Dr Eric Hoffmann was in its new home, he sealed the jar and hunted around in the wreckage of the upstairs bedroom for a sewing box. The tape measure was just what he needed.

He looked and listened carefully for some minutes before venturing out of the farmhouse. It was a beautiful spring morning, birds singing, and no sound of distant gunfire. He found a spade in an outhouse, measured exactly three metres diagonally from the corner of the farmhouse, and dug a metre-deep hole. It was a vegetable garden – the soil had been worked for generations and was light and friable. He set the jar containing his identity in the bottom of the hole, and contemplated it for a few moments. Its contents represented his whole life – the hours of study and driving enthusiasm that had left no time for girls or a social life; his examination results, accomplishments in his chosen field, references – all crammed into a glass jar. He started filling in the hole, wondering if he'd ever see the jar's contents again. He stood back, committing the farm's name and the location of the cache to memory.

As he expected, the hour's exposure to bright sunlight had caused the photograph of Dieter Muller to further darken so that finer details in his features had virtually disappeared. Some careful work with his razor before a broken mirror resulted in a passable match with the dead man's widow's peak. Brushing his hair straight back completed the simple disguise. Eric held up the photograph beside the mirror, comparing his face with the picture. It was far from perfect but was good enough to pass muster from a casual glance, and who looked like their identity card photograph anyway? The final gesture in assuming Dieter Muller's identity was to place his service ID tag around his neck and tuck it his shirt. The metal gorget plate hanging by its chain around his neck was an irritation but he would get used to it. One advantage of the uniform was that he now had plenty of pockets for his belongings, which was just as well because the saddlebag was nearly bursting.

An hour later, after pumping up the punctured tyre as hard as he dared, Eric set off across the field, wheeling his bicycle to the entrance at the far end, where the reason for the officer's presence in the field became apparent. A military police motorcycle and sidecar was stuck deep in a water-filled crater. No doubt Dieter Muller had thought it was merely a puddle caused by cattle. After the mishap, perhaps he had been heading for the farmhouse in the hope of finding a rafter to lever the machine out of the hole when the two SS men had accosted him. The presence of the machine was a nuisance because its discovery might result in a search that would lead to the dead officer being found in the farmhouse.

It was too late to worry about that now. Once on the road, Eric mounted the bicycle and pedalled east, the Feldgendarmerie gorget swinging and tinkling annoyingly against his tunic buttons. His plan was to skirt behind General Model's forces and then head south for about thirty kilometres before once again turning west in the hope of meeting up with the advancing Americans. The day passed without incident other than when he chanced on a small group of armoured cars pulled up in a clump of conifers, their drivers and crews brewing coffee and smoking. It was too late to avoid them, so he kept pedalling, his jaw set determinedly as though on an official mission with no time to stop and chat. War-weary soldiers eyed him with suspicion and seemed pleased that he ignored them. The Feldgendarmerie were disliked because they had more powers than the military police of most countries and had a reputation for officiousness.

'Hey, dog chain!' an NCO yelled – a disparaging reference to Eric's Feldgendarmerie gorget. 'We've got mud on our lights. How about a ticket?'

There was laughter. Eric continued to ignore them and kept pedalling. The rest of the day was uneventful. His new identity was proving a blessing; hitherto, once he had left the outskirts of his home town of Berlin and was in the countryside, he had holed up during the day, and only moved at night, sometimes taking to open fields and carrying his stolen bicycle in the vicinity of military activity. Now he could move freely and openly along roads in the daytime. No one saw fit to stop a Feldgendarmerie officer seemingly intent on his business. He prayed that he would never have to use Dieter Muller's sidearm – a Luger.

4

That night Eric found another half-destroyed farmhouse which had enough of its roof left to afford some protection from the rain. He wondered why so many scattered farmhouses had been destroyed by air attacks. Perhaps it was to prevent them serving as sniper outposts or machine-gun nests. It couldn't be to terrorize the population because most of the farms, their livestock, and villages in the area had been evacuated. It was a land bracing itself for the inevitable.

He was woken shortly before dawn by the sound of distant gunfire. The rain had stopped, so he went outside and used his pocket compass to fix the direction of the artillery fire. It was coming from the south-west. The rolling reports had that dull, echoing note that suggested they were a long way off. Perhaps as far as a hundred kilo-metres.

He resumed his journey at first light on what was to prove an uneventful day. At a village post office he posted Dieter Muller's letter to his sister and managed to buy a week-old loaf and a large jar of fish paste.

'I'd been saving it,' said the elderly shopkeeper. 'But you might as well have it. We're all being evacuated tomorrow and I've been called up to join the Volkssturm.'

Eric left the store and saw that his bicycle's front tyre was nearly flat again. The slow puncture was getting worse; he had to stop to re-inflate it every hour. He considered dumping the machine but, even with the puncture, it enabled him to make better progress than on foot.

The Feldgendarmerie gorget swinging back and forth on his chest got on his nerves. He stopped and reversed the chain so that the heavy metal plate hung down his back, under his jacket, as he had seen the Feldgendarmerie do at the research establishment when tinkering with their motorbikes.

The tyre finally announced its expiry at midday the following day with a loud report that made him jump, nearly causing him to fall off. If that wasn't unnerving enough, there was a sudden burst of wholly unexpected hearty laughter from a mechanized unit that was so well concealed under camouflage netting that he hadn't seen it.

'You'll need a mate if you're on your way to arrest General Patton and his Third Army,' said an infantry sergeant.

The infantrymen roared. The appearance of a military policeman armed with a Luger and a bicycle was a much-needed tonic. Mention of the US army alerted Eric. He wheeled his machine to where the crews of the two tanks and a self-propelled gun were playing cards using ammunition cases as tables and stools. There was a strong smell of frying sausages that made Eric's mouth water. 'Are the Americans near?' he asked, grinning around at the soldiers.

'Not yet. But I'm sure they soon will be,' said the sergeant affably. 'You're probably better equipped to deal with them than us, leutnant. You don't need fuel. Sergeant Paul Springer. Fifth Panzer. We're waiting to be re-supplied.'

'I don't think this bicycle's much use now,' said Eric ruefully, introducing himself and shaking hands. 'I don't have a puncture-repair kit.'

'I reckon we can deal with that.' The sergeant took the bicycle and shouted orders. The infantrymen seem glad of something to do. Toolboxes appeared and they set to work.

'This is very kind of you,' said Eric, sitting on an offered box and declining a cigarette. 'Any idea how far the Americans are?' He made it sound like a casual enquiry. The smell of frying was overpowering.

The NCO shrugged and nodded to the west. 'No one tells us anything. Probably because no one knows anything. At a guess, I'd say their front line is about fifty kilometres. They seemed to have stopped. Being re-supplied, I suppose.' He added bitterly. 'And probably having better luck than us.'

They were interrupted by the shattering roar of a lone jet fighter flying low, heading west. All the infantrymen stopped to watch

Willy Messerschmitt's much-vaunted Me 262 twin-engine fighter dwindling into the distance with astonishing speed.

'Fucking marvellous,' said the sergeant morosely. 'We spend millions of marks building a few of them fancy things while we're sitting here twiddling our thumbs because we haven't got enough bloody tankers. Maybe a couple thousand jets might've made a difference, but a few hundred cheap supply trucks at a thousandth of the cost would've made a hell of a difference. We could be meeting the Allies head on instead of waiting for them to make their move.'

'The Rhine's being heavily fortified,' said Eric. 'And they'd never take the bridges.'

The comment amused Sergeant Springer. 'I reckon that's a ruse. The Allies have left them alone, thinking that we'd waste our armour defending them. Do you think an army that can ship millions of tonnes of kit across the English Channel at its widest point is going to need bridges to cross a river? Nobody seems to have thought of that, just as they didn't think that keeping an army supplied is more important than wasting money on a few bloody prop-less jet planes.'

Eric could not think of an appropriate rely. The innovative versus the conventional was an argument that had dominated many stormy meetings he had attended.

'It was the same at Christmas in the Ardennes,' said Sergeant Springer, getting into his stride. 'We broke out and pushed the

Allies back. Remember how the wireless and papers were trumpeting about how we were going to retake Antwerp and drive the Allies into the sea? Maybe we would've done it, too. Christ – old Runny Rundstedt had over twenty divisions. But there we were, out of fuel, no re-supplies, a few of those stupid jets prancing around doing fuck all while hundreds of bloody Mustangs were swarming all over us once the weather cleared.'

Eric glanced at the soldiers gathered around, listening, and realized how exhausted and emotionally drained they all looked.

'They'll roll over us easily enough,' Sergeant Springer continued bitterly. 'Maybe that will make them over-confident for when they meet the SS units. The SS don't go without.' He broke off, sensing that he had said too much.

An infantryman announced that the repairs to the bicycle were finished but they wanted the inner tube's patch to cure in the sun for an hour first. Eric accepted Sergeant Springer's invitation to share their lunch after his reservations about their food stocks were brushed aside. 'We've got to eat up all these sausages today. They won't keep much longer,' the NCO assured him.

Two hours later, satisfyingly full of beans and sausages, Eric bid a grateful farewell to his benefactors and continued his journey.

He passed several more armoured units during the rest of that day and the following day, all dug in and camouflaged as best they could, but stranded, unable to re-group owing to lack of fuel. They would be easy meat for General Patton once he began his thrust on the Rhine. Eric felt guilty about their plight as he recalled the times he had argued passionately for the funding for research on a project that he now realized had been a complete waste of time and resources.

A Mustang roared overhead from the west. They had never shown any interest in Eric, so he no longer hid from them, guessing correctly that they were on photo-reconnaissance sorties. That he had not seen any RAF aircraft for several days convinced him that he had travelled far enough south to be abreast of the American lines. He consulted his cycling club touring map and worked out a route that would take him west.

Three hours later, dazzled by the setting sun, the doubts returned to torment him.

'Whatever you do, don't give yourself up to the Tommies – they'll hang you. You must find the Americans.'

The road was a minor route across a broad plain of beet fields, little more than a lane. Its surface was reasonable provided he kept a sharp lookout for potholes. It was long and straight, arrowing west. The front tyre remained hard thanks to the infantrymen's repair. He was making such rapid progress that his nerve continued to fail him and he found himself unconsciously slowing his pace. There was no sign of ruts or plough marks across the fields. It was hard to believe that this land was locked in a deadly battle.

The only consolation was that if he did fall into British hands, they wouldn't expect him to give any information other than his name, rank, and service number. He had already taken care to memorize his number because it was the one thing every serviceman knew by heart. His grandfather had known his service number even after forty years from when he had served with a German colonial regiment in east Africa. He had told his wide-eyed grandson about terrible atrocities perpetrated by the British against the Boers. The memory of those stories further weakened Eric's belief that all he had to do was stick to name, rank and number. If the British suspected anything, if records fell into their hands, as seemed inevitable, and they discovered the truth about his identity, then it would be a brief trial, a priest, and a hangman's noose.

'Halt!'

Eric had been so wrapped up in his thoughts while concentrating on the road to avoid tyre-punishing potholes, that he didn't see the quarter-track reconnaissance vehicle until he was almost upon it. It was parked across the road. An 11-tonne Daimler-Benz type KM – a large, lightly armoured general-purpose vehicle. Eric was familiar with the model because he designed some specialized towing gear for them the previous year. This one sported a business-like quadruple-barrelled 20mm anti-aircraft gun mounted on its rear platform. It bore Waffen-SS unit markings.

The captain in charge of the four-man crew strode towards Eric, unbuckling the flap on his holster. His face black with anger. 'What are you doing here?' he demanded, his glare raking Eric.

'Obeying orders. Checking on outlying farms,' Eric replied promptly. His apparent boldness and determination was lost on the SS officer.

'Liar! No farmers have returned! You're deserting! Going to give yourself up to the enemy!' The SS officer levelled his Luger at Eric. He was almost shaking with fanatical rage, his finger white and trembling on the trigger. 'Traitorous filth!'

The SS officer, the two soldiers manning the anti-aircraft gun and the driver were staring at Eric and didn't see the black dot, low in the sky, that was swelling rapidly from the west. The pilot of the approaching Mustang saw the quarter-track Daimler-Benz and banked towards it.

The purpose of the Allied hit-and-run 'rhubarbs' using hedge-hopping lone fighters was crude, simple and effective. They were to destroy any hardware that was likely to be unenthusiastic about extending a warm welcome to the advancing Allied forces. Quarter-tracks toting multi-barrelled anti-aircraft guns fell into that category.

The startled SS captain wheeled around. His two strides towards his vehicle took him into the path of the Mustang's blazing cannons as their rounds stitched dirt and clods across the field and raked the quarter-track, killing the two men on the gun instantly. The Mustang's pilot was experienced, his shooting deadly. The fighter climbed and turned. Screams of agony prompted Eric to yank the driver's door. He was about to drag the man out of the vehicle when it was suddenly engulfed in a fireball. Even the camouflage paint burst into flames. Eric was driven back by the heat. He saw the Mustang coming in for another attack, flaps down to kill its speed, and ran, his only thought to put distance between himself and the stricken vehicle, but the fighter held its fire and roared east in search of more targets.

Eric stood transfixed, staring at the blazing pyre – the four barrels of the anti-aircraft gun pointing out of the flames in impotent defiance at the sky. The crack of exploding 20mm ammunition reminded Eric of the danger he was in. Also the column of black smoke was certain to attract unwelcome attention from his own forces. He grabbed his bicycle and pedalled furiously, pausing only for a few seconds at the top of a rise to glance back at the pall of black smoke. He resumed hard cycling and kept up the pace for half an hour, sweat streaming into eyes, until the smoke was a distant smear across the sky. He rested for a few minutes, drinking from his water bottle, reflecting that the SS unit had been crazy to stop in the middle of a field without cover.

By late afternoon he started to keep his eyes open for a possible night shelter. The open nature of the countryside depressed him. The few buildings that might offer shelter for the night looked too conspicuous, too undamaged, too vulnerable, so he pressed on for longer than usual until nightfall when the land became more wooded, and exhaustion eventually forced him to seek the best shelter he could find: a corner of a field with high hedges where rhododendrons had taken over.

He fell into a fitful sleep in which he dreamed that he was hooded and handcuffed, being led along an echoing corridor with a priest following, intoning the last rites. He kept waking to experience little waves of elation at the realization that it was only a dream, but the return of sleep merely took him a few steps further along the same corridor.

5

The orderly, solemn ritual of a hanging dissolved into chaos; there was bedlam at the end of the prison corridor. The roar of powerful diesel engines drowned out the droning of the priest. Eric tried to struggle up but was too paralysed with cold to move. All he could manage was to force his hand up to tear at the hangman's hood. It was a spare pullover that he had wrapped around his head to help keep him warm although his neck now felt as if mischievous creatures of the night had removed his head and put it back in the wrong position before encasing his neck in concrete. Not three metres from where he had burrowed into the hedge men were shouting orders, laughing.

'For Chrissake, you dumb lugs! Go easy with that goddamn winch!'

Eric's English was good enough to recognize American accents but he had to be one hundred per cent certain.

The screech and clatter of heavy machines being moved. Not only were his vertebrae locked but every joint had been welded into immovability by the cold, yet Eric's heart was free to pound in unison with the throbbing diesels as he forced himself to sit up, blinking and befuddled by the bright sunrise.

Boots. Heavy chains being dragged. Yelled curses. More engines starting up. The uproar and the fumes were appalling. He rolled on to his chest and used his elbows to thrust himself further into the hedge but all he could see through the tangled undergrowth, thick at the base, were boots, and huge caterpillar tracks.

A few metres to his left the hedge was thinner. He stumbled towards the narrow gap, clutching his Allied fighting vehicle recognition booklet and peered cautiously through. There was no mistaking the American-built Sexton self-propelled gun that completely filled his limited field of view. It resembled a tank but the turret, with its snub barrel gun, was set further forward than a tank's turret. He risked pushing his head further forward. The slight bend in the road enabled him to see a line of them, at least ten, all mounted on huge Pioneer articulated tank transporters. And there were soldiers milling everywhere.

US soldiers!

The racket was due to the Sextons being winched down the transporters' ramps and their noisy air-cooled radial engines starting up. Some were already grinding their way to the head of the convoy, the harsh grating of their tracks adding to the uproar.

His stiffness forgotten, Eric fumbled to pull a few belongings from the bicycle's saddlebag, and set off on foot towards the entrance that was at the far end of the pasture. The previous night he had camped as far from the entrance as possible. He kept close to the hedge, his ears straining to catch the occasional smatter of dialogue above the infernal racket of the massed diesels. He passed the end of the convoy when he was within fifty metres of the entrance. The gate was difficult to open because he had lifted it on its worn hinges the previous night to ensure that it was securely closed. Before setting foot on the road, he pulled a white handkerchief from his pocket and clutched it tightly, ready to wave it at the Americans. He gulped several deep breaths in the hope of stilling his racing heart, and took a pace into the road.

He was so shocked by the sight of the soldiers in khaki battledress and brimmed helmets that he forgot to raise his handkerchief. He stood rooted in horror.

Tommies!

Captain William Fry of the 2nd Battleon Royal Engineers saw Eric first. He was standing on top of the last Sexton in the convoy, supervising the unloading of one of the ten replacement self-propelled guns which the Americans were supplying to the 90th Field Regiment of the Royal Artillery.

Eric saw the British officer produce his sidearm. He had been so excited by the discovery of what he thought was a US armoured column that he had forgotten to unbuckle his Feldgendarmerie-issue Luger and holster. He was about to wave the handkerchief, saw the British officer take aim and realized that he was still armed. In his confusion he didn't think to merely hold his hands up high, but dropped them to the gun belt's buckle with the intention of unfastening it.

Captain Fry thought the German soldier was going to take a shot at him and got one off first.

The round ricocheting off the road within a metre of Eric panicked him. Convinced that the British officer was going to shoot again, he ran into the field and raced down the slope with the vague notion of getting out of small-arms range and then waving the handkerchief. Or maybe the British wouldn't consider a lone soldier was worth chasing after and he could return to collect his bicycle when they were gone.

'Corporal Wilkins!' Captain Fry barked, pointing. 'Get up here and stop that Jerry!'

The NCO had won awards at Bisley for his shooting. He climbed nimbly up beside Captain Fry, his jaws working rhythmically on some chewing gum he had scrounged from the Americans, and brought his rifle up. He hardly seemed to take aim at the running figure. He fired his Lee Enfield once.

The bullet hit Eric in the back, immediately over the heart. He pitched forward, struck his head on a rusting tractor wheel and lay still.

'Nice shooting, Wilkins,' Captain Fry

complimented. 'You better take some medics and a stretcher party and bring him back. Find out if his unit is in the vicinity.'

'No point, sir,' said the corporal laconically. 'He's dead meat. I got him smack in the heart.'

'I asked you to stop him.'

'And that's what I've done, sir.'

The officer raised his field glasses and stared at the still form in the middle of the field. 'Was it necessary to kill him?'

'Seems like a good way of winning wars, sir.'

Captain Fry had no ready answer to that. He nodded. 'Very well, Wilkins. You'd better go and collect his ID disc.'

The corporal saluted and acknowledged. He jumped to the ground and set off across the field. At no time during the incident had his jaws stopped chomping on the wad of chewing gum.

6

Britain was the host nation, therefore it fell to Lieutenant-Commander Ian Lancaster Fleming, RNVR, looking resplendent in a new uniform made for the occasion, to rise and formally greet the Allied naval intelligence delegates seated around the conference table. He had to raise his voice to be heard above the thunderous rain beating down on the hotel ballroom's roof. It was real rain – Kingston, Jamaica non-negotiable rain that meant business. The large bucket of water catching drips that a waiter had to replace at intervals was in keeping with the faded, threadbare splendours of the Myrtle Bank Hotel's colonial past.

'Good morning, gentlemen,' said Fleming. 'Welcome to Jamaica, and you're all more than welcome to the Myrtle Bank Hotel.' All thirty-three delegates laughed. They warmed to the suave, debonair British naval officer immediately.

'Like most of you,' Fleming continued, 'this is my first visit to Jamaica and my first thought on entering this hotel, the best hotel in Kingston I've been assured, is that the place smells of mushrooms. This is due, apparently, to ... mushrooms. I've already found some in the corner of my room. But rest assured – according to the chef, they're edible.'

More laughter.

'But I must sound a warning note. The chef has a strong German accent, so it might be prudent to treat his opinion with caution.'

Fleming's easy-going bonhomie and his acerbic sense of humour struck a chord with the delegates. They were seated at a circular table that consisted of a ring of velveteen-covered dining-room tables. Americans, Canadians, French, Australians – all the Allied powers were represented. The six American intelligence experts were the largest group.

'I'm a stranger here,' said Fleming, 'only just arrived, but my London colleague, Johnny Benyon,' he indicated the solemn-looking man on his right, 'is married to a lady who has a house here and he knows Jamaica well. He says that there's a saying on the island that when it's raining, the sun is never far away. The cryptanalysis experts among you will, no doubt, be able to decode that as also meaning, when it's sunny, the rain is never far away.'

The laughter was infectious. Even the two stone-faced English-speaking Soviet naval intelligence officers managed a faint smile.

'Johnny also insists that it's not true that there's nothing to do in Kingston. There are three things one can do and do well: one can get wet, one can get muddy, and the third is one can get blind drunk on rum.'

Johnny Benyon laughed loudest at that.

'He also assures me Jamaica has two seasons: the wet season, and the fucking wet season. This season, he assures me, is the former. Luckily his intelligence on U-boat matters is more reliable. He says the rain will clear by this evening. We're here for three days – plenty of time to devise adequate punishment if he's wrong.

'First things first, gentlemen. We need to appoint a chairman to keep us in order if we're to get through this agenda in three days. I'm happy to serve as acting chairman until you've decided.'

'Aw, hell, Ian,' said Lieutenant Mike Roscoe from the US Navy's Torpedo Research station. 'I say we all vote for you and be done with it.'

Fleming grinned at his old acquaintance. He always admired the Americans for their no-nonsense cut-to-the-chase let's-get-on-with-it approach. It got things done. The show of hands for Fleming was unanimous so he got straight down to business by telling the Royal Marines sergeant-at-arms that the conference was underway and that the hotel and its dank, dripping gardens were to be secured. Packs of photographed and numbered documents were passed around.

'First item in the British papers deals with the supposed threat from German one-man U-boats,' said Fleming. 'The so-called human torpedoes. They were used in significant numbers during the D-Day landings and proved ineffectual. Document 3 shows a type Biber U-boat that failed to release its torpedo.'

One of the photographs showed what looked like two torpedoes, one on top of the other. The upper hull had a small blister-type canopy over a tiny cockpit – it could hardly be called the bridge.

'The canopy was shattered by small-arms fire,' Fleming continued. 'The craft flooded and sank immediately. It was recovered and sent to the Royal Navy dockyard at Portsmouth for appraisal. As you can see, their conclusions are that the craft, although well-designed, has suffered from shoddy, hurried workmanship and short cuts. His Majesty's Government is of the opinion that no resources should be diverted to finding and attacking manufacturing facilities, and that the Bibers should be dealt with as and when the need to deal with them arises.'

'That's pretty well our conclusions, too, Mr Chairman,' Mike Roscoe commented. 'They're not a serious threat. If anything, they're a greater danger to their one-man crews than they are to us.'

The Soviet senior delegate was not happy. 'Our forces are having to cross more rivers, and estuaries and canals than any other force. These Bibers are very small and can operate in shallow water, docks and canals where attacks are not expected.'

'Then tell your guys to expect them,' a Canadian officer commented unsympathetically. 'The canopy is made of some sort of brittle plastic. It shatters easily into nasty splinters.' He added sarcastically, 'A cross-eyed Boy Scout with a .22 can knock out a Biber.'

'They're only vulnerable if the canopy is above the surface,' the Russian said frostily. 'These are miniature submarines and like all submarines, miniature or otherwise, you will doubtless be astonished to learn that they can submerge.'

Fleming was more diplomatic and intervened quickly. 'You're quite right to be worried,' he said to the Russian. 'It doesn't matter what a torpedo is launched from – it's still a torpedo therefore your concern, which I'm sure we all share –' he shot a warning glance at the Canadian – 'is understandable. The problem is that bombing the production facilities at this late stage in the war, assuming they could be found, is unlikely to make that much difference to the supply because Germans probably have considerable stocks awaiting despatch or in transit. The Bibers are very small. Unlike U-boats, they can be built in ordinary, hard-to-find workshops. Perhaps it would be best if we all handed over what information we have on the Bibers to our Soviet comrades so that they can use their remarkable ingenuity to devise countermeasures which they will, hopefully, pass to other forces.'

'Soldiers who can shoot straight are the best countermeasure,' the Canadian officer couldn't resist slipping in, more taken back by the Russian's perfect English than his attack.

The Soviet delegation knew that Fleming's proposal was the best deal they were likely to get and voted with the majority to ignore the Bibers unless the situation changed.

The note Johnny Benyon passed to Fleming complimented him on his batting.

The next item on the agenda was the very real menace of the Kriegsmarine's new Type XXI U-boat, and this the Americans were very interested in, and with good reason. Fleming provided a briefing with the aid of large drawings on an easel. It was hardly necessary – most of the delegates knew all about the Type XXI U-boat menace but the representatives of recently liberated Belgium, Holland and France needed to catch up.

'The standard 750-tonne Type XIIC U-boat is really a fast surface attack craft with the ability to dive,' Fleming began. 'It spends most of its time on the surface. We know from *U-570* and other captured boats that its best top speed submerged is around five knots – a speed that can flatten its batteries in under a couple of hours. Whereas its surfaced speed using its diesels is around seventeen knots. The most devastating U-boat attacks have always been massed surface attacks – wolf packs – at night on convoys. Under such circumstances sonar and other means of detecting submerged U-boats are futile.

'We first received intelligence in 1942 that the Germans had built an experimental 2000-tonne U-boat – three times the size of their operational boats.'

Fleming turned a sheet over on the easel to show an outline drawing of a long, sleek-looking submarine. 'Length: approximately three hundred feet.' Fleming paused. He was a good speaker and had his audience's full attention. He tapped the drawing with his pointer. 'This, gentleman, is a damned big boat. And it's not some freakish one-off monster such as the British were fond of building with their M-class and X-class submarines, or the French favoured with their huge *Surcouf*,' he nodded to the French representative. 'These are operational boats being built in great numbers as a replacement for the Type VIIC workhorse. Our intelligence failure is that we discounted these boats at first because we couldn't see how they could be mass-produced. Not only are the Germans' main construction yards being frequently bombed, but the Germans have no construction sheds and launch facilities long enough for the Type XXI. Then, our photo-reconnaissance interpreters noticed these odd things that kept cropping up all over Germany. In freight yards, on railway wagons, road transporters and barges.'

Fleming's next picture was a huge enlargement of a photograph that showed three egg-shaped structures standing upright on a barge. 'These are cross-sections of the Type XXI's hull, gentlemen. Albert Speer has done exactly what we British did with aircraft production. The boats are being made in pre-fabricated sections and he's dispersed their manufacture in factories across Germany, making it impossible to disrupt production by bombing. The sections are sent to Krupp and other yards at German ports, where they can be bolted together and fitted out in a matter of days instead of weeks or months. And we have plenty more pictures as you will find in your packs.'

The delegates stared in silence at the grainy enlargements as Fleming turned the sheets. One picture showed a man standing inside one of the oval structures. He was standing on the lowest of three decks – staring in alarm at the aircraft that must have been diving towards him.

'This picture gives you an idea of the Type XXI's considerable cross-sectional size,' Fleming observed. 'It's huge. If that lower deck is stuffed full of batteries, then it's possible that the boat will have enough battery capacity to remain submerged for days at a time with a submerged cruising speed of seventeen to twenty knots – possibly much higher.'

'Mr Chairman,' the Soviet spokesman interrupted. 'Surely this boat has come too late to have any effect on your operations in the west? So why has the rest of this morning been allocated to it?'

Mike Roscoe caught Fleming's eye.

'I'll let our American colleagues complete the picture,' Fleming concluded, and returned to his seat.

'The Type XXI has no deck casing, and no deck gun. She's smooth,' Roscoe began. 'That means she's designed solely for submerged operations. So it could be that she's a whole lot faster submerged than the British estimate. If you look at plate 3 in our section, you have a picture taken of a half-constructed Type XXI at Bremen on the River Weser. Plate 4 was taken two weeks later and the Type XXI has gone, and another one is having its sections set up. Plate 5 is a wide shot of the entire yard with Type XXI sections ringed and looking intact despite bombing. There's enough there for three more boats which I daresay have been completed and launched by now. There could be five of these new boats at sea and unaccounted for while we're yakking. Our intelligence sources are that one of the new boats was loaded with construction drawings and key personnel a month ago. Now who the hell is likely to be the beneficiary of such information? There's only one country. Japan. The Japanese are brilliant production engineers and their industrial base has been hardly scratched despite Mitchell's raids. If they can get these goddamn bolt-together Type XXIs into production, and fast, and there's no reason why they couldn't – hell, we've been bombing the shit out of the German yards and we haven't stopped them – then the Japanese will have the means of resupplying their remaining key bases in the Pacific. They could build Type XXIs without the six bow torpedo tubes. Stripped to the bone as cargo boats, they're capable of carrying a thousand tons or more per trip. We could be fighting this fucking war for years. Thank you, Mr Chairman.'

The unexpected use of an expletive by the soft-spoken Roscoe and the blunt nature of his speech brought home to all the delegates the depth of America's concern.

'The picture is even bleaker than that,' said Fleming slowly. He returned to the easel and exposed a vague oblique shot of a Type XXI under construction. The paraphernalia of cranes, derricks and buildings made the lines of the craft difficult to pick out, so a photo-analyst had highlighted them.

'This is the best picture from a set of covers we obtained only last week, and I only received them just before I left London. The RAF flew a particularly dangerous photo-reconnaissance mission to obtain them. That Type XXI U-boat is nearing completion. Look very closely and you'll notice what appears to be a strange-looking cylindrical container on the boat's hull forward of the conning tower.' Fleming traced the vague outline of the container with his pointer. 'Plate 23 in our information papers.'

There was a shuffling of papers as delegates found the print and pored over it, some using magnifying glasses.

'The dimensions of the container are given on the interpretation document. Anyone like to hazard a guess as to its purpose?'

'It appears to be flared at one end,' ventured the Soviet.

'Well-spotted,' Fleming complimented. 'The flaring is to accommodate stabilizer fins. That container, gentlemen, matches the dimensions of a V2 rocket perfectly. Look very closely and you'll see what can only be hydraulic rams for elevating the rocket to the firing position once the container has been opened.' Fleming paused. 'The boat has now gone. A test firing mission perhaps. We don't know. What we do know is that the consequences of V2s with chemical or gas warheads falling on New York, California, Sydney, Cape Town, would be catastrophic.'

This was shattering news to all the delegates. A sea of shocked faces confronted Fleming.

'As far as we're concerned,' said Fleming grimly, 'this is irrefutable proof that the Germans are planning the deliberate annihilation of densely populated civilian areas. And when we catch those responsible for devising such a hideous concept, we'll hang them.'

7

Fleming set down his coffee, lit his thirtieth cigarette of the day, and stared longingly across the lush jungle that tumbled down to a brilliant white sandy cove. It was evening at the end of the conference's first day. As Johnny Benyon had predicted, the skies had cleared and the low sun was shining out of a clear sky. The jungle and coffee plantations shone with a green so brilliant that it almost hurt the eyes.

Fleming, Benyon, and his leggy 45-year-old blonde wife, June, were sitting on the veranda of Bellevue – June's magnificent, if a little faded eighteenth-century colonial mansion. As June explained, it had been somewhat neglected during the war years. June was a wealthy Bostonian widow whom Benyon had met two years previously during a posting to New York.

Dinner had been cleared away by the servants and the three were enjoying an animated chat when, in a vivid flurry of beach-towel colours, an adult macaw flapped down from a palm tree and perched on the veranda rail. It screeched macaw abuse at June and Benyon.

'Hallo, Percy,' said June, rubbing the bird's poll. She opened a tin and held out a brazil nut. The macaw inspected the offering with great caution before deciding that it was acceptable, whereupon it hooked its ridiculous beak around the nut and set it down on the table for an even closer inspection. It noticed Fleming and fixed him with a beady eye.

'Fuck off, you stupid cunt,' it said with great clarity.

'Percy!' June exclaimed, mortified with embarrassment, and tried to shoo the bird away.

'Your mother swam out to troopships,' Percy informed Fleming. It picked up the nut and returned to a nearby palm tree to collect a fearful scolding from his wife. Feathers drifted down. Benyon received similar treatment from June.

'Don't lie!' she raged. 'I've heard you teaching it. Ian – I really am most dreadfully sorry. It's all his fault, and he will be severely punished.'

Fleming laughingly assured her that he found the incident hilarious.

'Macaws became extinct in Jamaica,' said Benyon in answer to Fleming's enquiry. 'Those two are the offspring of a quite successful attempt to reintroduce them. They seem to like it here.'

'I can't say I blame them,' Fleming answered as the dispute between the two birds degenerated into a row of such scorching ferocity that it gave both parties grounds for divorce. 'This place is paradise.'

'Even though you've seen the rain?' asked June.

Fleming waved his hand at the magnificent vista. 'It's the rain that makes all this glorious jungle possible. This is a wonderful place. And this view is out of this world.'

'Hemingway thought so, too,' said June.

Fleming was astonished. 'Ernest Hemingway's been here?'

'About two years ago. His chunky great cabin cruiser came chugging around the headland. What was it called, Johnny?'

'The *Pilar*,' said Benyon. 'It was just after Pearl Harbor. He'd bought this ugly fishing smack, really hideous, mounted a machine-gun on the bow, and was going around the Caribbean hunting U-boats and marlin.'

Fleming couldn't help laughing incredulously. This was a piece of naval intelligence he was unaware of. 'You're kidding?'

'It's true,' June insisted. 'He dropped anchor in the cove, rowed ashore, and nearly drank the place dry in the two hours he was here. Look him up in the visitors' book. When I asked him to sign it, he said that the view was so stunning that he wanted to stay. But there were U-boats to be hunted, and an onshore wind was getting up.'

Fleming shook his head at the crazy story. 'I think Hemingway's taste matches mine,' he said at length. He stared across the limpid, reddening sea, trying to imagine Ernest

Hemingway swashbuckling around the Caribbean in a private gunboat. He greatly admired men of action. His voice became serious. 'This is where I would like to build a house and spend the rest of my life.'

June laughed. 'You say the funniest things, Ian – you, the London socialite with your love of creature comforts, living here?'

'It would be a very fine house,' said Fleming earnestly.

'And your fine Jermyn Street shirts would rot in the humidity,' said Benyon ruefully. 'Even the ones made from Caribbean cotton.'

'And what would you do when it's raining?' June asked.

'Write books.'

Benyon grinned. 'That will mean writing a lot of books, Ian.'

'I intend to. Even a children's book, as I once promised Beatrix Potter.'

'She died last year,' June commented.

'The year before,' Fleming corrected. 'She was a great writer.'

'Her stuff is all a bit simplistic,' said June dismissively.

'That's what made her a great writer,' Fleming replied; the ready humour crinkles around his eyes were gone. 'Much like Hemingway. If something is easy to read, it's hard to write; if something is hard to read, it's easy to write. I want everything I write to be easy to read. I shall want every word to count. If it's described as simplistic, then I shall consider that a compliment.'

Johnny and June were silent for a moment, both sensing that they were being allowed a brief insight into a side of Ian Fleming that he rarely showed.

'Forgive me for being blunt, Ian,' said June. 'But I think that suddenly deciding to live somewhere on an impulse, on the basis of misleading first impressions, is extremely foolhardy.'

'It's no impulse but something I've been thinking about for some time,' Fleming replied, the humour creases returning. 'Moreso now that this war seems to be on its last legs. Johnny, do you remember that operation in 1941 when we made initial plans to deal with the defence of Gibraltar in case the Germans decided to grab it with a seaborne operation launched through Spain or Portugal?'

'As I recall, you got all the foreign trips,' said Benyon without rancour. 'Typical,' he said to June. 'Any sniff of a bit of cloak and dagger work and he was off.'

Fleming's laugh was good-natured. 'We scrounged a Hudson and went for a flight from Gib along the Spanish coast, looking for likely landing spots that the Germans might use. Now and then there were lovely villas with gardens reaching down to the sea. I thought then how wonderful it must be to have a home in such a setting.'

'So buy a place in Spain or Portugal,' June suggested. 'It'll be easier to reach than here.'

Fleming shook his head. 'Too dry. No lush

jungle. That's what makes this place so magical.' He turned to June. 'How long are you here for, June?'

'About a month. I want to get the painters fixed up to do this place. Then I'll visit my son in New York – he's at Columbia – and then I'll rejoin Johnny in London.'

'Could you buy me a plot of land please, June? About fifteen acres, overlooking the sea, no road in the way, and with access down to the beach – preferably a little secluded cove. A fabulous view like this. Facing west or south-west. The conference is going to take up every minute. There won't be time to look around. And land prices might rocket when the war's over.'

June was about to treat the request as a joke but she saw that Fleming was serious. 'Well – yes – of course. I'd be pleased to, Ian. But how much are you prepared to spend?'

Fleming considered. 'I could go to two thousand pounds.'

'Two thousand pounds will buy you the best plot in Jamaica on the North Shore,' Benyon commented. 'Even more stunning than this.'

'Then that's what I'll want June to buy for me. I'll wire you the money as soon as you've found somewhere.'

'I'll be delighted to do it, Ian. But we'll have to arrange restricted power of attorney for me to act for you. We could fix that up in Kingston tomorrow during lunchtime.'

Fleming beamed happily. 'You married an

angel, Johnny.'

The phone rang in the house and the angel went to deal with the call in response to the housekeeper's request, leaving the two men to chat. Their conversation ended a few minutes later with the onset of a minor uproar in the house as June's voice could be heard chivvying and haranguing servants. She reappeared on the veranda looking flustered.

'You'll never guess who that was,' she said.

'If we'll never guess, there's no point in your keeping us in the dark, old girl,' Benyon reasoned.

'Your boss.'

Benyon was puzzled. 'Which one of us do you mean?'

'Both of you,' said June patiently. 'Listen carefully. Repeat my words to yourself. Move your lips at the same time if it helps. The man on the phone was your boss.'

Now Benyon was really baffled. 'You mean Admiral Godfrey?'

'My God – he's finally got there. Yes – Admiral Godfrey!'

Both men looked astonished. Fleming was the first to speak. 'Admiral Godfrey checking up on us! Via a radio-telephone link? He'd never do such a crazy thing.'

'He's not in London,' said June. 'He's here. In Jamaica. That was him at the airport. He arrived on the Miami evening flight.'

They all started talking at once.

'Of course I'm sure!' June insisted. 'He said he wants to see Ian.'

'Christ – it's got to be something serious,' said Benyon. 'You haven't nobbled his daughter or something, have you, Ian?'

'I didn't even know he had a daughter,' said Fleming worriedly. 'I know he spends a lot of time in Washington now, but what the devil's he doing here? Didn't he give any indication of what he wanted? No – he wouldn't, of course. Not him.'

'He's after your head on a plate by the sound of it,' was Benyon's unhelpful contribution. 'I did warn you that rounding sixpenny taxi fare tips up to a shilling on your expenses would all end in tears.'

Fleming was not amused. 'That's not even remotely funny, Johnny,' he snapped.

'I agree,' said June, tossing car keys on the table. 'And for that he can go and collect him. The only respectable hotel's closed for your get-together so I've told Harriet to prepare the room Nelson used when this house was his HQ.'

Benyon took the keys and turned to leave. 'Good idea. The crusty old bastard will like that.' He paused at the top of the steps and frowned. 'By the way, Ian, what was the name of that operation that had you hobnobbing around Spain and Portugal? I've been racking my brains.'

'Goldeneye,' said Fleming absently. 'Operation Goldeneye.'

8

The first sound to reach Eric was of someone sobbing. The pitiful sound drifted in and out of his consciousness. Puzzling whether it was a man or woman suffering such anguish seemed to occupy a century. Towards the end of it he become aware of other sounds. Womens' voices. Fast French or was it Flemish? The clatter of boots. The sensation of being in the centre of a whirl of activity.

He opened his eyes. He was lying on his side in a hard bed. Rough sheets. No pillow-cases – bare ticking. A feather was pricking his cheek. He rolled on to his back and the sudden pain made him cry out. A woman's ageless face appeared above him. She seemed to be wearing a dead albatross on her head. When he focused his eyes he realized that it was the white starched flare of a Sister of Mercy's wimple.

'You will be more comfortable on your side,' she insisted in slow German. Eric offered no resistance as she eased him on to his side. The pain subsided. Eric mumbled his thanks but she was gone, her habit rustling between beds packed so closely together that there was only just enough room for her to move. The young man with the bandaged eyes who had been crying was so close that Eric could almost touch him. His face was turned towards him. He was blond, aged about 20 and could have been even younger.

'Hallo,' said the young man. There was a note of quiet despair in his cultured, educated voice. 'Sorry if I woke you. I get these bouts now and then and can't help myself. What happened to you?'

Eric had a vague recollection of running across a field when there had been the crack of a rifle and a sudden, terrible pain in his back. One by one the memories dropped into place and arranged themselves into a logical sequence of events.

He cautiously pushed himself higher up on his pillow and took stock of himself and his surroundings. There was a bandage around his head and uncomfortably tight bindings around his chest. He was in a high-ceilinged room with about twenty other beds crammed in. On the opposite wall was a blackboard. A section of wall was missing, so that he could see into a busy corridor, crowded with more occupied hospital beds. To his left was a window protected with an outer wall of sandbags. The panes of glass were a mass of sticky tape. All around patients were coughing, some reading, some dozing. The neatly folded uniforms on chairs beside the beds were all German.

'I think I was shot in the back,' said Eric in

answer to the young man's question.

'You were. I heard the doctors talking. They were amazed by your luck. There's something hanging on your bed that tinkles when there's a draught. They were saying that it saved your life.'

Eric felt behind him. It was the Feldgendarmerie gorget, hanging by its chain. He unhooked it and stared at it in amazement. The metal plate was bigger than it should be because it had been splayed out by the impact from Corporal Wilkins's .303 rifle round.

'What is it?' the young man asked. 'Some sort of armour?'

'Almost, it seems,' Eric replied, and explained what had happened. The two men introduced themselves. The young man was Leutnant sur Zee Mark Schiller, the only son of a veterinary surgeon who owned a small farm. He was only 18.

'I was given my own command,' said Mark when they had shaken hands. 'My father was very proud.'

'An eighteen-year-old junior leutnant given a command?' Eric queried.

'It was a one-man U-boat. A Biber. Have you heard of them?'

'Vaguely.'

'Training at Kiel was fun. You sit in a little cockpit with your head in a plastic blister. The water rushes at you even though you are only doing about five knots. I once saw some fish when I was submerged. My first mission was the port of Antwerp and to use my torpedo against the biggest supply ship I could find. But I had trouble with the boat's depth-keeping controls. The hydroplane kept jamming. In the end I had to flood my ballast tanks and sink to bottom of the dock. I managed to dump my torpedo but the boat shot to the surface. I don't think the tanks had flooded properly. Then there were shots...'

The young man stopped talking. His hand sought Eric's wrist and gripped it tightly. There was a sob in his voice when he resumed. 'The canopy seemed to explode ... There was a terrible stinging in my eyes. My compass was the last thing I ever saw.'

The young naval officer was unable to continue for a few moments. Two other patients were watching but Eric decided that he didn't give a damn if they thought it unmanly that he should hold this boy's hand.

'The doctors here are mostly Flemish. They're very good even though we are the enemy. An eye specialist looked at my eyes. Something about corneal lacerations, perforations of the anterior chambers. They had to remove the lenses.'

'So you're blind?'

'Yes. But they saved my eyes, so at least I won't look like a freak unless infection gets in and they have to remove them. They've stitched down my eyelids to keep infection out.'

Two nurses rushed by in uniforms Eric didn't recognize.

'What is this place, Mark?'

'Part of the Tozefotraat military hospital. The British have annexed this school for POWs. They've turned the assembly hall into a mortuary because there have been so many civilian casualties from the V2s.'

Eric's heart pounded. 'V2s?' he echoed.

'They're bad, Eric. No warning. They can come down anywhere. Even the main St. Tozefotraat military hospital was hit. That was very recent – March 6th, I think. Many were killed and injured. Just before Christmas one hit the Rex Cinema. Nearly six hundred dead. They were wheeling bodies past for hours. A lot of British servicemen. And some Queen Alexandra nurses from here. There was a funeral service for them. We all went if we could. They were such lovely, caring girls. I got to know them by their footsteps. There was one...' He fought hard to keep control. 'God – I wish I was with her now.'

'Was that the worst V2 incident?' asked Eric.

'I think so. There were others. Shopping streets. That was the terrible thing. There was no warning. No sound. Just a sudden tremendous explosion. Why was that, do you suppose?'

'They were travelling faster than sound,' said Eric stonily.

'There haven't been any for about two weeks now. The BBC German language news is saying that the war will be over in a matter of days. We'll all be going home. I haven't seen my father for nearly a year. My mother died two years ago.'

'So what is this place?' Eric demanded.

'I told you. The Tozefotraat military—'

'That means nothing to me,' Eric interrupted brusquely. 'Where are we? What town?'

'Antwerp,' said Mark, puzzled by Eric's tone. 'From what I've heard it's the Allies' main supply port. On the news they were saying that over six hundred V2s have fallen on Antwerp. That's more than have been fired at London.'

9

A bath, a light supper, and some fine brandy with the promise of more because a bottle had been placed before him, put Admiral Godfrey, the Director of Naval Intelligence, in a better humour than when he had first arrived at June's mansion. But the senior officer's better humours were a long way short of good humours, especially when his company was Ian Fleming, and particularly when his subordinate officer was indirectly responsible for his having to make this trip. He had once been stationed in Jamaica and had no great love for the place. June and Benyon had withdrawn, leaving the two men alone.

He regarded Fleming frostily. 'So you fixed yourself chairmanship of this damned conference? Well done.'

'I was railroaded into it by our American friends, sir.'

Admiral Godfrey grunted. 'Benyon says you handled the Russians well.'

Fleming turned on his most disarming smile. 'They're not exactly eating out of my hand just yet, sir, but I'm working on it. I don't mean to sound rude, but why are you here?'

'Because some wretch in our Washington embassy worked out from timetables that I could be here by this evening. Everyone's running around like headless chickens because they've discovered that the Americans are running a little operation to round up all the German V2 scientists that they can lay their hands on, and any caches of V2s. We know that they've already found about twenty on a goods train at Verden and they want a lot more. Operation Paperclip they now call it. It was Overcast. You're wanted to ferret out what you can from the US contingent here. You'll have to look smart because you have only two days.'

Fleming looked doubtful. 'They're mostly our opposite numbers in naval intelligence, sir.'

'Exactly what I said before I was sent on

this ridiculous wild-goose chase. God knows why, but there are some who think rather highly of you, Fleming.' The admiral sipped his brandy appreciatively. 'There's more.' He felt in his pocket and tossed an envelope on the coffee table. 'Take a look.'

Fleming unfolded the four pages of foolscap typescript. The heading and the opening paragraphs jumped off the page at him:

BUILDING A NEW GERMANY

> The first objective is, of course, to win the war and destroy National Socialism. It is suggested that the second objective should be accomplished as quickly as possible and that is to put a democratic government in place in Germany, by Germans, for Germans because history has taught us that governing by garrison inevitably fails. We need Germans of integrity and determination. Luckily there are plenty of them but they have to be identified.
>
> This is not a post-war operation, to be put hurriedly into place when Germany is defeated, with all the attendant risks of doing important things in a hurry. Fortunately the programme is already well-established and working well. It started in 1940 with the screening of German POWs. Interrogations at the various cages sorts prisoners into com-

mitted Nazis, who are sent to the so-called 'black' camps; the borderline cases, who are sent to 'grey' camps; and those POWs who, although not necessarily disloyal to their fatherland, have no taste for Hitler and his policies. These POWs are subjected to more careful interrogation and are sent to the 'white' camps. Officers considered 'white' camp candidates are sent to a special camp for officers at Grizedale Hall in the Lake District. These people are what we would call the cream of German society. The intelligentsia. They are the future. They are our hope for peace in Europe. We should capitalize on this careful and expensive segregation work by looking to such men to form the backbone of the governance of a new Germany.

I suggest that Erin Rommel is approached to head an interim government following German's collapse.

Admiral Godfrey chuckled at Fleming's expression. 'I wager you never expected to see that again.'

Fleming nodded. 'I wrote it in my flat nearly three years ago during a boring, wet weekend, sir, and submitted it to you as a loose minute.' He paused and tapped the sheaf of documents. 'This was little more than my thinking aloud, sir – just to show you that there's a thoughtful side to my nature and that I don't spend all my free time chasing after women.'

'Just most of it?'

Fleming gave one of his sudden, disarming smiles. 'About ninety per cent, sir.'

'Anyway,' said Admiral Godfrey. 'Because there's some sound reasoning in it and it was positive because it assumed victory, and because it doesn't read like a Dashiell Hammett thriller – like your usual reports – I decided that it was worth referring up. Just to show that there's a thoughtful side to the N.I.D. and that we're not always chasing after intelligence.'

'May I ask to whom, sir?'

'You may not. But it went high. And from there it went even higher. High enough for a policy decision to be taken on the strength of it. Your recommendation of Rommel to head an interim government coincided with the thinking of the government, who felt that Rommel was the only German they would be prepared to deal with.'

'Damn shame about his death,' Fleming commented.

'You've been out of domestic work relating to intelligence-gathering from POWs for nearly two years, so I don't suppose you know what's been going on.'

'I'm very much out of touch,' Fleming admitted.

Admiral Godfrey continued, 'About two months after I submitted your report, Grizedale Hall was designated as a special category camp.'

Fleming was flattered and astonished by the news. 'I thought it had been closed down and all the POWs sent to Canada?'

'It wasn't, and they weren't. Some were at the beginning of '43 but most were kept at Grizedale Hall. Although its numbers are now only fifty-one.'

'Including Otto Kruger, sir?'

'He's still the senior German officer there. There are higher ranking officers than him at Grizedale now but none have had the courage or desire to usurp Kruger.'

'I'm not surprised. He can be a bit intimidating. But I'm glad someone has seen the sense in holding him back.'

'I've heard that the fellow was a trouble-maker,' Admiral Godfrey growled.

'You're thinking about that business when he refused to permit the handcuffing of selected POW officers? With respect, sir, Kruger isn't a trouble-maker – he's a fair-minded man but a stickler for protocol. A man of the highest integrity. That handcuffing order was wrong and he was prepared to stand up and say so, and he didn't flinch when Bren guns were pointed at him.' Fleming glanced through the report. 'On page 3, sir, I made the point that people of his character were exactly what was needed in Germany after the war. Men like Kruger, who wouldn't take any nonsense from us, certainly won't take any from the Soviet Union.'

Admiral Godfrey poured himself another brandy. 'It was the thinking behind that comment of yours, and other things you said, such as your Rommel suggestion, that made such a big impression, and the reason I'm here and not in an air-conditioned, comfortable room in a Washington hotel. I'm here to offer you a job. As soon as this conference is over, you're to scour Germany to find and secure all the best V2 brains and material that will be useful to us and deny them to the Soviets, and you're to help in the identification of all those Germans that can play a useful rule in the administration and rebuilding of post-war Germany. The two responsibilities dovetail neatly together. If you accept, a signal will be sent to your chief.'

There was a long silence as Fleming absorbed this astonishing offer. It held the promise of cloak and dagger work – something he adored. He kept his voice steady when he replied. 'I'm pleased to accept, sir.'

Admiral Godfrey grunted. 'Both tasks of equal importance, but priority must be given finding the rocket men. You'll have full co-operation at all levels. Shouldn't be too big a job for your ego to cope with, Fleming.'

Fleming's private view was that the men who planned unleashing horror weapons on civilians, particularly those behind the planning of launching V2s from U-boats, should be tried and hanged.

When they had finished talking, June turned the outside lights on so that Admiral

Godfrey could take a stroll around the garden before retiring. He returned from his constitutional somewhat disgruntled.

'Dammit!' he muttered to June and Benyon. 'I take a breather to admire the moonlight on the sea and a damned great parrot flew down beside me. Frightened the life out of me, it did. It told me to f—' He checked himself. 'It told me to leave, using indescribably obscene terms, and then cleared off.'

'Oh dear, Admiral,' said June quickly, her glare frying Benyon, who seemed to be having a choking fit. 'I'm terribly sorry. They pick up bad language from sailors.'

Admiral Godfrey fixed his eye on her. '*I'm* a sailor, madam, and I would never think of using such disgusting language. Damned parrot.'

'It was Percy. He's a macaw.'

'I don't care what damned highland clan he hails from, he was disgracefully rude!'

That night Fleming's bedtime reading was a favourite book that he found in the mansion's library. It was *Birds of the West Indies* by James Bond.

10

Over four years as a prisoner of war in Grizedale Hall had not been kind to Leutnant Willi Hartmann's waistline. He was not built for tracking down all the POW camp's prisoners scattered around the hall's extensive grounds. The only exertion he relished was his frequent toiling up to his little room on the top floor to add to his increasing hord of money behind a skirting board – the proceeds of four years as Grizedale Hall's ace swindler.

Willi was Grizedale Hall's most remarkable prisoner because he was the only one who had, according to Nurse Brenda Hobson's camp records, managed to put on a stone in weight during his captivity. This achievement was chiefly due to Willi's frequent sampling of his stock of confectionery he had amassed as currency during his incarceration. Mars Bars, Toblerone bars, slabs of chocolate and suchlike were as good as pound notes in food-rationed Britain. His stash of one-pound bags of sugar under the floorboards in his room was valuable but proving harder to barter owing to its bulky nature. Nevertheless it could traded at local sweet shops for liquorice sticks and other sweets. Willi was into sugar laundering.

The reason he had managed to acquire such a stock, and a useful sum of English money, was quite simply because he was a crook. In civilian life he had been a small-time crook. Then he joined the army, was sent to occupied France, and became a big-time crook, using his position as an army supplies officer to sell motor transport spares to a lucrative and grateful black market.

Willi's service life had been a catalogue of misfortunes, of which the most unfortunate entry had been his application of a moderate amount of blackmail to secure a flight in a Heinkel on a daylight raid on the Isle of Wight because he wanted to see England. The Heinkel had been shot down and for nearly five years Willi had been seeing more of England than he had anticipated. The only comfort was that at least he was beyond the reach of the Feldgendarmerie in France, who were anxious to discuss some of their beliefs and deep inner convictions with him: namely their belief that supplying garages around Chartres with army-issue tyres, petrol and other spares was taking the concept of maintaining good relationships with the civilian populace a little too far, and a deep inner conviction that Willi deserved ten years. But his relations with the British camp guards was good, with the possible exception of Sergeant Finch, who had once declared: 'That fat little Bavarian bastard has got his thieving, pudgy fingers into every pie, and one day I'm going to break them off one by one.'

'Commander Kruger wants all prisoners assembled in the courtyard at 1400,' Willi told two men tending their vegetable plot. 'It's like a roll-call but you're to wash, brush your hair, and generally make yourselves look presentable.'

'What's it about, Willi? Some sort of inspection?' asked a prisoner who was leaning on a rake.

'Something to do with the armistice,' another prisoner commented, busy weeding with a hoe.

'I don't know,' said Willi. 'Pass it on, please.'

'There's no one here to pass it on to, Willi,' the rake-leaning prisoner observed, glancing around. 'You'll have to find everyone yourself.'

'Will you help me?'

'I've got this weeding to do,' said the prisoner the hoe.

'And if I walk away, this rake will fall over,' added his companion. He looked over Willi's shoulder and his eyes widened in surprise. 'How did she get in? Looks like your Carol Bunce has come to see you, Willi.'

A look of panic came into Willi's eyes. Carol Bunce was a strapping wench of a land girl who worked on the nearby Spauldings Farm. Willi had first met her when he was on an outside working party. The mighty Amazon, who towered above the plump Barvarian, had fallen hopelessly in love with Willi and had even taken to waiting for him outside the main gate. On one occasion she had seized him in her brawny arms and whirled him around with a joyful exuberance that produced cheers and guffaws from the guards, and a diagnosis of a cracked rib from Brenda Hobson and tight straps that he had to wear for a fortnight.

Willi spun around, his eyes wide and fearful, but there was no one there. The gardeners roared with helpless laughter.

'Bastards!' Willi spat and set off, clutching his clipboard, with his fellow prisoners' mirth ringing in his ears. His breath made clouds of vapour in the bitterly cold air as he broke into a wobbly jog.

An hour later he had a pencil tick against every prisoner and returned to the hall to report to Kruger.

Following his capture after the ramming and sinking of his U-boat, *U-112*, Commander Otto Kruger had appointed Willi as his adjutant – the more official-sounding military term for general dogsbody. For nearly two years the hapless Willi had had to labour up and down three flights of stairs on his interminable errands for Kruger because the senior officer's office and quarters were on the top floor of the Lake District mansion. The situation had improved marginally when Kruger had transferred to a new office on the ground floor that the POWs had prepared for him.

That was at Christmas 1942 and since then, Willi's fortunes, like those of his homeland, had gone steadily downhill. From mid-1943 the stream of young, gullible junior officers to whom he could sell supplies such as pillowcases and extra blankets, which they were entitled to anyway, in exchange for the contents of their first food parcels had almost completely stopped. New arrivals were now mostly senior officers, wise in the ways of the world, who refused to accept any nonsense from Willi. What was particularly galling for Willi was that the new breed of prisoners generally came from well-off middle-class families who could afford to send their captured relatives generous parcels through the Red Cross.

Willi entered the great hall that the prisoners had restored and crossed to Kruger's office. He knocked.

'Come!'

Willi entered. It was a fine office. Hauptmann Anton Hertzog, the camp's artist, had been persuaded to set aside his passion for painting mighty, muscle-bound Rubens nudes to produce a large picture in oils of Kruger's *U-112* forging into Atlantic seas under a sullen sky. It had been painted directly on to the plaster. Kruger was in earnest conference with the two other senior officers: Oberleutnant Karl Shriver and Hauptman Paul Ulbrick. They were studying a document on Kruger's desk; their faces grim.

'I've notified everyone, Commander,' said Willi.

Kruger's intimidating, hawk-like features were as inscrutable as ever. He regarded his aide dispassionately. 'Thank you, Willi. One more errand and you can go and get cleaned up yourself. Would you present my compliments to Major Reynolds and ask if he would be good enough to meet me in the courtyard at 1400.'

'What shall I tell him, Commander? He's sure to ask.'

'Tell him what you like,' said Kruger irritably. 'Just make sure he comes.' He glanced up at one of Dietrich Berg's cuckoo clocks that had been presented to him – the only one that the young army officer and his team of craftsmen had ever made that kept reasonably good time. 'You have fifteen minutes, so you had better look lively.'

Willi wasn't built for looking lively but he scuttled across to the camp's administration block and stated his business to the guard outside the camp commandant's office. A minute later he was allowed into Major Reynolds's office. It was smaller than Kruger's office, the floor covered with Ministry of Works brown linoleum instead of the fine Axminster that Willi had scrounged for Kruger, and it was akin to an angler's workshop. Reynolds's prize catch, a huge carp that he had caught in one of Cathy Standish's tarns, was in a glass case mounted on the wall.

Major James Reynolds, DSO, Canadian Army Corps, was not the sort of man whose ego needed propping up by continuing to write when he had a visitor. He set down his pen and regarded Willi with his lone eye – he had lost his left eye at Dunkirk.

'If it's about repatriation of POWs, Willi, then I know no more than I told you all at roll-call yesterday evening.'

'Commander Kruger sends his compliments, sir,' said Willi – nearly five years in England and Kruger's classes had improved his English. 'And requests that you meet with him in the courtyard at 1400.'

Reynolds frowned. 'Did he say what it was about?'

'No, sir. But he has ordered all German officers to assemble in the courtyard.'

'Strange.'

'Perhaps he thinks you should hold a roll-call?'

Reynolds looked worried. 'Why? Has there been an escape?'

'I don't think so, sir.'

'Very well. My compliments to Commander Kruger. I'll see him in ten minutes.'

11

Nurse Brenda Hobson (Sergeant) of the Queen Alexandra's Royal Army Nursing Corps was wheeling her bicycle across Grizedale Hall's courtyard when prisoners started assembling in the courtyard, forming into lines. It was a measure of Kruger's strict discipline that although many of the German officers gave the attractive blonde apprecia-tive glances, none made any suggestive noises or gestures. She had been tending the men's medical needs for five years on her regular visits to the hall and always felt safer with them than with the patients in the military hospital at Barrow. Having been nursing men and women for five years and seen the horrors of this hateful war at first hand, she was elated that it was over.

It was a war that had taken her husband, David – the father of her six-year-old son – from her in November 1941 when the battleship HMS *Barham* had been torpedoed in the Mediterranean by a U-boat. After three-and-a-half years the wounds of that terrible loss were only just beginning to heal.

She left her bicycle outside and entered her

sickbay. She went to the window to see what was going on. She was cross with herself because her heartbeat quickened when Kruger appeared. She told herself it was because the tall, aloof, mysterious German officer reminded her of Mr Darcy in Jane Austen's *Pride and Prejudice* – her favourite book, and Fitzwilliam Darcy her favourite hero.

The guards liked hovering around her sickbay when she was on duty. One of her admirers was Private Knox, a former journalist who now worked in Reynolds's outer office and knew a good deal about what was going on. She had once steered their conversation around to discussing Kruger. Brenda was curious about the disdainful and always very correct but private man.

'He writes to his parents now and then,' Knox had said. 'Hard to believe, but there's a woman he writes to.'

'Oh? Who?' Brenda had asked, hoping the query sounded casual while she pretended to be intent her record cards.

'Someone called Alice.'

'I find it hard to imagine Otto Kruger pouring out his heart to a woman.'

'He doesn't. Never a word of endearment according to the censors. Long rambles about how the vegetable plots are doing – that sort of thing. All fits, I suppose. There's no warmth in the man.'

'And yet he's got a heart,' Brenda had said.

'A lump of Coniston granite, more like.'

'My husband was killed just before Christmas, 1941,' Brenda had said quietly. 'Otto Kruger got Dietrich Berg and his team to make lots of wonderful toys for my boy, Stephen. He still adores his big engine. And every Christmas there have been more toys. Just left outside the sickbay door with a note to wish us a happy Christmas. And there's always an extra present and a card for Stephen's birthday which is on New Year's Eve. I mentioned it once to Kruger in passing and he's never forgotten.'

'A man of mystery,' Private Knox had concluded.

As Brenda gazed out of the window at the assembling POWs, she couldn't help recalling that conversation with the former journalist. Nor could she help that little tremble she experienced when Kruger took his place at the head of the parade and stood to attention. She turned from the window, hating herself for what she perceived as disloyalty to the memory of a beloved husband.

Major Reynolds and his senior NCO, Sergeant Finch, left the administration block and stared in surprise at the scene before them in the courtyard. The prisoners were paraded in tidier than usual lines, all wearing their uniforms, all looking clean, well-scrubbed, hair combed. At the head of the parade was Kruger, resplendent in the Kriegsmarine uniform that the British had made for after his capture so that they could present him to the world on newsreel films to show that the German U-boatmen and their U-boats were not invincible. His Knight's Cross and swords gleamed at his throat. Shriver and Ulbrick flanked him. In front of Kruger was a cloth-covered trestle table and some chairs. A large object on the table was covered with a cloth.

Never certain what to expect from 'them bloody Jerries', Sergeant Finch directed ten guards to take up positions on each side of the parade. Reynolds turned up the collar of his greatcoat against the biting wind and approached Kruger. The two men exchanged formal salutes.

'Thank you coming out, Major,' said Kruger. 'In accordance with instructions we've received from the German High Command, we are gathered to present our surrender. Hostilities are over between us.'

Reynolds gaped. 'You're what?' he spluttered.

Kruger repeated his statement.

'But that's not necessary!' Reynolds expostulated. 'The German forces have surrendered on your behalf anyway!'

Kruger was unmoved. 'Although the formal general announcement of the armistice was yesterday, we received instructions this morning that all operational units, including warships and U-boats at sea, are to cease hostilities immediately.'

Reynolds began to wonder if Kruger had been reading too many Kafka novels. 'I don't understand you, Commander. You're not an operational unit.'

Kruger regarded the Canadian officer coolly. 'Since my arrival here, Major, this camp has been an operational unit as far as I'm concerned. Our main function had been the dissemination of intelligence and forwarding it to the OKM.'

One of us is going mad, thought Reynolds. And I'm damn certain it isn't me. 'What intelligence?' he blustered. 'How—?'

'We've sent the OKM reports from new arrivals. Information on Allied interrogation techniques; information on Allied U-boat hunting techniques and probable new weapons; snippets of information gleaned from all the US newspapers and magazines that relatives and sympathizers have sent us, in case our own intelligence units back home missed them. We've had more time than most to study such sources in detail. A considerable amount of valuable information, Major. The last report was sent only two weeks ago.'

'But how? It's not possible. All letters from POWs are subjected to intensive scrutiny by War Office censors. Every word pattern analysed!'

'My many chatty letters to "Alice",' said Kruger, giving a faint smile. 'And her letters to me.'

'The letters were encoded?'

'Indeed they were.'

'How?'

Kruger considered the question carefully before answering. Well – the war was over and he was required to cooperate with the victors. 'The information was not embedded in the words,' he replied, 'but in the gaps between the words, and between the letters. Gaps that you would never notice unless you knew what you were looking for. The "Ireland" letter code was devised by Admiral Doenitz for use in the event of our capture. Willi became an expert at writing and decoding them.'

Reynolds was speechless for a few moments. Some of the POWs in earshot were smirking. Shriver and Ulbrick were struggling to keep straight faces. The Canadian officer glanced at Sergeant Finch. The British army NCO was glaring at Kruger with more than the usual measure of hate in his expression.

'I knew it, sir,' he muttered. 'I just knew it! Didn't I always say that they were up to something?'

'But how could you have received orders about the surrender?' Reynolds wondered aloud.

Kruger stepped forward and removed the cloth that was covering the object on the table. It was an extensively modified domestic radio receiver without its wooden cabinet. Extra brackets had been fixed to the main chassis to support the mass of coils and tuning capacitors that obviously weren't part of the set's original design. The homemade tuning wheels were beautifully marked with frequencies.

'We always monitor 500 kilocycles – 600 metres,' said Kruger. 'The surrender orders are broadcast every two hours in Morse in the clear.'

Reynolds and Sergeant Finch gaped at the strange radio in astonishment. 'How long have you had this?' Reynolds demanded, his face pale with shock.

'Four years,' Kruger replied. 'It's now yours, but I would respectfully request, Major, that we're allowed to keep it now that the war is over.'

'Four years!' Reynolds gasped.

'I was right all along about that, too,' Sergeant Finch declared, his face red with anger. 'I knew they had a wireless.'

Reynolds rounded on him. 'And you never found it in four years, Sergeant!' he rasped.

'We've found several crystal sets, sir.'

Reynolds was about to blast Sergeant Finch but checked himself. He had no wish to berate a British army NCO in front of the POWs. The truth was that crystal sets were easy to make. They required no external power, not even a battery, and a piece of coke could serve as a detector. Furthermore, they weren't selective and were therefore useless as short-wave receivers. He turned to Kruger. 'So where has it been hidden all these years?'

Kruger pointed to Grizedale Hall's roof. 'Last chimney stack on the left. In the roof space where the stack passes beside the water tank. Bricks have been removed to provide a large opening with dummy bricks to cover it. The closeness of the water tank made it impossible for Sergeant Finch's men to tap the stack properly in order to find hollows. The aerial wire runs along under the eaves on the outside of the roof, tucked out of sight.'

Reynold's black mood faded as he began to see the humour in the situation, especially when he saw Sergeant Finch's thunderstruck expression, but he kept his face straight. 'And you want to be allowed to keep it?'

Kruger gave a little bow. 'Our orders are to hand over all our equipment. But the wireless is difficult to use. We are no longer at war, neither myself or my men will offer any form of hostility towards you, therefore we would appreciate being allowed to retain the set on loan.'

'It doesn't have transmitter capability?'

'I give you my word that it doesn't.'

Kruger's word was good enough for Reynolds. He could see no objection to the prisoners keeping their radio set. Kruger expressed his thanks.

'And I also have to hand over these,' said Kruger. He felt under the cloth and produced a pair of long-handled croppers. 'Wire cutters, Major.' He held them out to Sergeant Finch. 'Made from two leaf springs removed from the rear suspension of your car several years ago, Sergeant Finch. I do hope their loss did not affect its performance.'

Sergeant Finch had bitter memories of the time when the rear axle on his car had collapsed. He snatched the tool, examined it, and glared in unconcealed anger at the

German officer.

'And now the surrender,' said Kruger. He sat at the table and indicated for Reynolds to do likewise. He produced an envelope containing carefully hand-lettered documents.

'This one,' said Kruger, placing the first document on the table, 'is our acceptance of the broad terms of the surrender instructions as issued by Reich Chancellor Grand Admiral Karl Doenitz. All the prisoners have signed it.' Kruger added his signature to the foot of the sheet and handed it to Reynolds, who accepted it as though the document were part of an unreal fantasy.

'And if you would initial this receipt, please, Major.'

Reynolds read the wording, decided it was innocuous and scribbled his initials.

'And this document,' said Kruger, 'is a full transcript of the terms of surrender transmitted to all U-boats by OKM – the German Naval High Command – in Morse code on standard U-boat frequencies. Reception conditions have been poor, therefore we have compiled the text from several transmissions. I would appreciate it if you would read it, please, Major.'

Reynolds did so.

ANNEXURE 'A'

SURRENDER OF GERMAN 'U' BOAT FLEET

1. Carry out the following instructions forthwith which have been given by the Allied representatives:

(A) Surface immediately and remain surfaced.
(B) Report immediately in plain language your position in latitude and longitude and number of your 'U' Boat to nearest British, US, Canadian or Soviet coast W/T station on 500 kc/s (600 metres) and to use call sign GZZ 10 on one of the following high fre quencies: 16845 – 12685 or 5970 kc/s.
(C) Fly a large black flag by day.
(D) Burn navigation lights by night.
(E) Jettison all ammunition, remove all breach-blocks from guns and render torpedoes safe by removing pistols. Allmines are to be rendered safe.
(F) Make all signals in plain language.
(G) Follow strictly the instructions for proceeding to Allied ports from your present area given in immediately following message.
(H) Observe strictly the orders of Allied Representatives to refrain from scuttling or in any way damaging your 'U' Boat.

2. These instructions will be repeated at two hour intervals until further notice.

Reynolds finished reading the document and looked up at Kruger across the table. The German's officer's angry expression puzzled him.

'Is there a problem with this order, Commander?'

'Condition "C" is unacceptable,' Kruger replied coldly. 'A black flag is a pirate flag. To treat U-boat crews as pirates is a gross humiliation and is therefore contrary to the terms of the Geneva Convention relating to the treatment of prisoners of war.'

Reynolds was lost for words for a few moments. 'So does this mean that you're not surrendering?' He knew there was madness in the question but it was all he could think of to say.

'Certainly not. We've already signed the instrument of surrender. What it means is that the U-boatmen among the prisoners are demanding an apology from the Allies for this disgraceful slur. And we will not move until we receive it.'

Reynolds stood and surveyed the ranks and files of the prisoners. 'But you haven't got a U-boat. The prisoners don't need to fly any flag.'

'That is immaterial. Treating U-boats at sea and their crews as pirates is a slur against all U-boatmen.'

'So what do you propose doing about it?'

'We will remain here until we receive an apology.'

'What – just stand here?'

'Indeed. We will offer no resistance if we're forcibly removed. But we will always reassemble.'

'Luftwaffe and Heer as well?'

'All German servicemen are united in this matter,' Kruger replied impassively, rising from the table.

'All day and all night?'

'If necessary.'

'We'll move them, sir,' said Sergeant Finch grimly.

'No,' said Reynolds after a moment's thought. 'I hope that that won't be necessary. Dismiss your men, Sergeant.'

The NCO looked as though he were about to protest but he thought better of it. He scowled at Kruger and the prisoners and ordered the guards to disperse.

Reynolds stood staring at Kruger, not doubting that he and all the prisoners would do exactly as he said. He shrugged, exchanged salutes with the German officer and turned to leave.

'I would remind you, Major,' said Kruger politely, 'that we now have nothing. We are defeated. We have lost everything and we have surrendered everything. All we have left is our pride, and we were not required to surrender that.'

Reynolds nodded and returned to his office. He sat at his desk for some minutes, reading Kruger's surrender acceptance document, and eventually came to a decision. One of the perks of the war had been conveying bad news to Captain Moyle, General Somerfield's humourless aide at North-Western Command HQ. He picked up his telephone and told Private Knox to put a call through to him.

He was speaking to him a few minutes later. 'Ah, Captain Moyle. Good afternoon. Reynolds, Grizedale Hall.'

'Good afternoon, Major,' said Moyle cautiously. Calls from Reynolds invariably spelt trouble. 'What can I do for you?'

'I have some good news for General Somerfield. The Germans have surrendered.'

There was a brief silence. 'I think the General is aware of that, Major Reynolds.' A harsh note crept into Captain Moyle's voice. 'In fact, Major, we're all aware of that. It happened yesterday!'

'No. You're talking about Doenitz's general surrender of all German forces to General Eisenhower and the Soviets. So you've heard about that? Well, I'm glad to hear that North-Western Command HQ is keeping up with major events. I'm referring to *our* Germans – the POWs at Grizedale Hall. You may recall that we're looking after some.'

'What the hell are you talking about? You mean there's been a disturbance? Why haven't you reported it?'

'No disturbance, Captain. All our POWs have surrendered. I have the instrument of their surrender before me.'

'But they don't have to surrender!'

'They do if they're an operational unit.'

'How can POWs in a POW camp be an operational unit?' Moyle howled.

'It's a long story,' Reynolds replied. 'The problem is that although the POWs have surrendered unconditionally, the Kriegsmarine prisoners are objecting very strongly to the requirement that U-boats should fly what they consider to be a pirates' flag – a black flag.'

'But they haven't got a U-boat!'

'I'm sure you're right. Sergeant Finch would've found it by now if they had.'

Private Knox put his head around the door and tried to catch Reynolds's attention. He was waved away. Winding up Captain Moyle was a dish to be enjoyed alone.

'This is madness,' Moyle declared. 'Complete and utter madness. I suppose Kruger's behind all this?'

'There's no putting anything past you, Captain,' said Reynolds admiringly.

'They should've all been sent to Canada like the others. I sometimes wonder why they weren't.'

'It's something I wonder all the time,' Reynolds replied equitably. 'I wouldn't mind being sent there myself.'

'So what does Kruger want?'

'I think an apology will suffice. They're all standing on parade and will, I fear, remain so until an apology is received. They see the whole thing as the humiliation of POWs contrary to the Geneva Convention.'

As usual, the conversation got quite acrimonious and ended, as usual, with Captain Moyle losing his temper and, as usual, slamming the phone down.

Private Knox stuck his head around the door and got in with a quick, 'They're here, sir,' before giving Reynolds a chance to tell him to clear off.

'Who are here?'

'The press, sir. Two car loads. Waiting at the main gate. On time, too.'

Reynolds groaned. He had forgotten all about the press visit that North-Western Command had agreed to. The local papers had been clamouring for a chance to talk to German POWs, to sound out their opinions on the armistice, because the POWs were the only German servicemen that were to hand.

'Some of the locals are going to rack up some nice lineage fees from the nationals over this glorious mess,' said Private Knox with relish. 'They all string for the nationals. "'WE'RE NOT PIRATES,' SAYS U-BOAT ACE" – just the sort of headline I'd like to write. I can't wait to be de-mobbed and get back into it, sir.'

Reynolds rested his elbows on the desk and clapped his hands despairingly over his temples. 'Oh my godfathers.' He looked up at the private. 'Knox – you keep them waiting for ten minutes and I'll write you a reference that'll land you a top job on the *Daily Mirror*. Move!'

Private Knox promptly disappeared. Reynolds pulled on his cap, left his office to face Kruger, and was accosted by Brenda Hobson, her face drawn and angry.

'Sir,' she began without preamble. 'I've just learned about this latest piece of nonsense,' she gestured at the parade. 'Leutnant Alex Todt is out there. He's only just been discharged from the sickbay. He's been very ill for two weeks and is very weak. This is his first parade for two weeks. The cold will kill him!'

Reynolds could only groan inwardly. As if he didn't have enough problems. The father of Alex Todt, Iron Cross, was the late Fritz Todt – head of the Todt Organization. Alex Todt's elder brother had been killed on the Russian Front making young Alex one of the biggest landowners under Allied control in the west. Unlike his father, Alex had had nothing to do with the Nazi party. Early reports said that all the tenant farmers on the Todt estates liked the personable young man and would be pleased to co-operate with him. Food production in post-war Germany was going to be a key issue. Alex was viewed as an important prisoner and North-Western Command had notified Reynolds that the young man was to be treated with care.

'I'll do what I can,' he promised the anxious nurse and crossed the courtyard to Kruger.

Kruger came to attention and returned Reynolds's salute.

'Your insistence on an apology is understandable, I suppose,' Reynolds began. 'The question is, what level do you expect this apology to come from?'

Kruger hadn't thought about that. 'From a senior level, Major.'

'Very well,' said Reynolds. He raised his voice to address the parade. 'On behalf of the British Army's North-Western Command, I wish to apologize to the Kriegsmarine, its officers and men for the order that required their U-boats to hoist black flags as a mark of their surrender. We recognize that such an order was a mistake and should never have been given. I shall enter the details in the camp log and sign it myself. I will stand by that come what may. I trust that will suffice?'

It took only a moment's reflection for Kruger to realize that the Canadian officer had taken a courageous stance. 'Thank you, Major. That will suffice. The apology is accepted.' Kruger turned to face the parade and gave the order for the men to fall out.

Reynolds was entering his office when two cars loaded with reporters and photographers rolled into the courtyard. Private Knox watched their eager arrival, wondered about feeding them a headline – ALLIED OFFICER SAYS SORRY TO GERMANS – and thought better of it.

12

Eric lay on his stomach on the hospital bed while the Flemish doctor, the third one in two weeks, carefully felt his ribs. 'This is good,' said the doctor in English – a language he had in common with Eric. 'Your head has healed. Two ribs were badly shattered by the bullet but they are healing well, I think. We will know tomorrow for sure.'

Eric heard the clink of a chain as the doctor took the Feldgendarmerie gorget plate off the corner of the bed. The now splayed and distorted metal plate that had taken the impact of a British soldier's .303 round had become a talisman. Now you're going to say what a lucky escape I had, thought Eric.

'Incredible,' said the doctor. 'Quite amazing, Leutnant Muller.'

By now Eric was getting used to being addressed as Leutnant Dieter Muller – the name of the murdered Feldgendarmerie office whose identity he had stolen.

The doctor went back to his prodding and questioning about pain spots.

'It doesn't hurt so much now when you do that,' said Eric. 'And I can now turn on to my back for short periods. But why tomorrow?'

'We should be getting a supply of X-Ray plates. We have put your name down for one.' He studied Eric's notes. 'From these observations it seems that none of your internal organs are harmed. This is very good. We do not have facilities to test your urine, you understand. Everything destroyed by your V2s. But it looks good and smells good.'

'Skol,' muttered Eric.

The hard-pressed doctor and his entourage squeezed past the packed beds to move to their next patient.

'Doctor!' said Eric, trying to twist around. He pointed to the empty bed beside him. 'What has happened to Leutnant sur Zee Mark Schiller? He's been gone two hours.'

'I think he has been taken to the main hospital to have his eyes examined by a specialist. Some of the stitches that hold his eyelids closed will have to be removed. That is all I know.'

Eric eased himself on to his side and started reading a book, pretending to be engrossed. It deterred other patients in the crowded former classroom from engaging him in conversation. People in close conversation got to know each other's faces. The other patients had soon learned to leave the taciturn officer alone. That he had spent most of the time in the makeshift hospital on his stomach helped. But his feelings towards the young, blinded navy officer in the bed next to him were very different. During the long nights he had often sensed when Mark was alone with his thoughts and in need of support and comfort, even if it was only an offered hand for the young man to grasp in the darkness.

The door opened and Mark appeared, supported by two nurses. His eyes were covered in fresh bandages. The young man's legs seemed to have no strength as the nurses steered him to his bed. Eric suddenly realized how difficult it was for a blind man in unfamiliar surroundings to get exercise. The nurses settled him down, told him that he was to obey the doctors by keeping his head as still as possible, and rushed off to answer an emergency call.

'Dieter?' said Mark after a few minutes. 'Are you there?'

'I'm here,' Eric answered. 'Don't say anything for a moment. Give yourself a chance to unwind.'

Hearing the older man's voice reassured Mark. He was silent for some moments. 'My corneas aren't healing,' he said at length. 'Unless they heal, they cannot look at my eyes because of the danger of infection. So they stitched down my eyelids again.'

Eric understood. In Mark's case, the corneas, the tough outer skins of transparent tissue that covered the eye, the only part of the human eye in physical contact with the outside world, had been badly lacerated by splinters from the plastic canopy of his Biber. Until they healed, the doctors could not risk exposing the young man's eyes to possible infection, so they kept his eyelids stitched shut because eyelids made admirable dressings that kept out bugs.

Mark banged the side of his bed in angry frustration. 'Why aren't they healing?! Why?! They are so painful all the time!'

Eric sat on the edge of his bed – the movement was less painful now – and took hold of Mark's wrist. 'They will heal, Mark. Give them time.'

'But it's been over a month! The pain in my left eye is very bad.'

'These things take time. My back still hurts like hell if I lie on it for too long.'

'Even if they do heal,' said Mark despondently, 'what good will my eyes be? They had to take the lenses out. I couldn't see anything just now. I could just about tell where a window was but nothing else. And I could see the light from the doctor's torch thing. But no detail. Nothing when he held up his fingers.'

'If you can see lights and where windows are, it must mean that your retinas and optic nerves are OK. That must be something.'

'But my eyes aren't healing! They're hurting. The pain goes on and on. And they keep telling me not to make any sudden movements with my head. As if I could, Dieter. I just lie here day after day, getting weaker and weaker. Not only will I be blind, I'll be a cripple as well.' Mark's body started to shake.

Eric patted him reassuringly and said that

he had to go to the toilet. Walking was getting easier each day. The assistant matron's office was at the far end of the corridor. Eric was surprised because until now there had always been a British soldier standing guard at the exit at the end of the corridor. Now the door was propped open by a chair to admit a pleasant breeze.

Sister Theresa looked up and smiled with pleasure when Eric tapped on her open door. 'Good to see you getting about, Leutnant Muller.'

'May I have a brief word, please, Sister?'

The nun indicated a chair in front of her desk. Eric sat. 'What happened to the guards?' he asked.

'Oh – all the security is being relaxed now. It's a lovely spring day – so nice to get some air in the place. The patients need it.'

'I've come to see you about Leutnant Mark Schiller in the bed next to mine.'

Sister Theresa's expression softened. 'Such a terrible thing to have happened to such a nice young man.'

'I think he needs some exercise, Sister. Would it be all right if I took him out on little walks around the grounds to get his strength back?'

'That would be an excellent idea if you would, Leutnant Muller. We're so busy that we don't have time to deal with our patients' physiotherapy needs. Just a little walk morning and afternoon. You mustn't overdo it, and you must make sure that he takes it very easy – no jarring of his head.'

'No running,' said Eric, grinning.

'Definitely no running,' Sister Theresa replied. 'There is another small matter before you leave, Leutnant Muller. I have no next of kin on your record card.'

'I gave my name, rank and number,' said Eric guardedly.

'Yes, I appreciate that. But surely there is someone you'd like to get in touch with?'

'There's no one, Sister,' said Eric curtly, and turned to leave.

The following morning after breakfast Eric took Mark up and down the corridor for a trial walk. It was less than fifty metres. It tired Mark but he was eager to try again in the afternoon.

'Down a step, about ten centimetres,' said Eric to Mark who was holding on to his forearm. 'Half a step forward and there's another step down, about ten centimetres. OK we're now in what was the kids' playground. It's all on one level now.'

'I can feel the sun,' said Mark excitedly.

'OK. We'll go around the edge of the playground. It's about two hundred metres right round. Think you can manage it?'

'I'll try, Dieter.'

'You'd better because I don't want to have to carry you with my back.'

It was the first time that Eric had ever seen Mark smile, and he felt as elated as the young man.

'There's no debris to worry about,' Eric

continued as they set off. 'I borrowed a broom and swept a path clear after lunch.'

'Tell me what you can see, please, Dieter.'

'Not much really. The school is in a residential area. Most of it is surrounded by a high wall. There's some damage to a nearby house, which must be where all the bits of roof tiles came from.'

'The V2 is a terrible weapon, Dieter. The people who designed and built it, and those that fired it so randomly into civilian areas must be monsters.'

'Like those that bombed Dresden?' Eric queried. To change the subject he said, 'You're better off than me with those bandages because there's a lot of masonry dust about. Those pneumatic drills we can hear in the distance must mean that they've started rebuilding the place. All the guards seem to have gone now that we've all given our parole – not that you and I are in any state to go rushing off anywhere, and where would we go?'

They continued their slow walk for some minutes.

'What's in the little muslin bag tied to your wrist?' Eric asked when he shifted his grip on Mark's arm and saw the bag. 'A talisman?'

'Splinters – bits of the plastic canopy that the doctors removed from my face and eyes. They thought it would be a good idea if I kept it with me in case other doctors wanted to see them.'

They walked in silence for another five

minutes. Mark's paces slowed, and his weight on Eric's arm became more noticeable.

'I'm sorry, Dieter. But I need a breather.'

'There's a big water tank straight ahead. Another ten metres.'

The two men sat on the water tank for five minutes before they returned to their ward.

That day set the pattern for the rest of that week. On the third day Eric commented to his charge when they were sitting on the water tank, 'Well that's two circuits without your having to park yourself on this bloody cold thing.'

'It's good of you to take all this trouble, Dieter. I don't know how I can ever repay you.'

'There's nothing to thank me for. If I wasn't looking after your worthless self, I'd be sitting around bored to death.'

Mark laughed.

Two days later, unaware that Sister Theresa often watched their progress from her office window, Mark managed to break into a stride for a short distance, and the day after that Eric found him a walking stick so that he could practise finding his way along the perimeter wall, unaided but under Eric's watchful eye. After that Mark's confidence improved, so that he could find his way along the corridor to the lavatories without calling for a nurse or a hospital orderly. His proudest moment came when he fetched Eric a glass of water. After that they and other POW patients were allowed to leave the hospital but they had to wear a tracksuit-like garment with an orange spot on the back. 'And no posting letters, remember,' was the army captain's warning.

Eric thought that the populace would show resentment towards servicemen from the country that had caused them so much suffering but there was very little other than the occasional hostile stare, which was surprising because Eric was astounded by the damage that the A4s had caused around the waterfront. They chose a morning for their first trip when there had been rain to keep down the brick dust. Grabs and bulldozers were at work, clearing rubble which was being used to repair the moles and quays. The great port of Antwerp had made a determined start on rebuilding itself. Ships were unloading cement to feed the roaring concrete mixers. German POWs, watched by British soldiers, were filing up a gangplank to board a ship. Antwerp was the neck of the Allies' giant funnel, the vital beachhead feeding men and supplies in and out of Europe.

Eric kept up a constant description of what was going on for Mark's benefit while all the time looking out for American servicemen who might be able to direct him to their headquarters. He would be giving himself up to another of the Allies, so he did not consider that such a move could be considered a violation of his parole. But the only US servicemen he saw looked more likely to be interested in the whereabouts of the red-light district. The British military police were everywhere. They made Eric uneasy because the peaks of their caps were drawn down over their eyes so that it was impossible to know what they were looking at. Two of them stopped the POWs and examined the blue passes that the army captain at the hospital had issued. Their faces were hard and unfriendly. The sergeant stared at Eric as though he were examining his innermost secrets.

A letter was awaiting Mark when they returned, which Eric read to the young officer. The news caused Mark to give a loud whoop of joy. The letter was from his father. He said that his American hosts had agreed to take him to Antwerp to visit his son the following Friday – in two days' time.

'What does he mean by his American hosts?' Eric queried.

Mark had no idea.

Eric's next task was to find a safety razor for Mark.

'He's hopeless with an ordinary razor,' he told Sister Theresa. 'He'll cut his head off and he wants to smarten up for his father's visit.'

The nun promised to locate one and produced it the following day, when she found, much to her surprise, that Eric and Mark were playing poker.

'Pin pricks,' Mark explained, showing Sister Theresa his hand. 'Dieter's idea. He's made one pin prick at the top of the card for clubs, two pin pricks for diamonds, and so on. The pin pricks down the side are for the card's value.' He smiled happily. '*And* I'm winning.'

'It's because I can't see his face under all those bandages,' Eric growled. 'It gives him a huge advantage. He's won all the boiled sweets the hospital visitors gave us.'

'He refuses to admit that he's a lousy poker player,' said Mark, grinning.

'I'm not sure I approve of gambling in my hospital, gentlemen.'

'Don't worry, Sister,' Eric replied sourly. 'I'll steal them back when he's not looking.'

Mark found this very funny and flopped back on his pillow laughing. Laughter was something the nun never expected to hear from the young naval officer. She gave Eric the safety razor and moved around the ward, making some of the patients more comfortable. She paused at the door to watch the two happy gamblers in the corner beds before returning to her office, her face drawn in thought.

The next morning was spent with Eric helping get Mark looking presentable for his father's visit at midday. Mark had never used a safety razor but he insisted on learning to use it without Eric's help and bundled him out of the lavatory, saying that the lack of mirrors wasn't a problem.

The cuts on Mark's face and the tufts of unshaved beard provoked so much laughter from the other patients when he returned to the ward that a nurse bustled in, cleaned

Mark up, and ordered the two men back to their beds.

Sister Theresa entered the ward and told two cleaners to sweep up as best they could around the crowded beds. They were even required to polish everything in sight and clean the windows. The nurse went around straightening bed covers and arranging pillows.

'What's all the fuss about?' Eric asked her.

'VIP visitors, I think.'

'What VIPs?'

'How should I know? They'll be here in an hour. No one is to mess the place up or Sister will kill me.'

'But my father's due soon,' said Mark anxiously. 'He won't be stopped from seeing me, will he?'

'I've no idea,' said the nurse. 'You'll have to ask Sister Theresa.'

To allay Mark's worries, Eric went in search of the senior nun. She wasn't in her office and he was ordered back to his bed by a beefy Queen Alexandra's nurse noted for her short temper. All the POW patients were a little scared of her. Eric obeyed. He shrugged at Mark and settled down in his bed to read a two-day-old copy of the London *Times*. At least his injuries had healed sufficiently for him to be able to use a back rest. He had been told that he would most likely be discharged from the hospital within the next two or three days and transferred to a holding camp to await repatriation. Repatriation where? But he had been warned that it would be a slow process, perhaps as long as a year, which meant that the problem could be postponed for the time being. Another problem that couldn't be postponed much longer was to tell Mark that he would be leaving soon.

There was a commotion in the corridor shortly before noon. Voices, laughter, and to Eric's alarm and the amazement of the other patients, several photographers backed into the ward, popping their flashes at a tall, rugged man in his fifties, wearing a suit that clashed with his leathern, weathered features. He was accompanied by Sister Theresa. She pointed to Mark's bed. 'There he is, Mr Schiller. Mark – here's your father to see you!'

Eric sank out of sight behind his *Times*. Photographers! What the hell was going on? Two pressmen carrying 16mm movie cameras crammed into the ward in time to capture Max Schiller pushing his way to his astonished son's bed.

'Dad!' said Mark tearfully, reaching out his arms in the direction of his father's voice. 'It's so wonderful to see you!'

'Doesn't look like you are seeing me, Mark,' Max Schiller boomed cheerfully. 'Wonderful to see you, too, boy. Looks like you've been in the wars!'

The big man sat on the bed and hooked a brawny arm around his son's shoulders. The camera shutters went crazy. There were American-accented yells from the photographers telling Mark to look at the cameras.

'He can't see the damned cameras,' said Mark's father good-naturedly.

'Can your son speak English, Mr Schiller?'

'Better than me!'

'Well, get your son to speak in English, please.'

Mark turned his head from left to right in bewilderment to capture the source of all the sounds as flashes popped and movie cameras whirred. Everyone seemed to be talking at once. 'Dad! What's happening? Who are all these people?'

'Press. These guys have got everything wrong, as usual,' said Max in English.

'Your pa's a hero,' said a voice, speaking in a slow Texan drawl. 'So you're Mark? Can you follow what I'm saying, Mark?'

'Yes, of course,' said Mark, replying in English.

'Well, just after Christmas your pa hid the crew of a crashed B-42 in the cellar of his farmhouse. He set the navigator's broken leg, too.'

'Easier than animals,' said Max dismissively. 'You get told where the pain is.'

The newsmen laughed. Eric sank deeper behind the security of his newspaper, his mind racing. He desperately needed to contact the Americans but to do so here, with newsmen and under these bizarre circumstances, would be impossible.

'By the end of the war he had ten USAAF airmen hidden from the Nazis.'

'I'd heard that the scum were shooting some they'd captured,' Max explained. 'I didn't particularly like the American airmen dropping bombs on me but I was damned if I was going to let the SS get their hands on them. That would have been wrong.'

There was more laughter. More flashes.

'But surely they searched for them?' Mark exclaimed, forgetting to speak English for the moment.

'Nearly every day,' said Max Schiller with feeling. 'Remember the old cellar under the big barn? In there. And I put the pigs in the barn. All of them. Those SS didn't like getting pigshit on their fancy uniforms, so they didn't look too hard. Then one day there are Sherman tanks everywhere, chewing up my fields, so I hand the airmen over to their fellow countrymen, and then all this nonsense happens.'

'But supposing you'd been caught!'

'Well, I wasn't.'

Sister Theresa clapped her hands and told the press that it was time to leave Mr Schiller alone with his son for a while. The photographers snatched their last pictures as they were shooed from the ward and peace was restored. Max Schiller sat on Mark's bed with his back to Eric. The two men were in deep and earnest conversation. Eric caught the occasional sentence. 'There's an American colonel, I met,' Max said, raising his voice. 'Very high up. I'm going to see him and see what can be done about you.'

'Please don't make a fuss, father. They've been good to me here.'

'You'd be better off with the Americans looking after you. This isn't a proper hospital.'

They talked for a few more minutes. Max Schiller's mention of the Americans and that he knew a senior US officer set Eric's mind racing.

'Mr Muller?'

Eric lowered his newspaper. Mark's father grasped his hand in a powerful grip and shook it. 'Mr Muller – Mark's been telling me about all you've been doing for him. I want to thank you from the bottom of my heart.'

'It's nothing, Mr Schiller. Really.'

'Well, that's not how Mark sees it. And nor do I. I aim to do something about it.'

'I'm glad to hear that, Mr Schiller,' said Eric earnestly. 'Forgive me, but I overheard you say that you knew a high-ranking American officer who might be able to help Mark.'

'That's right. I'm going to find him as soon as I leave here.'

'Try to get him to come here to see the conditions at first hand,' Eric urged. 'The staff are fantastic – one cannot fault their dedication, but the conditions ... The overcrowding ... Well – you can see for yourself.'

'That's a good idea, Mr Muller. While this press mob is following me about, there's nothing that the Americans won't do.'

When all was quiet again in the makeshift ward, Eric reflected that it been one of those two paces forward days.

13

'We can cross Dornberger off our "A" list,' Johnny Benyon announced when Ian Fleming walked into his dusty, paper-strewn office and perched on the corner of a desk. 'We've got him.'

Benyon had agreed to accept a short-term posting from London to run Fleming's Antwerp office, which was on the top floor of an undamaged repository that served as a British HQ building. Benyon was a first-class analyst of German documents, with a remarkable memory and an eye for detail that had served him well as a journalist, and even more so as an intelligence officer. Since joining Fleming's unit he had already identified several important V2 production engineers, and three designers who had worked on the experimental Walther gas-turbine U-boat. Being near the border, Antwerp was the focal point for key German weapons personnel fleeing from the Russians and seeking the United States forces.

Fleming looked surprised at the news and

with good reason. General Walter Dornberger was the Head of the German Army's A4 rocket research programme. He was the organizational genius who had formed and welded together the team of brilliant scientists headed by Wernher von Braun who had produced the V2. 'When you say "we", Johnny, I take you mean the Americans have got him?'

'No, Ian. *We've* got him. I don't have the details of his capture yet, but it seems that he blundered into the 44th Infantry near Oberammergau. He's kicking up a stink, demanding to be handed over to the Americans and saying that he refuses to work for the British.'

'Sounds like a sensible man.'

'By all accounts he's a prickly bugger, but there are more important matters to deal with, Ian. I've scrounged a War Office issue Primus off the army and I have some real coffee.'

'Now that's definitely on top of the immediate action basket,' said Fleming. 'How did you manage that?'

'Antwerp may be half-flattened but it's a city that likes proper coffee. You ought to do some shopping while you're here.'

Benyon rose. In the corner of the office was an antique Primus stove. He pumped up the pressure, lit it, and placed a kettle on the burner ring. 'How's Berlin?' he enquired.

'Exciting,' said Fleming with relish. He was enjoying his job even though it was delaying his plans to build a house in Jamaica on the land that June Benyon had bought on his behalf. 'There's a sweaty, hair-trigger tension about the place. Everyone eyeing everyone one else in suspicion. Like the countdown to a gunfight in a Western. The Russians fought hard to take Berlin and don't like the Allies horning in. They're suspicious, surly and just plain bloody-minded. They make the most marvellous villains.'

'There's plenty of suspicious eyeing up and down going on here,' said Benyon, adjusting the Primus. 'The Americans are pushing for more access to our POW cages. They're putting everything into their Operation Paperclip.'

'Do they know we've got Dornberger?'

'Yes,' said Benyon seriously, straightening up from the Primus that was refusing to provide a strong flame. 'We've got a slight problem there, Ian. I've learned that this job involves a lot more than just catching them, there are vexed political problems of what to do with them when we've caught them. Some lawyers from public prosecutions have already been to see Dornberger to question him. I tried to block them from poking their noses in but was too late. My bet is that they're toying with the idea of hanging civilian charges on him: waging war on civilians, or something like that.'

Fleming crossed to the window and stared out at Antwerp's waterfront devastation. 'Letting the public prosecutions office loose on him at this early stage might be a mistake,' he mused. 'They'd have to prove that his object was to wage war on civilians. And I'd certainly want to find out if that is true and also if he was behind the plan to launch V2s from U-boats.'

'Exactly,' said Benyon. 'Dornberger is a serving army officer. He has to be treated as a prisoner of war. The Red Cross have already been giving us problems with the few technical officers we've nabbed so far. It would be sensible to hold Dornberger as a prisoner of war until there's a solid civil case against him. You can be bloody certain that the Americans aren't reacting like us.'

'You're right,' said Fleming slowly, weighing up the political furore that might follow if Dornberger were treated as a criminal. 'Our best bet is treat him as a POW, and to treat him well. That way no one can jump on our backs.'

'That means not sending him to one of the cages we've set up here,' said Benyon. 'They're pretty grim. And not that Island Camp Farm hellhole in Wales where the idiots have sent Rundstedt. Haven't we got any POW holiday camps in England? What about that place in the Lake District?'

Fleming grinned. 'That's what I like about you, Johnny. The problems you highlight in good time for them to be dealt with quickly are always accompanied by practical suggestions and solutions for ways of dealing with them. I'll see what can be done about

Dornberger.' He reached forward and picked up some photographs from an empty desk. The first was of a fleshy faced, fair-headed man. He was in a group. His arm was in a sling and held horizontal by a supporting cradle.

'Wernher von Braun,' Benyon commented when Fleming held up the picture. 'Now an American guest of honour. A major catch for them.'

'So who's at the top of our "A" list now that we've got Dornberger?' Fleming asked.

Benyon sorted through some papers on his desk. 'A civilian. Dr Eric Hoffmann. He's at the top of the American Operation Paperclip list, too.'

'Why?'

'Hoffmann is a big fish. Before the war he was a member of the same rocket society that von Braun belonged to. I've found a few articles he wrote for German science magazines about schemes to go to the moon.'

'Another dreamer,' Fleming mused. 'Peenemunde seems to have been full of them.'

'Hoffmann's been mainly based at the V2 production facility at Nordhausen in the Hartz Mountains for the past two years,' said Benyon. 'He had a lucky escape in the big RAF raid on Peenemunde. It seems he's good at sorting out problems and coming up with fast solutions. He had a mobile workshop and drawing office which he used to bring out to the V2 launch batteries near here that were firing on London and Antwerp. He'd sort out the problem, produce modification drawings and send them back to Nordhausen.'

'Sounds like a clever chap.'

'He's certainly that, all right. But trouble-shooting isn't his speciality. He only did that because he was available.'

'And what was is his speciality?'

'Regenerative cooling.'

Fleming frowned. 'What the devil's that?'

Benyon nodded to the kettle that was just beginning to sing. 'That kettle's made of aluminium and it's sitting on flames that are hotter than the melting point of aluminium. The kettle doesn't melt because the water keeps the aluminium cool. The combustion chamber and the big thrust nozzle on a V2's rocket engine have to withstand temperatures far higher than the melting point of the aluminium they're made of. Cooling them works in the same way as the water in that kettle, but in V2 engines the coolant used is the actual fuel – liquid oxygen. On its way to being burnt in the combustion chamber, it's first pumped around the combustion chamber's outer skin so that it forms a cooling jacket that conducts the heat away.'

'Sounds damned dangerous,' Fleming observed.

Benyon smiled. 'It is. Failure of the cooling system and the chamber walls caused some spectacular blow-ups during test launches. But, from what we've learned, Eric Hoffmann's designs soon had the problem under control. My contacts in Army Intelligence have unearthed some interesting drawings showing that Hoffmann was working with von Braun on the combustion chamber designs of a very large rocket engine – one that could deliver a one tonne warhead over 2000 kilometres – about 1200 miles. They also had the idea of putting a small rocket on top of a big rocket so that the smaller rocket could fire up and carry on when the parent rocket was spent. That little theoretical nasty had a range of twice that.'

'Hell,' Fleming muttered.

There was silence in the office apart from the kettle's preliminary hiss.

'Has anything come up to link him with the plan to launch V2s from U-boats?'

'Not yet, Ian.'

'And the blighter seems to have disappeared without trace?' Fleming queried.

'Just before the Soviets overran the place, Dornberger visited Nordhausen and advised all his senior technicians and heads of departments to head west and give themselves up to the Americans. We know that Hoffmann hasn't done so yet, and that no one answering his description has been found because we get the daily lists of intakes into the civilian cage. We also know that Hoffmann was clever, fit, and resourceful. The chances are that he took the shortest route between Nordhausen and here like his colleagues. He's somewhere in the vicinity and he'll be found.'

'Let's hope we find him first,' said Fleming.

Benyon busied himself with the kettle to make coffee. 'Would you like to take a close look at a V2, Ian? The Royal Artillery have got one – complete with a mobile launch vehicle and its original battery team – all POWs. They're putting on a launch set-up demo tomorrow for some brass.'

Fleming brightened. He loved the mystery and aura of futuristic secret weapons. 'I'd love to,' he enthused.

14

'*B*,' said Mark.

'Try again,' said Eric patiently.

Mark ran his fingertips over the raised dots that Eric had made by pushing a pin through the piece of a get well card that he had cut into small squares. The two men were sitting outdoors. The water tank in the grounds of the hospital had been cleared away by workmen. In its place was a park bench.

'*Y*!' Mark exclaimed. 'I got the bottom dot round the wrong way.'

'Very good. And this?' Eric placed another card in the blind officer's fingers.

'*E*.'

'Try again.'

Mark felt the single dot. 'Well, if it's not an *E*, it must be an *A*.'

'It's an *A*.'

'Dieter – how can I tell the difference between an *A* and an *E* when there aren't other letters beside them?'

Mark had a valid point. The Braille cell consists of six dots arranged in three rows of two dots each like the dots for 6s on dice. The individual letters of the alphabet are achieved by variations in the configuration of the raised dots. In American Modified Braille, which Mark Schiller was learning, the letters *A* and *E* consist of single dots and are the simplest Braille characters of all because they are the two most frequently occurring letters in English. The problem that Mark described was because the dot for the letter *A* was on the top row of the cell, and the dot for an *E* dot was on the bottom row. Without adjoining letters to provide a position reference, it was impossible to determine which letter a single dot represented.

Eric took the card, checked the Braille reference card that one of the nurses had found for him, and added two dots with his pin. He gave the card back to Mark. 'OK – try again.'

'It's two letters – *R* and *A*. Two dots is an *R* so it's *R* and *A*. No it's not! No it's not!' Mark bit his lip as he concentrated hard on the information he was receiving from his fingertips. 'The two dots are at the bottom of the cell ... It's a capital *A*, Dieter!'

'Brilliant!' Eric exclaimed in genuine admiration. 'You really are a fast learner.' He looked at his score card. 'You got 72 per cent that time. The highest yet.'

'Another test, please, Dieter.'

This time Mark scored 81 per cent. He gave a whoop of joy and hugged himself in pleasure when Eric gave him the result.

His triumphant cry attracted Sister Theresa's attention when she entered her office. She watched the two men through her open window, picked up a large volume, and left her office.

Mark stopped concentrating on his test card and said, 'Sister Theresa cometh.'

Eric looked up and was surprised to see the elderly nun approaching. The nun was equally surprised when Mark greeted her by name without prompting from Eric.

'You're getting too clever, young man,' she commented. She picked up one of Eric's homemade test cards and admired the neatly positioned dots.

'I've just scored 81 per cent, Sister,' said Mark happily.

'Only three days, too,' said Eric. 'He's learning fast, Sister. The only thing that worries me is that I'm not a trained Braille teacher. I'm probably doing everything wrong. He might have to unlearn everything.'

'What does it matter so long as I can read?' said Mark emphatically. 'Dieter's been wonderful to me. I couldn't have had a better teacher.'

'Well, this might slow you down a little, young man,' said the nun, placing the book in

Mark's hands. 'It's Volume One of two. It's surprising just how big books in Braille are.'

Mark seized the book eagerly and ran his fingers over the cover. He found the large Braille title cells and read them without undue difficulty. '*T-R-E-E* – no – it's an *A. S-U. Treasure Island*! I used to love this book. Thank you so much, Sister.'

'I'm sorry but it's in English.'

'It doesn't matter! It really doesn't matter! It's a book.'

Mark opened the book and found the first line of text. His jubilant expression faded as he ran his fingers several times along the opening lines. 'Oh hell – sorry, Sister – this is going to be much harder than I thought.'

Sister Theresa beckoned to Eric and led him a few paces away. 'I've heard nothing from his father about any Americans coming to see him,' said the nun quietly.

'But they will come?'

'I've really no idea, Mr Muller. Why is it so important that you see them?'

'I need to tell them about Mark's needs.'

Sister Theresa watched the young man struggling to read. 'Perhaps you'd better write everything down, Mr Muller. My reasons for not discharging you are certain to be overruled any day now. The patient numbers are going down in the main hospital as servicemen patients who can travel are being sent home. This emergency hospital will close soon because the locals want their school back. You will be sent to one of the POW cages to await repatriation. I'll do my best but I can't guarantee that you and Mark will be kept together. I'm sorry.'

The nun smiled and returned to her office.

'Dieter! Listen to this!' said Mark excitedly and began reciting, his fingertips sliding hesitantly across the page. '"I remember him as if it were" something "as he came" something "to the inn door, his tea-chest following behind him in a hand-farrow."'

'Sea chest,' Eric corrected absently. 'And it's hand-barrow – not farrow.'

'I can now do something that you can't do, Dieter,' said Mark happily.

'Oh? And what's that?'

'Read in bed after lights out.'

Sister Theresa heard the laughter of the two men as she entered her makeshift hospital.

15

Fleming gazed up in wonder as the hydraulic rams on the V2's huge launch trailer gradually elevated the rocket to the vertical and lowered it gently to the ground. Clamps around the body of the weapon were released when one of the POWs – a former member of the Wehrmacht's Gruppe Nord Batterie 444 artillery team – shouted an OK. His clearance was signalled to the operator of the hydraulic controls in the cab of the big Damiler-Benz KM half-track towing vehicle. Three other POW members of the team pulled the clamps clear and shouted the all clear. The driver engaged gears and drove the half-track several metres, leaving the graceful weapon standing upright on its four stabilizer fins in the centre of the car park.

The Royal Artillery officer in charge of the demonstration raised a megaphone to address the small crowd of civilians and servicemen gathered in the car park of Antwerp's Rex cinema in the Keyserlei.

'As you can see, ladies and gentlemen,' said the army officer, 'any junction or crossroads could serve as a launch site, which is why the V2 was so dangerous and why they were still being launched against London and Antwerp up to within a month of the armistice. By comparison, the Luftwaffe's V1 flying bombs required large concrete ski-sites for their launching which were vulnerable to air attack. The next stage was to fill the weapon's tanks with fuel.'

A second KM half-track appeared, hauling a trailer loaded with large, wire-bound spheres. Working quickly and efficiently, the POW team dragged heavy hoses from the trailer and connected them up to charging points behind hatches set in the V2's skin.

'Those spherical tanks contained liquid oxygen – the V2's propellant fuel, ladies and gentlemen,' the Royal Artillery officer continued. 'At the height of the V2 offensive this team of POWs, all members of the German army's Batterie 444, were firing ten weapons each day – entire trainloads of V2s were keeping them supplied. Their battery commander, Oberleutant Anton Kessling – the POW in the blue tracksuit – says that they could've fired more but for shortages of liquid oxygen.'

When the demonstration was over, there followed a short service conducted by an army chaplain to commemorate the deaths of the 567 Allied servicemen and women, and civilians, who perished when a V2 scored a direct hit on the Rex cinema on 16th December 1944. Flowers were placed on a temporary memorial. Each member of the notorious Batterie 444 stepped forward in turn to add their posies and salutes. The service ended and the Germans returned to their V2, towering above the small crowd, and set to work to lower it back on to its transporter. The police allowed the crowd to mill around, asking the POWs questions.

Fleming crossed to the temporary memorial and studied the long list of names. Benyon joined him.

'Depressing,' was all he could think of to say.

Fleming was suddenly uncharacteristically animated. 'If they'd done this a few years ago – back in '41 or '42, Johnny – I could've understood. But they didn't.' He gestured at the V2. 'They starting firing that obscenity at London and then here *after* the D-Day landings, when they knew that all was lost, and when they knew that these things could not affect the outcome of the war.'

'Unless they'd found a way of giving them atomic warheads.'

'Which they didn't. They put everything into stepping up production at Nordhausen for the sole purpose of waging war on civilian populations. We're going to get them, Johnny. All of them. And we don't let lawyers near them to queer cases until the evidence against them is so strong that we won't need lawyers.'

Fleming walked away. Making his way through the crowd gave him time to think, to calm his anger. He approached the senior officer of the group of POWs who were lowering the V2.

'Good afternoon Oberleutnant Kessling. You were this battery's commanding officer, were you not?'

Anton Kessling turned and stared in surprise at the British naval officer who had addressed him in fluent German.

'Commander Ian Fleming, Royal Navy Volunteer Reserve,' said Fleming, holding out his hand.

Puzzled, the German army officer shook the offered hand and agreed that Fleming had the right man.

'An amazing weapon,' said Fleming, shading his eyes and gazing up at the V2's slender needle-like tip. 'It has a look of beauty and grace about it.'

The POW made a guarded, non-committal comment.

'I understand you have been extremely helpful since your capture,' Fleming continued. 'Perhaps you'd be so kind as to help me. I'm trying to find a fellow countryman of yours who is missing. We're concerned about him.'

Fleming produced a group photograph that included General Walter Dornberger and Wernher von Braun. Most of the men in the picture were smiling at the camera. 'Do you recognize any of these men, Oberleutnant? I believe it was taken at Peenemunde in 1940.'

The German officer took the picture and studied it closely. He pointed. 'That's General Dornberger. I met him once at a test firing in Poland. And that's *der Chef* himself –

Dr Wernher von Braun.'

'And the man on the right?'

It was a tall, dark-haired man, with a drawn, serious face. Aristocratic, haughty features. He was the only one in the group not smiling.

'Dr Eric Hoffmann,' said the artillery officer without hesitation. 'He was Dornberger's Mr Fixit. If we had a problem, he'd come out with his mobile workshop and two engineers, and he would come up with a design modification on the spot. He was a good man. Not like some of the dummies.'

'When did you last see him?'

'It must've been just before Christmas. It'll be in the battery's war diary.' He added pointedly, 'Which I've already handed over to the British.'

'Could you identify him if you were taken around to the POW cages?'

'Maybe ... If you can promise me that he's not wanted on civilian charges.'

'I can make no such guarantees,' said Fleming flatly. 'But we would appreciate your help in finding him.'

The German officer considered. So far co-operating with the victors had paid off; the British had treated him and his men well. He came to a decision. 'I'll help in any way I can, Commander Fleming. Now you must excuse me, please.' He jerked a thumb at the V2. 'Taking one of these down isn't as easy as setting one up.'

'Why is that?' Fleming asked.

The artillery man permitted himself a faint

smile. 'We don't have so much practice at taking them down. Once set up, we used to fire them, and then they became someone else's problem.'

The two men exchanged salutes and the German returned to his team.

As Fleming looked up at the majestic V2, it occurred to him that a story about a power-crazed maniac having such awesome weapons at his disposal would make a good thriller. He checked himself with the realization that this had already happened.

'One last thing, Oberleutnant,' Fleming called out. 'Did Dr Hoffmann ever talk about a plan to launch these things from U-boats?'

The German artillery officer shook his head. 'No, Commander.'

Someone clapped him on the back.

'Ian!' boomed a well-educated New York accent. 'Well, I'll be damned! What in hell are you doing here?'

It was Lieutenant Mike Roscoe, the US naval intelligence officer whom Fleming had first met in New York and again at the Jamaica conference.

'Mike!' Fleming exclaimed, genuinely delighted to see the big, amiable New Yorker, pumping his hand. 'What are you doing in Antwerp?'

'I was about to ask you the same question,' said Roscoe. 'Knowing your love of cloak and dagger stuff, I thought you'd be in Berlin, busy compromising Soviet top-brass with beautiful blondes.'

'I'd like to be,' said Fleming with feeling.

The American took Fleming's arm. 'Come on. The Keyserlei Hotel's got a well-stocked bar and there's some colleagues I'd like you to meet.'

Fleming was always eager to widen his circle of contacts, so he made his apologies to Benyon and willingly accompanied the American. Five minutes later he was relaxing in the hotel's undamaged American Bar, drinking pink gin and listening to Roscoe's account of the capture of the missing Type XXI U-boat that had been on its way to Japan.

'*Kentucky* picked her up on her radar five hundred miles east of Toyko,' Roscoe was saying. 'She was sitting on the surface. A fire had swept through her midships battery compartment and gutted everything. Her control room – radio room – the works. They couldn't dive because the batteries were still making chlorine gas. The poor saps didn't even know the war was over.'

A group of USAAF officers entered the bar, laughing and joking. Roscoe made the introductions.

'Fleming?' echoed a young lieutenant. He shook Fleming's hand, sat down and ordered a beer from the waiter. 'Ray Osborne. 101st Airborne Division press office. I've been in touch with your War Office with a problem. They said that you'd be the one here in Antwerp to help out.'

'I'll do what I can,' said Fleming guardedly.

'Have you heard of Max Schiller?'

'Can't say I have,' Fleming admitted. 'Why?'

'A big story back home,' said Roscoe.

'Max Schiller is looked on as a hero,' said Osborne. 'He's a German farmer – a vet – who hid some crashed USAAF airmen from the SS and the Gestapo.'

'Yes – I remember now.'

'The problem is that Max Schiller's son is a POW in a British-run POW hospital here in Antwerp,' Osborne continued. 'He's only eighteen. Blinded when he was captured. Pa wants his boy shipped off to England to receive proper treatment for his eyes. Your War Office is acting all officious and bloody-minded saying that all POWs are receiving equal treatment, and the best possible medical treatment at that, and that it would be wrong to single out one POW for special treatment. Blah blah blah.'

'Are his eyes treatable?'

Osborne shrugged. 'I don't know.'

'I know how the civil service mind works in such cases,' said Fleming. 'They don't like the unprecedented.'

'We think that a German farmer taking appalling risks without regard for his own life to hide crashed US airmen is pretty unprecedented,' said Osborne seriously. 'Some of the editorials back home are getting pretty hostile towards what they see as hidebound British bureaucracy. They want young Schiller sent home to the US to receive proper treatment.'

'Now that would have minor Whitehall bureaucrats manning the barricades,' said Fleming wryly. He thought for a moment. 'Could this story blow up?'

'It's already pretty big. It could go even bigger if I say it could,' said Osborne mildly.

'Can you give me twenty-four hours?'

'To achieve what?'

'A good, old-fashioned English compromise.'

'We're talking about a young man's eyesight – the son of a hero as far as the American people are concerned,' was the service pressman's reply. 'But OK. Twenty-four hours.'

16

Brenda Hobson made a minute adjustment to the balance's sliding weight, read Willi's weight, and entered it on her record card.

'Willi,' she said reprovingly, prodding his paunch. 'Another pound since last month.'

'How much is that, nurse?' said Willi, who knew perfectly well. Much of his black-market dealings during his four years as a POW in Grizedale Hall had been in pounds and ounces.

'About half a kilo. We're going to have to put you on a diet.'

'But our rations here *are* a diet,' Willi protested.

'Nonsense. You get the same amount of food as everyone else. Probably more if you're fond of your stock.' She cocked her head on one side and smiled. 'I suppose I could always have a word with Carol Bunce, Willi. Get her to chase you around the camp every morning. The pounds would roll off.'

Willi was far from amused but held his peace.

'All right, Willi. You can get dressed now.'

Willi felt much more secure once he had scrambled into his underpants. He finished getting dressed and left the sickbay. There was a line of POWs standing outside in the corridor for the monthly weigh-in. Some looking apprehensive at the ordeal of having to strip off for Nurse Hobson, and some, like Leutnant Walter Hilgard, a giant of a man who had been the leading chef on the *Bismarck*, actually relishing the ritual. 'A chance for these prissy English tarts to see what a real man looks like, and what they're missing,' was his proud boast.

'Next man,' said Willi to the man at the head of the queue and scuttled off to visit his money.

The routine and conditions at Grizedale Hall had changed dramatically since the armistice. The main gates were now permanently open and guarded more to keep the curious out rather than the POWs in. Subject to certain parole conditions, such as not being allowed to travel more than ten miles from the hall, or post letters that didn't go through the censors, and having to be back in the camp by 1800 each evening, and not wear uniforms outside the camp, the majority of the prisoners enjoyed considerable freedom while they waited for their repatriation papers: some with great eagerness, and some, those whose homes were now under Soviet domination, less so. Occasionally there were POWs who were not allowed out of the camp. They were those under investigation into serious charges but such prisoners were rare.

Many even got casual jobs on local farms and formed more than casual relationships with Women's Land Army girls whenever the opportunity presented itself. Willi was the notable exception. He would venture out to visit his buyers only when he had made certain that Carol Bunce wasn't waiting for him. The demobilization of the British army was proving a slow process, which meant that German POWs were still the only young men in the area who were readily available. Sergeant Finch's guard had been reduced to ten men.

Other than the morning and evening roll-calls, there was one prison-camp routine that was unchanged: every month Nurse Brenda Hobson supervised a shivering procession of naked POWs on and off her sickbay scales. She also looked for nits in their scalps and pubic hair, and grasped their scrotums while requiring them to cough. The slightest lewd comment from a POW during the latter process was reported immediately to Otto Kruger who gave the offending prisoner a verbal roasting in his office. Not even Leutnant Walter Hilgard dared make a comment even though his scrotum resembled two medicine balls in a cricket bag, obliging Brenda to use both hands to make her mysterious diagnosis.

'Willi!'

The combination of the imperious cry and Willi's permanently guilty conscience conspired to pull him up short as he trotted across the courtyard. At least it wasn't Carol Bunce. He gave a sigh of relief when he saw that the caller was the harmless Private Knox.

'Willi – do you want to make a bob or two?' It was a singularly stupid question to put to Leutnant Willi Hartmann.

'Maybe,' said Willi cautiously.

'I need a birthday card, Willi. A really nice birthday card. Not those awful pulp cards that the local shops sell – they're nothing more than a sheet of folded paper.'

'Birthday cards usually have messages inside them,' said Willi. 'Who's it for? Mother? Father?'

'For the sweetest, most wonderful girl in the world,' said Private Knox dreamily.

'Ah. Nurse Hobson?'

'Who else. She means as much to me as Carol Bunce means to you. She's such a lovely girl, Willi. She has a wonderful warm heart.'

‘And cold hands. Two quid.’

Private Knox was shocked. It was an outrageous amount and he said so. ‘Girls are paying that sort of money for nylon stockings and silk underwear. Not bloody cards.’

‘Look,’ said Willi patiently. ‘Two quid gets you an American scented card in a box that will have a satin-covered heart on it. She’ll fall swooning into your arms.’

‘Do you really think so, Willi?’

‘I know so.’

‘All right. Two pounds.’

‘When do you want the card by?’

‘Well – her birthday’s on the 1st of July.’

‘How do you know?’

Private Knox looked pained. ‘Willi – I’m a journalist.’

That gave Willi three weeks. No problem for his principal stationery supplier – the lady who owned the general stores at the nearby village of Satterthwaithe. She could get fancy prices for Willi’s bags of sugar and small bars of Toblerone and use one to bribe a stationery sales rep. With luck, Willi reckoned, he’d make fifteen shillings on the deal. ‘I’ll get one for you by the end of next week,’ he promised, and they shook hands on the deal.

‘You’re a pal, Willi.’

‘Is that right about girls paying two pounds for silk underwear?’

‘That’s what my cousin was saying she paid for a pair of French knickers. Oh – I nearly forgot, Major Reynolds would like to see you in his office.’

The news alarmed Willi. 'Have my repatriation papers come through?' He was wanted in his home town by the police for questioning in connection with their enquiries about a thousand Swiss watches that had disappeared from a warehouse in 1937. Willi knew that the Bavarian police were unlikely to allow a war to interfere with their investigations.

'No. I don't think so, Willi.' With that, Private Knox went off to see if the love of his life had finished weighing and doing other things to her POWs that he wished she'd do to him.

With his mind feverishly at work on French knickers and such items of women's underwear, although his thoughts were not motivated by any sexual interest, Willi tapped cautiously on Major Reynolds's office door and entered. He blinked in surprise at the good-looking, hard-faced Wehrmacht officer in an immaculate full-length leather overcoat who rose to his feet as Willi entered. All thoughts about exotic underwear fled when he saw from the stranger's collar tabs that he was a major-general.

'This is Leutnant Willi Hartmann,' said Reynolds. 'Commander Kruger's adjutant. Willi – will you please escort General Dornberger to Commander Kruger's office.'

'Let's hope this place is more agreeable than the dump I was sent to in Wales, Leutnant,' said Dornberger aggressively, thrusting a valise into Willi's hand that nearly dislocated his shoulder with its weight. 'You can take this to my suite and run me a bath.'

17

The smell of coffee attracted Fleming from Benyon's outer office, where he had been administering a mild upbraiding to an apologetic Wren signals clerk. The charm Fleming could apply ensured that the girl was pleased to receive a ticking off. On balance he was pleased with his Antwerp office now that it was set up and running smoothly. Just a few hiccups to iron out and he could return to Berlin.

Johnny Benyon looked up from his desk, which was strewn with American newspapers. Another WRNS girl was making coffee.

'Problems?' Benyon queried.

'Nothing serious. My signal suggesting that Dornberger should *not* to be sent to Island Farm Camp was sent as a suggestion that he *should* be sent to Island Camp Farm. Caused a bit of a flurry in Wales. Hate at first sight between him and von Rundstedt. They fought like cats.'

Benyon grinned. 'So you blamed one of my

girls and not your bloody awful handwriting?'

'A bit of both, old man.'

The girl gave each officer a mug of coffee and withdrew. She had made it black and strong, the way Fleming liked it. He sipped it appreciatively and idly turned over the pages of one of the American newspapers on Benyon's desk. 'So you've taken to reading American comic pages in government time?' Fleming observed. 'Don't you know there's a peace to be won?'

Benyon grimaced. 'Those newspapers are a present from your friend Lieutenant Osborne in the 101st's press office. All about Max Schiller and how he's been treated as a hero. And how his son, Mark, is being denied proper treatment for his eyes by the British authorities in Antwerp. Bloody unfair if you ask me. I've checked – he's had three trips to the eye clinic in the main hospital.'

'So what actually happened to Schiller junior's eyes?'

Benyon picked up a paper. 'He was trying to pilot a Biber midget submarine into the port here and his canopy was shattered by rifle fire. Splinters wrecked his eyes. They've removed the splinters but they'd punctured right into the poor sod's eyes and wrecked the lenses. They had to removed. To make matters worse, his corneas aren't healing and there's bugger all, if anything, that can be done until they do.'

'Ironic,' Fleming mused. 'Remember how the question of the Biber midget U-boats was on the agenda of the Jamaica conference? It was decided that they were a bigger danger to their one-man crews than they were to us.'

'That lot's now our biggest danger,' said Benyon, indicating a pile of signal flimsies. 'The London hospitals are inundated. Working flat out round the clock. None of them can squeeze in another case, and certainly not a POW because they're already having to put our own servicemen on long waiting lists.'

Fleming examined a newspaper photograph that showed a beaming Max Schiller sitting on a hospital bed with his arm around a younger version of himself with heavily bandaged eyes. He read the story. Mark Schiller was only 18. Fleming experienced a wave of anger towards a regime that had sent mere boys into battle with shoddily made weapons. Something about the picture interested him. He picked up another newspaper and examined the pictures taken in the ward of the temporary hospital.

'Notice anything odd about these pictures?' he asked.

Benyon looked at the newspaper Fleming was studying. 'No. Why? Should I?'

'All the other patients in the ward are gaping at the cameras, as well they might – it must've been quite an invasion. Yet the chap in the corner bed is hiding behind a newspaper, not showing any interest. A dog that's not barking.'

'Eh?'

'Sherlock Holmes,' said Fleming. 'His point on a case was that the dog *didn't* bark. Hospital routine is deadly boring and yet this gentleman isn't showing any interest. It's the same in every photograph. Odd.'

'So what are we going to do about this Mark Schiller? Try sending him to Switzerland or something?'

'Good God, no. That could cause a hell of a row.' Fleming thought for a moment and had an idea. 'Are the phone lines to London OK, Johnny?'

'Still a bit pot-luckish but getting better,' Benyon replied. 'You just have to take a chance.'

Fleming picked up the telephone on an empty desk and requested a call to room 39 in the Admiralty, London. The connection was made a few minutes later and he exchanged a few opening pleasantries with his secretary. 'Listen, Sally,' said Fleming after the girl had answered his enquiry about her mother's health. 'We've got a little problem. Nothing desperately urgent but one I'd like cleared up and out of the way because we've got better things to do.' He briefly described the problem with Mark Schiller and his father's fame in America. As Fleming expected, Sally grasped the political implications immediately.

'So what do you want me to do, sir?'

'Can you dig out the Grizedale Hall file, please. If memory serves, there was an incident, in 1941 I think, in which a POW built a wireless transmitter. Something blew up in his face when he was bending over the wireless and he was sent to a hospital's eye people to have some poisonous stuff removed from his eyes. If I remember, they did a first-class job.'

'You want the name of the hospital, sir?'

'And anything else you can find out, please, Sally.'

'I'll call you back in two hours, sir,' Sally promised.

'That girl's an angel,' said Fleming, replacing the handset.

Sally was as good as her word. The phone was ringing when Fleming and Benyon returned from lunch. Fleming signalled Benyon to listen in on his telephone.

'Have you got a pen and paper ready, sir?'

Benyon tossed Fleming a writing pad.

'OK, Sally. Fire away.'

'You were right about 1941, sir,' Sally reported. 'I have a copy of Major James Reynolds's report. 'It was Wehrmacht officer Hauptmann Dietrich Berg.'

'That's the fellow!'

'He's still at Grizedale Hall, sir. What happened was that he'd converted a domestic wireless to work as a transmitter. Doing so meant overloading the set considerably. This caused an electronic – correction – an electrolytic condenser to explode in his face. He was taken to the general at Barrow-in-Furness. Their ophthalmic department did the best they could to remove all the particles from Berg's eyes but they couldn't be sure what post-operative treatment was best because they didn't know what the material was, and Hauptmann Berg wouldn't tell them. Whatever it was, it was causing a nasty reaction. Once Commander Kruger was told that Berg could lose his eyesight, he admitted that the component that had exploded was a wireless condenser. The stuff was tantalum – a toxic heavy metal used in electrolytic condensers. Once they knew this, the hospital was able to save Dietrich Berg's eyesight.'

'Excellent, Sally,' said Fleming writing quickly. He clarified a few points, corrected his notes, and said, 'I'm very grateful. You've done well. So it seems that Barrow-in-Furness general knows its stuff. Right – my next task is to see if they'll take on young Mark Schiller.'

'They will. I hope you don't mind, sir, but I took it on myself to speak to the eye department's registrar. Mark Schiller will be admitted as an out-patient under Sir Marcus Welling – the noted ophthalmic surgeon. Mark Schiller is now outpatient number 4455. I thought that all that would look good in the press release, sir.'

Fleming and Benyon were astonished. 'Good!' Fleming echoed. 'My God, Sally – you've performed a miracle! This Welling is a top eye surgeon?'

'Well ... According to the registrar, he must be ninety now and they haven't seen him for several years. But he's still the boss. It's his name on everything. Here's something else that will look good in the press release: Mark Schiller's first appointment is for a week today at 1430 to see Mr Davison – the eye department's registrar. Am I right in assuming that Mark Schiller is still a POW?'

Benyon looked as though he were about to faint.

'Yes,' said Fleming, numbed, wondering what the miracle worker in his London office was going to announce next.

'I thought so,' said Sally. 'I've called Major Reynolds at Grizedale Hall to warn him to expect him. Which means ... Excuse me a minute while I check my list. Yes – which means that everything's taken care of at this end that I can do. I thought I'd better leave drafting the press release to you, sir.'

The line went quiet.

'Sir?'

'Yes, Sally?'

'Was my taking all that on OK? Only it seemed that the whole thing was worrying you so much that I thought—'

'You've done wonderfully, Sally,' Fleming interrupted to reassure her. 'Everything is perfectly OK and I can't thank you enough. It's just that you've given me a lot to brood on. I'll call you tomorrow and let you know what's happening.'

Fleming and Benyon replaced their respective receivers and stared at other, both temporarily lost for words.

'You know,' said Benyon at length. 'That

girl really is something. Did you ever feel that she might've done your job in the N.I.D. better than you did?'

Fleming smiled wryly. 'She was always a bit like you, Johnny. Good at seeing problems and having solutions ready.'

'Well I don't have a solution to the next problem.'

'Which is?'

'We have to get the boy to the Lake District.'

'We can raise the necessary travel warrants and his documents.'

'I wasn't thinking of that. He can't see. He's blind. He's going to need more than just an escort. He's going to need a permanent guide. How do we convince the army that we'll need at least two soldiers to look after him full time? Three shifts – a total of six soldiers. I had the devil of a job getting that Primus stove out of them.'

Fleming bit his lip as he turned the problem over. 'We'll jump through that hoop when we come to it. The first thing is for you to get over to the hospital and give the lad the news.'

18

General Dornberger marched into Kruger's office without knocking.

'That man is a crook,' he announced angrily.

Kruger looked up from his desk. 'Who is a crook, General?'

'That damned adjutant of yours!'

'You mean Leutnant Hartmann?'

'The fat one. He charged me a bar of shaving soap for an extra pillow, and a packet of safety razors for a bedside lamp. I've just learned that officers of my rank are entitled to them anyway. He's said I can have a larger room for two pounds in English money. This behaviour is outrageous.'

'Willi does tend to take his job as camp supplies officer seriously. But he has redeeming features – not many, but a few. He always knocks on doors before entering, for example.'

The General wasn't listening. 'It's not his job to swindle fellow officers,' he snapped. 'That he gets away with it, and is fat and overweight, is a general symptom of your lax discipline.'

Kruger rose, his expression cold. 'When you

arrived here, General, I offered to step down immediately as senior officer. You declined, saying that you didn't want trifling responsibilities. Your decision carried with it acceptance of the responsibilities of a prisoner of war towards his senior officer. Those include observing common courtesies such as knocking on doors before entering. Regarding your entitlements due to your rank, you'll be pleased to know that you're entitled to, not one vegetable plot, but two. Plots 12 and 13. They've been neglected of late because the numbers of officers here has gone down. Willi will issue you with a spade, a hoe, and a rake and will require no additional payment for them. Because you're not allowed out of the camp, I'm sure you will glad of this opportunity to keep yourself occupied. I shall be inspecting the plots tomorrow and will expect to see that you've made a start on cultivating them.'

General Dornberger looked stunned. He was unaccustomed to junior officers who were not intimidated by his rank or bluster. He opened his mouth to speak, thought better of it, turned on his heel and strode out of the office without saluting. Perhaps some of Kruger's harsh words had registered because he left the door open instead of slamming it.

Kruger sat, regretting that he had to speak so sharply to a brilliant man who had done so much for his country, whose amazing V2 had nearly given it victory.

'Willi!' he yelled angrily, knowing that his adjutant would be hovering within earshot. Willi appeared in the doorway, his moonlike face a picture of worry. He was clutching a slim package under his arm.

'Commander?'

'Come in and shut the door.'

Willi obeyed.

'You've been upsetting General Dornberger.'

'I'm sorry, Commander, but—'

'Keep up the good work, Willi,' said Kruger brusquely.

Willi blinked, not certain that he had heard right.

'What's that, Willi?'

'What's what, Commander?'

'That paper bag you're trying to hide.'

'A birthday card, Commander.'

Kruger held out his hand. Willi reluctantly handed the bag over. Inside was a slender cardboard box which Kruger opened. He regarded the ornate card for moment and read the printed inscription inside. '"To the most beautiful creature in the world on your birthday". I'm sure Miss Carol Bunce will be very pleased with this, Willi. It must have cost a lot of money.'

Willi swallowed at the mention of the dreaded name. 'No – it's not for her, Commander. It's for Private Knox.'

Kruger frowned. 'I'm not sure I approve of such goings on, Willi. Whatever you and Private Knox get up to, please be very discreet and ensure that I never get to hear about it.'

Although Willi disliked having to reveal details of his shady black-market, under-the-counter dealings, on this occasion he felt that it was absolutely necessary.

'No, it's not like that, Commander. I got that card for Private Knox. He wants to give it to Nurse Brenda Hobson for her birthday.'

Kruger returned the card. 'I see.'

'I think he's infatuated with her.'

'A love that equals your love for your Miss Carol Bunce, eh, Willi? So Nurse Hobson has a birthday coming up?'

'I think so, Commander.'

'When?'

Willi had long recognized that knowledge was power that could often be turned into money – usually by blackmail. Something about Kruger's tone in his apparently offhand question alerted his money-detecting sixth sense. 'I don't know, Commander. But I expect a small bribe could find out.'

'Why not ask Private Knox? He must know, surely?'

'Army personnel are forbidden to reveal private details about other personnel to prisoners, Commander. He'd need a small bribe.'

'How much?'

'Five shillings ought to be enough,' said Willi promptly.

Kruger considered. He opened a desk drawer, took two half-crowns out of a tobacco tin and gave them to Willi. 'Bring me the change if you can get the information for less, Willi.'

Willi saluted and left the office. He went to his room, almost hugging himself with glee. He locked the door, removed the section of skirting board that concealed his hole-in-the-wall bank deposit and added Kruger's five shillings to his fund. He made an entry in the little pocket diary and gazed rapt at the new total. In nearly five years of cheating, lying, conniving, and black-market dealings, he had amassed the not inconsiderable fortune of ninety-eight pounds. His target of one hundred pounds was within sight. He replaced the skirting board and returned to Kruger's office.

'Come!'

Willi entered.

'That was quick, Willi. Did you get the information?'

'Yes, commander. Nurse Brenda Hobson's birthday is on the 1st of July.'

Kruger glanced at his wall calendar. Just over two weeks. 'Thank you, Willi. Any change for me?'

Willi looked regretful. 'Actually, Commander, I had to go to six shillings.'

Kruger sighed. He opened his drawer and gave Willi another shilling. 'Would you please find Hauptmann Berg and tell him that I'd like to see him.'

Willi needed to talk to Dietrich Berg anyway on business matters which had natural precedence over Kruger's orders. He found the technician in his workshop on the ground floor with three assistants putting the finishing touches to a batch of five cuckoo clocks.

If Berg had existed in fiction he would have served an aspiring writer well as a mad scientist although he was neither mad nor a scientist. He was an extremely clever, eager to please, young technician who happened to be accident-prone on a scale best described as monumental. He first blew himself up at the age of six with the aid of a children's chemistry set that its makers had guaranteed was harmless. At school he decimated a chemical laboratory in addition to losing two fingers during his first attempt at building a perpetual-motion machine. His three years at university were punctuated by an assortment of minor explosions and a number of major ones.

When asked by the army for a reference, his university authorities had recommended that Berg should be posted to a department dealing with some form of research – possibly explosives. The German army, with its remarkable ability to put square pegs in round holes – a talent it shared with the British army – sent Berg to an infantry regiment as a wireless operator because they discovered that he had been an amateur radio enthusiast until Hitler had revoked all 'ham' radio licences in 1936 on the day after Berg had been issued with his.

After that, Berg had to content himself with

blowing-up the odd radio valve here and there although he did succeed in shooting off his big toe during rifle drill.

The injury left him with a slight limp that contributed to his capture at Dunkirk. Not many German soldiers were taken prisoner at Dunkirk, therefore Berg's accomplishment in this respect was notable. Even more notable was the fact that two of the three boats Berg was bundled aboard in the evacuation of Dunkirk's beaches were sunk by Stuka dive bombers. The same limp led to him being run over by a Post Office van at Euston railway station while in the company of two guards who were escorting him to Grizedale Hall and were quicker on their feet than he was.

Berg's long incarceration in Grizedale Hall had been relieved by frequent periods in hospital. On one occasion, Nurse Hobson's scissors had slipped when she was removing a plaster cast from Berg's arm. The stab wound resulted in his return to hospital. A more serious accident, and one that had nearly cost him his eyesight, had been when an overloaded condenser in a clandestine radio transmitter had exploded in his face.

Despite his long catalogue of injuries and the loss of two fingers, he was an accomplished engineer and was Grizedale Hall's technical officer in charge of a small workshop and a team of ten craftsmen that officially produced cuckoo clocks and toys, that Willi sold unofficially, and unofficially produced virtually anything else to order.

Their sewing and embroidery skills had been used for the production of clothing for Kruger's rarely sanctioned escape bids.

'These look excellent, Dietrich,' said Willi admiringly, examining one of the cuckoo clocks. 'When will they be ready?'

Berg disliked making a fuss but on this occasion he had been pushed into speaking out by the other POWs in his team.

'Willi. There is something we have to discuss about the price you're paying us for these clocks.'

'Yes?' said Willi cautiously, sensing trouble.

'As we have more free time and can go out now, we all need more money. Prices have gone up and so have our expenses.'

Willi remained silent.

'Cost me four shillings to take a girl to the cinema,' a prisoner grieved. 'They don't reduce their prices for matinees like they do at home.'

Berg pressed on. 'It's just that Edward saw one of our clocks on sale in an Ambleside shop for four pounds. That's an absurd amount compared with what you pay us.'

'There are middlemen,' said Willi. 'Wholesalers, distributors. Lots of people and they all take a cut.'

'That's silly,' said Berg. 'How many middlemen can there be between here and Ambleside?'

'It may not have been one of your clocks.'

'Edward said that there was no doubt. He makes the cuckoos' doors, so he ought to know. I'm sorry, Willi, but we'd like another ten shillings each for our clocks.'

'But that will ruin me!' Willi protested. 'I've entered into contracts.'

'Yes – but surely they're only verbal contracts?'

'Which I treat as binding, and so do my – I mean, our, customers.'

'Surely they will see that prices have to rise?' Berg reasoned. 'After all, we've been supplying our clocks at the same price for at least two years.'

Willi didn't point out that he had put his prices up several times in the intervening period. In the austerity of wartime and post-war rationed England, frivolous, luxury goods were in demand and his buyer had agreed to the progressive price increases.

The two men haggled for ten minutes, with other members of Berg's team of craftsmen chipping in with their grievances. It ended with Willi reluctantly agreeing to pay an extra eight shillings for each clock.

'I'm ruined,' he declared. 'Ruined. By the way, Commander Kruger would like to see you in his office.'

Berg was dismayed. 'How long ago was this?'

'About half an hour ago, so you had better look sharp.'

The young officer raced through Grizedale Hall and tapped fearfully on Kruger's door.

'Ah, Berg,' said Kruger with uncustomary geniality, waving Berg to a chair. 'How's everything going in the workshop?'

'Well enough, Commander. It keeps us busy.'

'Even busier now that you don't have Sergeant Finch's snap searches to contend with?'

'We still get them from time to time, Commander.'

Kruger unfolded a beautifully embroidered silk handkerchief. It was a work of art. He spread it out on his desk. 'Remember this? You made it for my Christmas present in '42. I've never used it as a handkerchief. It's far too good.'

'Yes, Commander. Would you like some more? We've got plenty of silk left – parachutes are so big. General Dornberger has ordered four made-to-measure shirts. He's complaining that he's not allowed civilian clothes.'

Kruger frowned. 'Four shirts?' He made a mental note to have a word with Dornberger about that.

The sour note in his senior officer's voice emboldened Berg to say, 'I'm not happy with the idea. You had a rule that all requests for civilian clothes had to go through the escape committee for approval.'

'I'm still the escape committee, Berg, and the rule still stands. Your referral to me is very proper. I do not approve and I shall have a word with General Dornberger on the matter. He is not allowed civilian dress by the British, therefore you will do no work for him on civilian dress without my permission.'

'Understood, Commander,' Berg agreed, much relieved because the General's brusque manner had not endeared him to his team of craftsmen.

'And you say that you've still plenty of parachute silk?' Kruger smoothed the handkerchief on his desk. 'Surely this material is much finer than the original silk?'

'It is, Commander. But the yarn used is the best quality. For your handkerchief, we unwound the yarn from the original material on to a converted bicycle wheel, and rewove it on our small loom to produce material with a much tighter warp and weft resulting in a much finer silk.'

'It sounds a tedious job.'

'It is, Commander. Mind-numbingly so, which is why we've done it only for small items such as handkerchiefs.'

'Did you do this magnificent embroidery and stitching?'

'No, Commander. That was Leutnant Krantz.'

'It must've taken him hours.'

'It did, Commander. But it's the sort of work he loves.'

Kruger was lost in thought for some moment as he studied the fine handkerchief. 'Do you still have the bicycle wheel and the loom?' he asked.

'Yes, Commander. We've never made any attempt to hide them, therefore Sergeant Finch has never seen fit to confiscate them. I think he sells the occasional handkerchief we give him.'

Kruger smiled. 'I think I may have a task for your loom and Leutnant Krantz's skills, Berg. You like challenges, don't you?'

Berg cautiously agreed that he did although the nature of the challenge that Kruger spelt out during the next few minutes had his pulse quickening in alarm.

'So what do you think?' Kruger enquired when he had finished outlining his scheme.

'Well – I'm sure it would be possible, Commander.' Berg's eyes went to Kruger's dramatic wall painting that showed *U-112* punching into heavy Atlantic seas under a leaden sky.

Kruger saw the direction of his gaze and glanced at the painting. 'I imagine you could use Hauptmann Anton Hertzog's skills?'

'He is a most accomplished artist,' said Berg. 'We need only a few drawings or sketches. But we must have something to work to. And the drawings will have to be accurate.'

'Very well. I will have a word with him. Thank you, Berg. When will you make a start?'

The young officer knew the answers that Kruger liked to hear. 'We'll start the weaving right away, Commander.'

'Excellent, Berg. There is one thing you should know,' His gaze hardened and bored into the army officer. 'If word about this project leaks out to anyone other than those involved, you will incur my most savage wrath. You will impress that on your men.'

'Understood, Commander,' said Berg fearfully, moving to the door.

'By the way, Berg, I saw one of your cuckoo clocks in a shop window in Ulverston last week. You will doubtless be pleased to learn that they were asking seven pounds for it.'

19

Eric sat on a public bench near the Keyserlei Hotel and decided that it would be impossible for him to approach any of the senior US army officers entering and leaving the building without incurring the suspicions of the British military police. On one occasion he had tried to enter the hotel but the doorman had refused to let him enter, saying that the hotel was off limits for POWs. The incident had attracted the redcaps who demanded to see Eric's identification. The distinctive tracksuit he had to wear made everything so damned difficult. He had even hovered nearby in the hope of following an officer but they always used taxis.

Dejected, he returned to the hospital, having been out for most of the afternoon. He was feeling a little guilty at having left

Mark for so long. There were now only six beds in his ward, four unoccupied, he and Mark were the ward's last patients and there were now fewer than thirty patients left in the entire hospital. Most of them had been shipped off to the cages. There was a working party of POWs in the corridor dismantling and stacking beds.

'Dieter!' Mark exclaimed excitedly as soon as he entered the ward. It was uncanny the way the lad had learned to recognize footsteps. 'This is Lieutenant Benyon! We've been waiting for you!'

There was nothing in Eric's manner to betray the horror he felt when he saw the uniformed British naval officer rise from Mark's bed and hold out his hand. He even managed to match Benyon's smile as he exchanged handshakes.

'Leutnant Muller,' said Benyon warmly. 'Mark has been telling me all about you and what you're doing for him.'

Despite the sickness in his stomach, Eric was able to give a dismissive wave and sit nonchalantly on his bed. He complimented Benyon on his German.

'I'm being sent to England,' said Mark happily. 'I'm going to be seen by their top eye doctors in a big hospital. They've already made appointments for me!'

'I'm delighted to hear it,' said Eric, his mind racing.

'There is a problem,' said Benyon. 'Mark is going to need a guide. The hospital he's going to is somewhere in England – in the north, actually. He'll be housed in a POW camp, of course, and will have to make journeys, not only to the camp, but back and forth to the hospital once he's there.'

Oh, Christ, thought Eric, seeing what was coming.

'Of course, Dieter,' Benyon continued, 'you're a POW of the British and we can send you where we like, but it would save a great many problems if you'd agree to acting as Mark's guide. I must stress that we can't make you do that but it would help Mark enormously if you agreed.'

'And I'd be posted to the same camp as Mark?'

Benyon nodded.

'Please, Dieter!' Mark begged. 'Say you'll do it! I'd be terrified of having to go to England without you!'

It was ironic, thought Eric. Ever since he had set out from the V2 production plant in the Hartz Mountains, his sole obsession had been to avoid the British forces at all costs. Now he was their prisoner and they wanted to ship him off to England. If he refused to act as Mark's guide, they'd probably send him there out of sheer perversity anyway. He was trapped.

Or was he?

On one of his trips outside without Mark he had visited all of the main railway stations and was surprised to discover that services were getting back to normal. Antwerp was one of Europe's great trading ports and they intended for it to stay that way. The desire to get everything back to normal was a fever in the city.

The real Dieter Muller had a sister. From her letters that Eric had taken from the murdered Feldgendarmerie officer, it was obvious that brother and sister were very close. That she had not heard from her brother would worry her and she would, no doubt, carefully check the lists of prisoners of war that the Red Cross were publishing. Eric had already seen Dieter Muller's name on one such list. She would make inquiries and once she proved who she was, the chances were that the Red Cross would tell her where her brother was. Now that travel in Europe was returning to normal, it was only a matter of time before she turned up in Antwerp. He had been expecting her to walk into his ward any day now. Once she saw him, the game would be up.

But to get to England would most likely be difficult for a German national. There was a chance that he would be safer in the lions' den rather than remain in mainland Europe. Maybe his repatriation would come through quickly. All he had to do was sit tight and pick up the threads of his real identity and life when it did.

'I'd be pleased to be your guide,' he said. 'Someone's got to keep you out of trouble.'

Mark gave a whoop of pleasure. He slid off

his bed, felt for Eric's bed, and threw his arms around his friend. 'Dieter – you don't know what it means to me! You're such a good man – a true friend.'

'So that's settled then,' said Benyon, looking pleased. He opened his briefcase and gave Eric a bulky envelope. 'Those are Mark's travel warrants and ID documents. I'll have your papers sent around first thing tomorrow morning. You'll be travelling with a group of German POWs tomorrow. A truck will pick you both up at 1500, so be waiting outside before then. You'll be taken by ferry to Dover and then escorted to Euston Station in London. That's the mainline station that serves the north of England. From there you'll be unescorted and will have to find your own way north. Mark speaks English.' He looked questioningly at Eric. 'And you, Leutnant?'

'Yes – I speak reasonable English,' Eric replied in English.

Benyon beamed. 'Excellent. So getting about won't be difficult for you. All the details are in the envelope.' Benyon paused and added seriously, 'Don't forget you're both still under your parole. The MPs will be forever stopping you, so don't lose your ID cards and your unescorted travel permits, or your travel warrants. Although somehow I don't think that young Mark here is very interested in or physically able to indulge in escapes ... Well – I think that's all. All that remains is for me to wish you bon voyage and that I hope all goes well for you, Mark.'

Benyon stood and shook hands with the two men.

'I don't know how to thank you, Lieutenant Benyon,' said Mark.

'Thank your father. He's had us jumping about a bit. A remarkable and very brave man. I was glad of the chance to meet him.' Benyon moved to the door. 'One thing, young Mark. Spend that money he gave you carefully. Oddly enough, you can get things here that are virtually unobtainable in England. Shaving tackle, soap, clothes, shoes – that sort of thing. You can take whatever you can carry but your kit will be searched at the docks.'

And with that parting advice, the English naval officer left.

'Why did we have to fight that stupid war with the English?' said Mark bitterly. He touched the bandages that covered his eyes. 'What has it achieved? My left eye hurts so much.'

'Your father's been here?' Eric queried.

'He came to say goodbye,' said Mark, his smile returning. 'He's very pleased for me. Oh, Dieter, I'm so excited. The British doctors will be able to find out why my corneas aren't healing properly. And then ... Well – who knows?'

'He gave you some money?'

Mark groped and opened the drawer in his bedside cabinet. He produced a wad of US dollar bills. 'A hundred dollars, Dieter! Have you ever seen such an amount? What's this one?'

'Ten dollars.'

'And this?'

'Another ten dollars. It looks like they're all ten dollar bills.'

Mark flipped the cover open on a wrist watch his father had given him. He felt the hands. 'I suppose it's too late to go shopping now?'

'It is,' said Eric with feeling. 'I've been walking all afternoon – I'm beat.'

'We'll go first thing in the morning. And we'll ask a nurse to order us a taxi.'

Johnny Benyon's taxi dropped him outside the army HQ. He strode briskly into his office, asked for some coffee, and started on the paperwork formalities to have Dieter Muller listed as a special category prisoner and his travel documents to be prepared. Fleming put his head around the door when he smelt coffee brewing.

'Hallo, Ian. Have some coffee.'

'How did it go?'

'He agreed. In fact he's over the moon.'

'One problem less.'

'Several problems less, actually. I've found a guide for him. Remember the man hiding behind the *Times* in the newspaper photographs? You can put his reticence down to modesty. Leutnant Dieter Muller. A Feldgendarmerie officer until we caught him. He's been looking after Mark Schiller. Taking him out. Even taught him Braille. The matron thinks he's a wonderful man. Quiet. Retiring. Very unassuming, and that it's not surprising that he hid from the photographers. Anyway, he's agreed to act as Mark Schiller's guide. I'm just squaring his transfer with the army and arranging for him to be listed as a special category prisoner.'

Fleming nodded. 'Well done, old boy. Does this Muller speak English?'

'Excellent English.'

'You'd think Jerry would've made better use of him rather than shove him in the military police.'

'Aren't you going to tell me how clever I've been?'

'I tell you that when you've found this damned Dr Eric Hoffmann,' Fleming replied with feeling.

20

Eric's and Mark's first purchases the following morning on their trip to the centre of Antwerp were two large kitbags from a camping shop that had a surprising amount of stock. Eric had objected to any of Mark's money being spent on him but the younger man had insisted, saying that half the money was for him and that his father had promised to send more money once he had a forwarding address.

They spent an enjoyable hour buying toiletries, towels, pyjamas, shoes, shirts and trousers, and plenty of chocolate and coffee, which a British nurse had told them was better than money in England. Afterwards they sat in the sun at a pavement café drinking coffee.

'Blonde,' Eric reported. 'Twenty-five to thirty. About one-sixty. Very pretty.'

Mark turned his head to follow the progress of the girl as her high-heels clicked past. He liked Eric to describe all the girls. Eric also reported all the admiring glances that Mark received from them, never mentioning the occasional stares of sympathy.

'There's one coming up behind me,' said

Mark. 'She sounds petite. That means pert breasts and a tight little bottom.'

Eric looked over Mark's shoulder. 'You don't need eyes, you sex-crazed bastard. Yes – she's very petite and she's got pert breasts.' Eric's gaze remain fixed beyond Mark as the girl walked past. His interest had been caught by a tailor's shop. There was a sign outside in English proclaiming that the shop had all sizes of good-quality suits in stock at bargain prices, and that English was spoken.

'Got to find a lavatory,' said Eric, rising. 'Don't run away.'

Mark smiled and sipped his coffee.

Eric strolled to the tailor's shop and examined the suits in the window. He went inside. The manager took in Eric's tracksuit but wasn't concerned. The parties of POWs working on war-damage repairs seemed to be earning good money. He fussed around Eric with his tape measure and sorted out a matching pair of trousers and a jacket which he assured Eric would be a perfect fit. He talked Eric into donning the jacket.

'If you would just come to the front of the shop, sir. There's more light which is why we moved the mirrors. We never know when there's going to be a power cut. You see? A perfect fit. The trousers will be the same.'

Eric looked at his reflection. He had three of Mark's ten dollar bills in his pocket.

It would all be so easy!

With the suit and a new shirt and tie, he would be able to walk straight into the

Keyserlei Hotel without being challenged by the damned MPs. He would engage a senior American officer in conversation in the bar. He would give them the exact location of the farm where he had buried his credentials in the vegetable plot. Within a few days his real identity – Dr Eric Hoffmann – would be established beyond doubt and he would be on his way to America to start a new life. The Americans wanted rockets. They had made no secret of that. Intercontinental rockets. That would mean working on multi-stage rockets – the only type of rocket that would be capable of reaching the moon. His heart pounded, blood pulsed through his veins at the prospect. He would be working with Wernher von Braun again, making real plans for their moon rocket that they had discussed endlessly into the nights over beers and coffees at Peenemunde.

It would all be so easy!

The manager was hovering, holding the pair of trousers for Eric's inspection. 'If you would like to try these on, sir. I'm sure you will find that they're a perfect fit.'

The throng of shoppers cleared and Eric saw Mark sitting at the café table – what could be seen of his face was alight with hope. He told himself that the boy didn't need him. The British were obviously concerned about him, and even if they wouldn't do anything for him, the Americans would.

It would all be so easy, and yet it was impossible. He took off the jacket.

'I'm sorry,' he said to the manager. 'But I've changed my mind.'

He walked out of the shop and rejoined Mark at the café's table.

'We ought to find a bank, Dieter.'

'What you really mean is that *I* should find a bank,' said Eric with mock severity. 'So you want to rob a bank? Fair enough – you can drive the get-away car.'

Mark laughed. Eric realized that nothing gave him so much pleasure as seeing and hearing that laugh.

'To change some of the dollars into English money. My father said that I'd have no trouble changing it.'

'No trouble? How will you know you're not being cheated?'

'Because I'll have my good friend Dieter Muller with me to make sure I won't be.'

It was Eric's turn to laugh. He chucked Mark playfully on the side of the chin. 'Well, that's true enough, young man. Let's have some more coffee. Tonight we set sail and invade England!'

If Mark had been sighted he would have discovered that his companion's concerned expression did not match the cheery tone in his voice.

21

Hauptmann Anton Hertzog was sitting before his easel and intent on a watercolour at the approach road to Grizedale Hall. He pulled a handkerchief from his pocket and shook it twice. It was the signal to Willi to say that Carol Bunce had tired of waiting for him and had gone.

Willi was immensely relieved. He had two one-pound bags of sugar hanging down inside his trousers which would fetch four shillings at a sweet shop in Satterthwaite, and he had business to discuss in the pub with a buyer for Berg's cuckoo clocks. The village was a long walk for Willi but the money involved would make it a short walk. He emerged from the gatehouse and set off towards his lookout, who was cleaning his brushes.

'She's beautiful, Willi,' Anton exclaimed when Willi drew level.

'Who is?'

'Your Carol Bunce.'

'She's not mine.' Willi was quite emphatic about this point.

'But she adores you! She just told me before she got tired of waiting and went home. Willi

– you are so lucky. She's a magnificent creature! Such breasts! Such thighs!'

Anton placed a sketching pad on his knee. A few fast strokes with a charcoal stick and there were Carol Bunce's breasts.

'What I would give to paint such a woman,' he said as he worked. 'Reclining on a chaise longue. Her wonderful, full breasts spilling and heaving – swollen like the sails of a war galley speeding across a wine-dark sea.' A few quick smudges with his fingertip and the picture had shading and shadows that accentuated the voluptuousness of Carol's breasts.

'Her legs slightly apart, offering the promise of a sweet haven for exhausted sailors. Her belly a maelstrom of seething passions with her navel as its eye! With such a woman before me and a blank canvas, I would want for nothing.'

Willi wanted to be sick. Anton Hertzog's passion for painting robust, massively proportioned Rubensesque maidens was well-known, and they didn't come much more robust and massively proportioned than Carol Bunce.

Willi indicated the watercolour. 'A nice painting,' he said to change the subject. He was about to set off when Anton said something that stopped him like an Austin 7 receiving a Sherman tank shell through its radiator.

'General Dornberger commissioned me to paint this picture for his room.'

Transactions in Grizedale Hall that did not concern Willi concerned him very much.

'He did?'

'Just a small watercolour to start with. He's admired all my paintings in the hall. He's paying me five pounds for this watercolour.'

The sum electrified Willi. *Five pounds!* He had no idea there was such money in commissioned works of art. He suddenly became very interested in painting, his meeting forgotten.

'Willi,' said Anton earnestly, 'I've decided to become a commercial artist. Magazines, fashion, strip cartoons – I don't care – just so long as I can make enough money to pay magnificent models to sit for me so that I can paint pictures like the great Rubens.' He handed the sketch pad to Willi. 'Take a look.'

Willi leafed through the drawings. They were pencil sketches, and were very good. There were two of Brenda Hobson wheeling her bicycle across the courtyard and a quite funny, cruelly accurate cartoon showing Sergeant Finch bawling out a cowering guard.

'These are very good of Brenda Hobson.'

'A bag of bones,' said Anton dismissively. 'But she's a woman, she's around, and such skinny, wretched creatures are always the vogue, so I sketch her without her knowing. Now your Carol Bunce. What would I give to have her sit for me.'

Willi's mind went into overdrive. 'You would pay her to sit for you?'

'But of course.'

'Nude?'

'Absolutely.' His eyes became alive with hope. 'Willi! Could you arrange it? Would she agree? Two hours – that is all I would require for the preliminary sketches. And two hours with the final picture.'

'Ten shillings an hour?' Willi ventured. Even if he had to drop fifty per cent, it would still be a considerable sum.

Anton hesitated. That would take almost half the money that General Dornberger had given him. But the thought of Carol's heady voluptuousness spread before him drove the doubts from his mind. 'Yes!' he said eagerly. 'Ten shillings an hour.'

That Willi's mind was set spinning did not interfere with its innate cunning and ability to hatch profitable schemes. 'Listen,' he said. 'She's a sensitive girl. Let me handle everything. Whatever you do, don't mention that you're paying her otherwise she will get upset. You know what English girls are like. So you pay me and I'll get the money to her in a way that won't cause offence.'

'Yes – I see,' Anton agreed, not seeing at all but not wanting to jeopardize this wonderful opportunity that had presented itself. 'I won't breathe a word about money to her.'

'Willi!' a woman yelled.

'My goddess!' breathed Anton.

'My God!' breathed Willi.

Willi spun around and was gripped in a rib-crushing bear hug. 'Willi! My love!' Carol exclaimed. 'You came. I'd almost given up hope.'

'I was detained by the guards,' said Willi when Carol put him down. He gave her a sickly, calculating grin. Anton stared, entranced by breasts that were threatening to burst past the straining buttons of a gingham blouse.

'Aren't you pleased to see me, darling?'

'Overwhelmed,' said Willi truthfully.

Carol nearly dislocated Willi's arm when she seized him. 'We'll go to my secret den and you can say lovely things to me,' she announced and dragged her prisoner in the direction of Spauldings Farm, leaving Anton to marvel at the intoxicating movement of her globular buttocks before resuming work on his watercolour.

Carol's den was in an open-sided Dutch barn in a pile of loose hay beside a stack of straw bales. She hauled Willi up the bales and pushed him into a crater-like depression in the hay that contained her romance and true confessions magazines. She jumped in after him. Their combined weight made the depression deeper. Willi's depression also deepened but it was largely alleviated by the thought of money. Carol rolled on to her back, clasping her beloved to her like a playful kitten gripping a ball of string in all four paws. Her groping hands on the outside of Willi's trousers found the lump caused by one of the concealed bags of sugar.

'Oh, Willi, Willi. You're such a wonderful

man.'

For a while the cratered hay pile shook and trembled like Mount Vesuvius making up its mind whether or not its eruption of the previous year warranted an encore.

Carol sat up a few minutes later. 'Oh, Willi Willi,' she declared, flustered. 'You're so wonderful.'

'And I think you're wonderful, too,' Willi replied, gasping like a spent salmon that had just fought its way through several waterfalls and rapids.

'Do you? Do you really?'

'Of course. I think about you all the time. I would love to have you by my side, in my room but it cannot be. I would love a photograph of you but that would be in black and white and that would not do justice to the lovely colour of your hair and eyes.'

'Oh, Willi – you say such beautiful things.'

'So I have asked Hauptmann Hertzog – to paint a picture of you for my room.'

'The bloke at the easel?'

'Yes. He is a brilliant artist. A professional. To have a picture of you would fulfil all my dreams. But he refuses.'

Carol was indignant. 'Why?'

'He says that professionals do not paint from memory – only from real life.'

'Then I'd pose for him!'

Willi took her work-hardened hand. 'Would you really, my love?'

'Of course.'

'That's wonderful! I'd have you with me in

my room all the time. I'd be so happy.'

Carol crushed Willi's head between her breasts. 'You're so lovely, Willi,' she said dreamily.

'And I would want to see these always,' said Willi, fondling a small percentage of her total breast area with one hand. 'You wouldn't be complete without them.'

Carol laughed. 'If you don't mind another man seeing me naked, I'll pose for him with nothing on. Just for you.'

Willi was elated. His bank balance would pass the hundred pound mark! It had all been so easy and yet he sensed that this particular cow could be milked even further.

'You're wonderful, Carol,' he said. 'To think that you would do that for me.'

'Of course I would, Willi.' She held his head away from her. Willi was looking sorrowful. 'But why the long face?'

'Being a professional artist, he will only work on commission. I cannot afford his fee.'

'How much does he want?'

'The money doesn't matter. If it were a million pounds and I had such a sum, I would pay it.'

'How much does he want?' Carol repeated.

'Ten pounds,' said Willi sadly. 'But I don't have ten pounds, or anything like that.'

'You must let me pay it,' Carol decided without hesitation. 'I'll draw the money out of the post office tomorrow.'

'I could never let you do that!' Willi protested.

'Don't be silly, Willi.' Carol giggled. Her breasts wobbled. 'I want to do it. There's nothing to spend my wages on anyway.'

'I will always be your slave,' said Willi. 'But you mustn't mention his fee to him. He's very sensitive about money.'

'Like doctors and dentists?'

'Worse,' said Willi.

'Then I promise not to mention money. I'll give it to you so that you can pay him.'

'Then I will have you with me always,' said Willi. 'You're so wonderful, Carol.'

'You've got the real me now,' said Carol, encircling her powerful arms around her beloved Willi and pulling him close.

A bedraggled Willi emerged from Carol's haystack den an hour later and made his way unsteadily back to Grizedale Hall, leaving a trail of sugar, reflecting that to be paid by the artist *and* the model for a painting was no mean achievement.

While Willi was recuperating, sprawled on his bed, one mile away from the camp, Leutnant Raymond Krantz was crouching behind a drystone wall, keeping the backs of a row of small cottages under observation through one of Berg's cardboard-tube home-made telescopes. It was a crude instrument but it served his purpose as he examined washing on clothes lines, fluttering in the wind in the narrow back gardens of the little cottages at the foot of the steep slope. There was one particular clothes line he was interested in.

The shadows were lengthening. He could not risk leaving it too late before returning to camp. Satisfied that the twilight now offered reasonable cover and that no one was about, he vaulted over the wall and raced down the hillside. He worked his way along the fence across the ends of the gardens until he reached the garden he had selected. A quick check. There was no one about and no one at any of the windows. Climbing over the fence, hopping over the rows of vegetables, snatching the garments he wanted off the clothes line and returning to the security of the fence's far side was accomplished in a matter of seconds.

He stuffed the stolen items inside his jacket and became a sauntering prisoner of war out for a stroll. He quickened his pace when he was well clear of the cottages. Only when he was back in the camp's workshop did he dare remove the stolen items from inside his jacket to examine them. The quality was poor, which was only to be expected, but that didn't worry him. What he was interested in was the method used in their manufacture, how the individual pieces of material were cut and stitched together. His supposition was that all such garments, regardless of quality, employed much the same method of construction, and variations in quality was achieved by varying the quality of the material. He picked up a needle and a pair of scissors and began picking at and cutting stitches.

22

Nurse Brenda Hobson always weighed Kruger in his underpants because she had never been able to nerve herself to order him to completely strip. Nor did she ever subject the fastidiously clean German naval officer to the indignities of a nit search. The other difference in her treatment of him compared with her treatment of the other prisoners of war in her care was that she always attended to her hair and make-up before she was due to see him. It was stupid, schoolgirl behaviour, for which she always scolded herself, and yet she always did it.

'Amazing, Commander,' she said, entering Kruger's weight on her record card while he got dressed. 'In all these years your weight hasn't varied by much more than two or three pounds.' She was uncomfortably aware of his brooding eyes on her as he buttoned his shirt. Rather than have to meet that compelling gaze, she concentrated on sharpening her pencil. 'In fact, you're a pound and a half heavier now than the first time I weighed you.'

'That may be because I've had to stop smoking.'

'Oh – yes. I haven't seen you smoking for a long time.' She smiled. 'Those awful little black cigars. Was giving up difficult?'

'I had no choice. Commander Ian Fleming used to keep me supplied. You haven't changed either. A terrible war that has changed the world and yet you and I are unchanged.'

'But we've changed inside,' said Brenda, thinking of the loss of her husband.

'We all have,' said Kruger, tying his shoelaces. It was if he were reading her mind because he added, 'This war has torn us all apart inside. And you and your son especially so. A terrible tragedy for which I am deeply sorry.'

It was the longest speech she had ever known this strange man to make. She looked up and smiled.

'And in what way haven't I changed? Your weight has remained the same. How have I stayed consistent?'

Kruger gave an unexpectedly warm smile. 'If I were to answer that, I fear you would be embarrassed. I do not want that.'

Brenda wasn't sure how to reply to that, so she changed the subject. 'We have two new prisoners arriving sometime today.'

'So I've been informed.'

'Junior Leutnant Mark Schiller, who was blinded at the time of his capture,' said Brenda, looking at a file. 'And Leutnant Dieter Muller, who acts as his guide. Mark Schiller is only eighteen!'

'Major Reynolds informed me that the

young man is to receive treatment at the Barrow-in-Furness hospital.'

'Well – they've got a very good eye department. He'll be in good hands.'

'I'm delighted to hear it.' Kruger picked up a framed photograph from Brenda's desk that showed a group of ten children in school uniform. 'This is new.'

'Taken this term.'

'Which one is Stephen?'

Brenda pointed. Kruger studied the photograph. 'He's turning into a fine boy. How is he doing at school?'

'He's clever. Just like his father was.'

Kruger replaced the photograph. 'I do not know when I'll be repatriated. It could be tomorrow, or the day after. Who knows? I would've liked a chance to have met him but I realize that it cannot be.'

'Why not?'

'Well...' The question seemed to embarrass Kruger. 'The circumstances ... My branch of the Kriegsmarine. His father—'

'The circumstances are that the war's over. We cannot allow the past to nourish the future.'

'Gandhi,' said Kruger.

Brenda was surprised. 'Why, yes.'

'We cannot wish for a better teacher.'

'So let's make a start on his lessons tomorrow. Why don't you come around to my place and meet him?'

'Gandhi?'

'No, stupid! Stephen!' Brenda clapped her

hand to mouth in horror. 'I'm terribly sorry, Commander. I didn't mean to be rude.' To her amazement Kruger actually laughed. He was looking at her with a warmth that she would never have imagined was possible.

'I deserved it, Brenda. It was a silly comment. Yes – I would dearly love to meet Stephen. I would consider it a great honour.'

'Tomorrow? Four o'clock? I'll give you my address. It's not far – about twenty minutes walk. I know he'd love to thank you for all the toys.' Her hand trembled as she scribbled her address on a piece of paper and held it out.

Kruger's movements were so graceful and polished that there seemed nothing jarringly un-English about them as he clicked his heels, bowed and kissed the back of her hand as he took the note. 'Tomorrow,' he said. 'I will look forward to it.'

After Kruger had left, Brenda suddenly realized with a little start that he had called her by her first name.

23

Major Reynolds was uncertain about the two new arrivals sitting in front of his desk with Kruger beside them. Dealing with a blind man, and certainly one as young as this Junior Leutnant Mark Schiller, was outside his experience. And the older man had a bearing and a command of English that seemed at odds with his rank of military police officer.

'Well, if Commander Kruger gets his adjutant to show you around, fix up your quarters and so on, I'll hand you over to him. Commander Kruger?'

Kruger stood and signalled to Eric to follow him.

'Thank you for explaining everything, sir,' said Mark.

'One thing, Leutnant Schiller,' said Reynolds. 'I lost an eye at Dunkirk, so I've some idea of what you're going through.'

'Thank you, sir.' Mark stood, pulled on his cap, and saluted. He picked up his bulging kitbag and reached out the other hand. Reynolds was surprised at Eric's smooth movement to intercept the hand and place it on his forearm before guiding the young man out of the office.

Willi was hovering outside, of course. He was a little apprehensive because while he had been waiting, dying to find out what could be in those obviously new, capacious, well-filled kitbags, Sergeant Finch had approached him, gathered the front of Willi's blouse in a huge hand and drawn Willi's face close to his own. He had then advised Willi in the manner for which he was noted, that if Willi pilfered anything from the blind naval officer, or cheated him in any way, that he, Sergeant Finch, would insert his arm right down Willi's throat, grab hold of whatever he could grab hold of, and pull Willi inside-out. His reasons for threatening thus was because Sergeant Finch was of the opinion that Willi, whose fat Bavarian arse warranted kicking to Land's End and back, and again for good luck, was a lying, stealing, unprincipled dried dog turd and that Sergeant Finch would, having disembowelled Willi, derive great pleasure from making his loathsome, miserable hide into a darts board. Several darts boards, in fact.

The door to Reynolds's office opened. Kruger was followed by the new arrivals. Willi's eyes fastened hungrily on the bulging kitbags and went forward in response to Kruger's beckon.

'Commander?'

'Willi – take these officers' bags, please. Leutnant Muller acts as a guide for his comrade. It would be easier if you carried them.'

'Certainly, Commander.'

Kruger lowered his voice. It always worried Willi when his senior officer lowered his voice. 'Willi, we are going to find these officers a first-class room with plenty of space, are we not?'

'Yes – of course, Commander.'

'Excellent. And we're going to ensure that they're issued with the requisite number of sheets, pillows, pillowcases and towels etcetera to which they're entitled without any spurious and wholly fictitious additional charges. Are we also agreed on that?'

'Yes, Commander,' said Willi glumly.

'And anyone who does make such charges will receive a punishment from me so hideous that not only will they wish that they had never been born, but that their mother had never been born. And possibly her mother, too. Are we also agreed on that?'

Willi felt that he was being unjustly persecuted that day. 'Yes, Commander.'

'So what room will we allocate to them?'

'I suggest room 17, Commander. A large room on the first floor. It was originally occupied by six prisoners. It has good views and is next to General Dornberger's room.'

'Thank you, Willi. You will follow us, please.'

The party, led by Kruger, set off across the courtyard with Mark holding lightly on to Eric's arm. Willi brought up the rear, puffing under his arm-lengthening burden.

'Five up, fifteen-twenty,' said Eric to Mark

when they neared a short flight of steps.

Kruger turned and looked questioningly at Eric.

'A sort of shorthand we use for steps, Commander,' said Eric. 'Five steps up, roughly fifteen centimetres high with a tread depth of twenty centimetres.'

Kruger nodded in understanding and watched the two men enter the hall. He pointed out the sickbay and told Eric and Mark that they would have to report to Nurse Hobson after breakfast the following day for their initial medical check-up. The party made their way up a flight of stairs. They followed Kruger along a broad, uncarpeted corridor. He opened a door and stood to one side. Eric whispered a rapid description of the room that had Mark feeling for a bed. He found one and claimed it by sitting on it. 'You can have the one nearest the window, Dieter,' he said. 'The view is more use to you than me.'

'How do you know where the window is?' Kruger enquired as Willi staggered in and swung the kitbags on the beds.

'I can feel the coldness on my cheeks,' said Mark. 'Also there is a distinctive echo from glass.'

'Sometimes I don't think he needs me,' said Eric, grinning.

'Oh, but I do,' said Mark seriously. 'I've no idea where windows are when the curtains are drawn.'

Even Kruger smiled at that.

A big, black cat entered the room and jumped up beside Mark. 'A cat!' Mark exclaimed in delight, stroking it and rubbing its head in the manner that cats found acceptable. The cat responded with loud purrs.

'That's Hermann,' said Kruger. 'He may feel like a cat, he may sound like a cat, and even scratch like a cat, but he's not a cat. He's actually a stomach on legs.'

The new arrivals' laughter would have probably been a little louder had they known that a Kruger joke was something to be caught, killed, stuffed, and displayed in a glass case.

'Does he like chocolate?' Mark asked, reaching for his kitbag. 'I've bought tonnes from Antwerp.'

Willi wanted to faint at the mention of the priceless commodity.

'Herman likes everything,' said Kruger. 'Willi. Would you please fetch a new prisoners' information guide and both room keys plus the unofficial third key that Berg had cut for you and which I'm not supposed to know about.'

The little Bavarian officer trotted off, reflecting that there was precious little justice in the world.

'Dinner is at eight in the main hall,' said Kruger, turning to leave. 'You should have no trouble finding it. Just follow your nose. Dinner is when I formally welcome new arrivals. We haven't had many of late. Willi will show you where the lavatories and showers are. Make sure he gives you three room keys.'

Eric and Mark were unpacking when Willi returned with their room keys. It wasn't so much seeing Hermann crunching a priceless piece of Toblerone that Willi found so upsetting, but the huge display of goods on the prisoners' beds. The sticks of shaving soap and the shirts alone would have been enough to add at least fifty per cent to his hole-in-the-wall bank balance. The several dozen small tins of Nescafé instant coffee almost brought tears to his eyes. Hitherto most prisoners arriving at the hall owned little more than the clothes they were wearing.

'Your keys,' he announced.

'Thank you, Willi,' said Eric. 'Is it all right to call you Willi?'

'Everyone calls me Willi. Well – I hope you'll be comfortable and that General Dornberger's snoring doesn't keep you awake.'

'WHO!'

'General Walter Dornberger,' Willi amplified, too intent on Mark's new silk dressing gown to notice Eric's shocked expression. 'You've heard of him then? The guards call him Doodlebug. He gets very angry and shouts that he had nothing to do with the Luftwaffe's flying bombs. Yes – Grizedale Hall has its own celebrity.'

24

The second sketch on the pad was of Nurse Brenda Hobson talking to Private Knox. 'Amazing likenesses, Anton,' said Berg. 'Really remarkable.'

He turned the sheet over. The next picture was a rough outline of Brenda with no detail. The following sheet was montage of heads and shoulders of Brenda, crowded together because Anton could not afford to waste paper. Each one came in for some well-deserved praise from Berg.

'Bag of bones,' said Anton sourly. It was his favourite expression. 'No meat on her at all.'

'I've always thought that she was a lovely girl.'

Anton snorted. 'That is not a real woman.' He turned the sheet over for Berg. *'That's* a real woman.'

Berg goggled at the nude. It was a charcoal sketch that showed a massively proportioned young woman in a reclining position. 'She looks like that wench who's always hanging about outside, waiting for Willi. It's not her, is it?'

Anton took the sketch pad back. 'One has to draw what is available,' he said brusquely.

'Not that I'd ever get much work as a commercial artist drawing proper women. Bags of bones is all they want now if those American magazines are anything to go by. I suppose this nonsense might be of more interest to you.'

Anton unrolled a long drawing executed on the back of a length of wallpaper. He pinned it to the wall of Berg's workshop. It was a beautifully drawn picture of a slim young woman. She was nude, standing at a slight angle to the artist so that the picture was neither a profile nor full-frontal. Her face had been left blank. The drawing was annotated with dimensions.

'It's life-size,' said Anton. 'Accurate to within a centimetre. Height, bust, waist, hips – all spot on.'

'It's Nurse Brenda Hobson?'

'Well, of course it is. I would've liked to have saved this wallpaper for a life-size sketch of Miss Bunce but it's not wide enough. As it is, I've wasted it on that bag of bones.'

'What I mean is, how did you get her to pose for you like that? If it's as accurate as you say, how did you manage to measure her?'

'Come with me.'

Berg followed Anton outside to the main entrance that opened on to the courtyard. 'I used to sit over there with my easel, and she'd often spend several minutes, standing right here, close to the wall, chatting to Private Knox. By counting the bricks in the courses behind her in the wall, I was able to calculate her exact height. Private Knox often had his briefcase tucked under his arm. He let me measure it once. From the relative proportions, I was able to calculate her other measurements. On one or two fine days she didn't wear her uniform. Once she wore tight-fitting slacks and a thin jumper which enabled me to fill in many details. That drawing in your workshop is a spot-on life-size reproduction of that miserable bag of bones.'

25

There was a rap on Brenda's front door at 4:00 p.m. Not 3:59 p.m., not 4:01 p.m. – but on the stroke of four o'clock. It could only be Otto Kruger. She shooed Stephen into the kitchen to put the kettle on and, pausing only to check herself in the hall mirror, opened the front door.

It was Otto Kruger, with a large paper bag under his arm and a smile in place. He was wearing slacks and a roll-neck pullover. She gave him a warm smile and bade him come in.

'Stephen's just put the kettle on. Would tea be all right?'

'Tea will be fine,' said Kruger, looking

curiously around the low-beamed cottage as Brenda ushered him into the front room, where a table had been set for three. 'But please don't go to any trouble on my account.'

Stephen came in. The ten-year-old eyed Kruger warily from behind the security of his mother. 'And this is Stephen. Stephen – say hallo to Commander Kruger.'

But the boy chose to flee.

'I'm so sorry. He's a little shy.'

'So was I at his age,' said Kruger, smiling.

Brenda thought that in shedding his uniform, he had also shed much of his forbidding nature. He seemed more relaxed – more human. Maybe she had been wrong about him, just as Lizzie Bennet had been wrong about Mr Darcy.

'These are for you,' said Kruger, holding out the bag.

Inside was a box of Swiss chocolates the size of a manhole cover. Brenda thanked him profusely, adding that they'd make her fat.

'With a small boy to share them with?'

The kettle started whistling. Brenda showed Kruger to an armchair and bustled out. Kruger's gaze took in the neat, little room and settled on a photograph of a young man in naval uniform on the sideboard. In the fireplace was a model racing car that he recognized as one that Berg's team had made. There were cigarette cards strewn on the floor bearing pictures of the world's great ocean liners.

Brenda returned, carrying a tray laden with

cups and saucers and fish-paste sandwiches; Stephen followed with homemade cakes.

The tea went better than Brenda had dared hope. Kruger knew how to treat children. He made no attempt to overcome Stephen's initial shyness with efforts to befriend him.

'I imagined you would be living in some sort of nursing staff barracks,' he remarked.

'We bought this cottage in 1934 – just before we got married. Otherwise I probably would be.'

'It's a very pleasant cottage.'

Stephen whispered in his mother's ear. She smiled. 'Oh – all right then. Just one. That box of chocolates is tormenting him.'

The boy left the table and returned with the chocolates, ripping off the cellophane covering.

'Do you like chocolates, Stephen?' asked Kruger.

That the stranger had spoken to him alarmed the boy at first but it seemed a harmless question, so he nodded.

'How about sweets?'

Stephen nodded again.

'Then why don't you eat that one behind your ear?'

Stephen looked puzzled.

Kruger pointed. 'Just there.'

Stephen felt behind his ear. He looked to his mother for reassurance. 'There isn't one,' he said.

'But there is. You're not feeling in the right place. Look.' Kruger reached out and seemed to produce a sweet from behind Stephen's ear which he held out to him. 'What do you think that is, then? The *Queen Mary*?'

The incongruity struck just the right note to appeal to a small boy. He burst out laughing. 'That's silly,' he said, unwrapping the sweet and popping it in his mouth.

'If it's so silly, why is there another one behind your other ear? I think it's the *Queen Elizabeth*.' Kruger produced another sweet, much to Stephen's delight, and it became a companion for the first sweet.

'Stevie,' said Brenda. 'It's Commander Kruger who arranged for you to have all those wonderful toys. Aren't you going to thank him?'

Stephen saluted his new friend. 'Hank you, Commader Ruger,' he said with his mouth full.

Afterwards Kruger and Brenda sat opposite each other in armchairs while Stephen played in the hall.

'May I?' asked Kruger, producing a cheroot.

'Of course. So you've found a supplier?'

'Ian Fleming suddenly remembered me.'

'Is he still around?'

'I think he might visit us. I suspect the cheroots are a peace offering.'

'It'll be nice to see him again,' said Brenda.

'He's a bit of ladies' man?'

'He's certainly attractive.'

Kruger lit his cheroot and inhaled. 'Maybe I could become one now? I'm sure to lose that extra weight I've put on. You know, Brenda – may I call you Brenda? – I've just realized that this is the first time I've seen you when you're not in your uniform. And it must be the first time you've seen me without mine.'

'No – I've seen you out of your uniform lots of times.'

They both laughed together, and talked for another hour until Kruger looked at his watch and said that he'd be late for the evening roll-call. He rose and thanked Brenda for a most enjoyable time. Stephen accepted the offered hand and shook it solemnly. He was rewarded with another sweet – this time it was the *Titanic* from under his chin.

Brenda accompanied him to wicket gate of her cottage.

'It's your birthday soon,' said Kruger. 'July 1st.'

'Now how do you know that?'

'As you know, two officers received their repatriation papers yesterday and will be gone tomorrow. It could happen to me any time.'

'Do you want it to?'

The question caught Kruger off-guard. He hesitated before replying. 'I did.' He looked steadily at her. The usual coolness in his eyes was no more. His expression was sad. 'But now I'm not so sure. In fact ... No – I don't think I do so much now. But before that happens, I would like very much to take you out to dinner for your birthday.' He paused, and smiled. 'But being out in the evening is not permitted, so it will have to be lunch. I will greatly enjoy your company again, and it will be a chance for me to say thank you for your care over the years to myself and my men even though you have very good reasons for hating us—'

'No. I don't hate you, Otto. Or any of your men. Perhaps I did, but that was a long time ago. Not now. Gandhi, remember.'

'So a lunch? A special lunch in a place of your choosing. I think my funds will even stretch to taxis.'

'That would be lovely, Otto.' She frowned. 'But my birthday is on a Sunday and I always take Stephen to see his granddad. It would be better the following day – when he's at school.'

Kruger smiled and kissed her hand. 'July 2nd. I will count the days, my dear Brenda.'

26

General Dornberger answered the knock on his door. His eyes widened in shock when he saw who the caller was. 'Eric! What in the name of God are you doing here?'

Eric pushed past him and closed the door. 'I'm a prisoner of war, just like you, General.'

'But you're a civilian!'

'I *was* a civilian.' Eric sat on the bed without being invited. 'We've got half an hour before dinner. Is it always on time?'

'On the dot. Always.'

'Then we haven't got long. Firstly, I'm not Eric Hoffmann any more. I'm Leutnant Dieter Muller, Feldgendarmerie.'

'And you were captured by the British?'

'I would've thought that that was obvious. I'd better start right at the beginning – from the last time we saw each other.'

Dornberger sat beside Eric. 'I think you'd better.'

It took ten minutes for Eric to recount the entire story. The only detail he omitted was the location of the farm where he had buried his papers. There was a long silence when Eric finished talking. Dornberger was the first to speak.

'So you're absolutely certain that the British have no idea who you are?'

Eric nodded. 'By now I am locked into their system as Dieter Muller.'

'What about the Feldgendarmerie officer? His body will have been found by now.'

'I took all his means of identification.'

'What about his motorcycle? That is certain to be linked to him.'

'That's one thing that's been worrying me,' Eric admitted.

'And his sister. If you ask me, you're scraping by on borrowed time.'

'I just have to wait for my repatriation papers and hope that they come through first.'

'You're a fool, Eric—'

'*Dieter!* My name is *Dieter Muller*!'

'Do you think the British are sending prisoners of war home just when they feel like it? They carry out exhaustive checks. They make sure that returning soldiers have a home to go to. Food cards. That's why it's taking so damned long!'

'Even if they do discover who I am, I'm not sure that I have so much to fear from them now. You're being treated as a prisoner of war and yet you were in charge of the entire A4 project. They know who you are.'

'I'm not allowed out of this damned camp, and I had no say in the use of the A4 against civilian targets, as you well know!' Dornberger rasped.

'You can prove that?'

'If anything, Eri— Dieter – you were even more involved in that side than I was. You made field trips to the firing batteries launching A4s at Antwerp.'

'At the port and docks the Allies were using.'

'Military targets in the centre of a city? You think the British will accept that, given the known accuracy of the A4? It was far from accurate, as we all knew.'

Eric thought about the A4 that had hit Antwerp's crowded Rex Cinema.

'And those same batteries were also launching against London,' Dornberger added. 'The British will have all the battery war diaries.'

'Won't they show who the target lists were from?'

'None of them do. SS General Kammler had all war diaries and documentation linking him and his thugs with civilian targeting destroyed before the general armistice. Even the minutes of that meeting in which he spelt out that civilian targets were to become the number one priority for the A4s – terror weapons that would make the Allies surrender. Damned fools.'

'I was at that meeting, if you recall. There must some evidence?'

'Nothing so far,' was Dornberger's harsh reply. 'That murderer Kammler was efficient.'

Eric congratulated himself on his foresight in keeping a copy of those minutes – now buried in the Kilner jar. He broke the silence that followed. 'So what happened to you, General? After your exhortations about not falling into British hands.'

'Much the same as your story. It was unavoidable.'

'And yet you're here. Not in a civil prison. There have been no charges against you.'

'I thought there were going to be. I was kept under civilian arrest for a while and then sent to a frightful place in Wales. I kicked up a fuss and was sent here. They won't allow me out so it's obvious they are scratching about for evidence. When they find something that they think will serve as evidence, then they'll act. Against both of us if they find out that you're Dr Eric Hoffmann.' He paused and gave a sudden laugh. 'It's funny really. They and the Americans are probably scouring Europe looking for you.'

27

Ian Davison, the hospital's eye department registrar was a quiet, soft-spoken man who inspired confidence in Mark Schiller. Unlike the busy, often exhausted doctors who had examined him in Antwerp, Davison actually talked to him, sometimes adding seemingly inconsequential information to his commentary which was calculated to help build a good working relationship with his patient. Best of all as far as Mark was concerned, he had no objection to Eric being present. He was a friendly voice behind the powerful light of the big, floor-mounted ophthalmoscope in the darkened examination room. When he had removed the last suture holding Mark's left eye closed, he had asked him what he could see.

'Just a very bright light, Mr Davison.'

'Is there a haze around it?'

'Yes. It's like looking at a car headlight in dense fog.'

'Your English is astonishing. Are there coloured lights like a rainbow effect?'

'Yes.'

'Faint? Bright?'

'Very faint but they're there.'

'Mmm ... Well, that's good news. Your retina looks healthy. Luckily none of the splinters reached it. I'm sorry to say, Mark, that I can't say the same about the rest of your eye but it's not all bad news. The surgeon who removed the lens did a good job. He removed it through the side, through the sclera – that's the white of your eye – through an undamaged part of your cornea and the incision has healed well. According to your notes much the same was performed on your right eye but we won't be looking at that just yet. We've got quite enough on our plate with your left eye. We're looking at it first because that's the one you say is giving you the most pain.'

He switched the light on and off a couple of times. 'Well – your iris is working fine although there are lacerations to some of the collagen fibres. They're the tiny muscles that control the opening and closing of your pupil. Your eye doesn't like this light, so I'm going to put some drops in your eye to dilate the pupil. It's atropine – belladonna, meaning beautiful woman – the stuff Roman women used to put in their eyes in the belief that enlarged pupils made them look more alluring.'

'What is it made from, Mr Davison?'

'It's an extract from deadly nightshade, would you believe.'

Davison put some drops in Mark's eye and sat at a desk to write up his notes while the atropine took effect. He was not so talkative when he resumed his examination of Mark's eye. The ophthalmoscope's light tracked back and forth while the patient, lying back on the couch, did as he was told, kept his head still, staring fixedly up with a barely seeing eye. After ten minutes Davison called for a nurse to bandage the eye. She bustled in with a small trolley and set to work while Davison opened the blind and sat at the desk to write more notes. He put down his pen and drummed his fingers on the desk, deep in thought.

'Aren't you going to stitch the eyelid down?' Mark asked tentatively.

'No. There's no infection, Mark, for which we must be thankful. And, with any luck, there's someone I'd like to see you tomorrow. Excuse me. I have to make a phone call.' He left the room. The nurse finished her work and left with her trolley.

Eric moved his chair nearer so that Mark could clutch his hand. His grip trembled. 'What do you think, Dieter?'

'I know you've faced up to this already, but it doesn't look too promising.' Eric squeezed Mark's hand. 'Still – there's always the other eye and you've always said that it's your left eye that hurts the most.'

Davison returned, looking more cheerful. 'We're in luck. A most fortunate coincidence. Dr Harold Ridley is up here from London to give a talk on his ... er ... his unusual ideas. He specializes in eye injuries to fighter pilots due to their canopies shattering. He thinks your case sounds very similar to the sort of cases he's been dealing with. He's agreed to see you tomorrow afternoon before he returns to London.'

'That sounds wonderful,' said Mark. 'What's he like?'

'Experienced,' Davison replied. It would be unethical for him to point out that Dr Ridley was noted for a crazy theory he was fond of expounding that it might be possible to implant an artificial lens in the eye to replace lenses with cataracts or, as in Mark's case, lenses that had been removed altogether. His ideas attracted a good deal of ridicule from his colleagues. The notion of implanting foreign bodies in the eye was too absurd to even contemplate, given the manner in which the eye reacted to anything that didn't belong. Dr Ridley was regarded as a crackpot, but his experience in eye injuries due to shattered aircraft cockpit canopies was second to none.

'The matron's arranging for Grizedale Hall to be notified, so you don't have to go back,' he continued. 'I'm sure we can find beds for both of you for the night.'

28

Dr Harold Ridley was a small, business-like, dapper man, neatly trimmed moustache, a sly sense of humour. He talked more to himself as he worked and had a slight speech impediment that made it difficult for Eric to follow everything he said.

'Ah. Yes. Yes,' he said as soon as the dressings were removed from Mark's left eye and he had made an initial examination with a handheld ophthalmoscope. 'Severe lacerations of the epithelium which shows no sign of healing after nearly three months. Fascinating but only to be expected if there are particles from this young man's miniature submarine canopy embedded in the epithelium.'

'But no noticeable reaction?' Davison queried. 'I've looked for particles and couldn't see them. The lack of reaction symptoms suggested that all the particles had been removed.'

'You're thinking of glass particles?'

'Well – yes. Any particles.'

'Understandable. Understandable. You wouldn't believe the new plastics that have appeared in the last five years. If the canopy of this young man's miniature submarine was made of a new variety of this acrylic material, then you'd never find them. The stuff has the same refractive index as water. A few tears over the cornea and they vanish. Can you remember what your canopy was made of, young man?'

Mark held up his hand without moving his head. 'There're some fragments and splinters in this bag, sir.'

'There are!' exclaimed Harold Ridley. 'Why, that's wonderful. Why didn't you say?'

'I'm sorry, sir. But I forgot. They were saved by the doctors in Antwerp. The big splinter they removed from my arm.' Mark unknotted the little muslin bag. Harold Ridley almost snatched it from his fingers. He opened the blind, cleared a space on the desk and tipped the bag's contents on to a blank sheet of paper.

He picked up the largest fragment, a wicked sliver as long as his finger, and felt it, trying to scratch it with his fingernail. Davison found a magnifying glass for him.

'Definitely acrylic,' Harold Ridley announced, beaming. 'The question is, what sort of acrylic?'

What the hell does it matter what it's made of? Davison wondered. The stuff's fucked this young man's eyes.

'I expect it's a variation of polymethylmethacrylate like Perspex,' the doctor continued, stumbling over the long word. 'I hope so. I know how to find that stuff. We'll know when we've found out how it reacts to impact. Right – I need the following items: a small hammer, some black paper – a scrap of fogged X-ray plate will do fine; clean sheets of blank paper. It must be uncontaminated so if a new pad could be found please. Also about a pint of sterilized distilled water, a couple of sterilized beakers, and a few grains of potassium permanganate and a couple of stirring rods.'

'Wouldn't you prefer to use the lab, Doctor?' asked Davison. His colleagues were right: this man was mad.

'No need. No need. We can do it all here.'

While nursing staff were pressed into tracking down the items, Harold Ridley clapped his hands together in satisfaction and spoke to Mark. 'Well, young man. I think we're on the track of something here and we'll soon find out why your corneas aren't healing.'

Everything was found. Davison watched with interest as Harold Ridley folded the splinter carefully into a blank sheet of paper. He had never encountered a surgeon with a practical bent before and began to understand why everyone thought he was mad. Some were so vitriolic that they condemned him as a lunatic who shouldn't be allowed near patients.

Harold Ridley picked up the hammer and struck the spool of paper a sharp blow. There was an faint crunch as the encased splinter shattered. He carefully unfolded the paper and scraped the fragments of plastic on to the photographic plate with his penknife. He took great care and continued scraping methodically even though the paper appeared to be clean.

'I must try not to breath or sneeze,' he joked as he held the plate up to his eye. 'Ah yes. We're in luck. I'd say it's definitely a type of Perspex.' He positioned the desk-lamp and studied the particles of Perspex through a magnifying glass. 'Mmm ... That's the problem. Take a close look. Don't worry about the big bits – look for the small bits.'

Davison took the magnifying glass and peered at the plate. 'You means those particles? They look like grains of salt.'

'But much smaller?'

'Yes.'

'May I see, please?' asked Eric, approaching the desk.

'Certainly,' said Harold Ridley. 'That's how that stuff shatters. Big fragments like glass and specks you can hardly see. Watch this.' He poured some distilled water into a beaker, added one of the larger pieces of the canopy, and gave the beaker to Davison.

The eye surgeon held the beaker up to the light. There was no sign of the fragment of plastic.

'It's got the same refractive index as water?' Eric queried.

'Exactly. Add water and the stuff becomes invisible.'

'Hell,' Davison muttered. 'Specks smaller

than grains of salt? We'll never find them.'

'Oh yes we will,' said Harold Ridley. He added a single grain of the purple potassium permanganate to the beaker and stirred so that it dissolved and gave the water a faint blue tint. He repositioned the desk-lamp and held the beaker against it. 'Now you'll see it if you look closely.'

Davison was impressed. 'Change the refractive index of water by adding a dye to the tears in surgery and we'll find them?'

'Exactly.'

'Is that what you've been doing in London?'

'It seems that when this stuff shatters, it gives off lots of tiny specks which have the mass to penetrate the corneas's epithelium and arrest healing without causing reaction, but not enough mass and velocity to go deeper – causing permanent damage to the endothelium.' He rose and crossed to Mark. 'Well, young man. We now know why your corneas aren't healing.' He pulled up a chair beside the patient and sat. 'The cornea is made up of several transparent layers, all with distinct functions. The outer layer, the epithelium, is tough but very sensitive. A mass of nerves. That's why it hurts when we get something in our eye. Nature's warning. Luckily that outer layer usually heals readily. Any foreign bodies that actually damage it result in a pronounced reaction. But the presence of certain plastic materials, such as your canopy plastic, can cause damage, of course, and yet the eye doesn't react to the stuff as it does with other materials. Some fighter pilots brought to see me with eye damage caused by their canopies shattering suffered all the normal reactions and some didn't. Why some fighter pilots' eyes reacted and others didn't led me to do a bit of simple research. I discovered that those whose eyes didn't react were Spitfire pilots, and those whose eyes did react were Hurricane pilots. It turned out that the canopies of Spitfires are made of Perspex, and the canopies of Hurricanes are made of glass. Your eyes haven't reacted to your canopy fragments in them for the same reason – it's made of acrylic. Nevertheless, those tiny fragments have inhibited healing and we're going to find them and dig them all out. I hope you understood all that waffle. Sorry about the way I speak.'

'Yes, Doctor. Thank you so much. You've made everything clear.'

'When did you last eat?'

'Breakfast.'

'What time?'

'About eight thirty.'

Harold Ridley looked at his watch and said to Davison, 'Two hours until my train. Any chance of finding a theatre and an anaesthetist?'

'What now?'

'Why not? We might as well do both eyes while we're at it.'

Two and a half hours later Eric was dozing in the hospital waiting room when Davison sat beside him. He was awake and alert immediately.

'How is he, Doctor?'

'Mark is fine. He had no more gas than you get when you visit the dentist, so he'll be OK to go home. We'll give him another half hour to recover. Dr Ridley missed his train. He's getting a later one but he doesn't mind.'

'I'm sorry.'

'He really didn't mind at all. There were over a hundred particles of Perspex in Mark's eyes, nearly all embedded in his corneas' epitheliums. Dr Ridley was spotting them long after I gave trying to find them.'

'A remarkable man.'

Davison hesitated. 'Well, he certainly is that. Anyway, Mark has smart new dressings. See the girl at the desk and arrange an appointment for him to see me in two week's time. Dr Ridley is confident we'll see an improvement.'

'But will he be able to see again properly? Are there special glasses he'll be able wear?'

'Let's see how he is in a couple of weeks,' Davison replied, smiling warmly to conceal his lack of confidence in the strange techniques and beliefs of Dr Harold Ridley. All through surgery the London specialist had subjected Davison to a lecture on his crazy ideas about the possibility of intraocular lens implantation. Clearly a madman but an undoubted expert at finding and removing almost invisible particles in the human eye.

29

Sergeant Nurse Hobson, Brenda told herself, you are the stupidest woman in the world. But she couldn't help it; the expected knock on the door on the stroke of eleven had started her heart hammering even faster.

A final check in the mirror. It was a fine, warm day, so she had decided to wear the pretty pink cotton dress that David had liked. She had spent an hour that morning repairing a tiny moth hole in the hem, rummaging frantically through the intimidating tangle of her sewing box to find threads with matching colours. Most people wouldn't notice, but she had an uncomfortable feeling that Kruger's dark, brooding eyes missed nothing.

Unpinning her hair was a mistake. She was convinced it made her look cheap. The knock at the door was repeated. Damn! Too late do anything about it now. She fixed a bright smile in place and opened the door. Kruger, looking very smart in the same slacks and roll-neck pullover, was holding out a bunch of flowers. A taxi was waiting in the road. His initial surprised expression changed quickly to genuine pleasure.

'Good morning, Brenda. Many happy

returns but I am a day late. Will you take it amiss if I say how lovely you look without fear of punishment? Your hair like that is a wonderful surprise.'

Brenda took the bunch of flowers and the envelope he was holding out. 'Oh, they're lovely, Otto. Thank you so much. Just a minute – I'll put them in water.' She paused. 'What punishment could I inflict on you?'

'Well now – you could make me stand naked and shivering in the corridor outside your sickbay.'

Brenda laughed. Kruger took a brown-paper parcel from under his arm. It was bound with string and red sealing wax, ready for mailing. 'Could I please leave this here until we get back? I'm posting it for a guard but I forgot to ask the driver to stop at the post office. I'll post it when we return. I don't want to have to carry it about.'

'Yes – of course.' Brenda took the parcel and placed it on the hall stand. 'I won't be minute.'

She darted into the kitchen with the flowers and had to will her fingers to stop trembling as she filled a vase.

Get a hold, silly girl. You're not a teenager embarking on her first date. God – it feels like it. What *is* the matter with me?

'So where are we going?' Kruger asked, holding the taxi door open for her.

'The Star at Ulverstone.'

'What is it like?' he asked, sitting beside her in the back. The taxi moved off.

'Oh, very nice. Very olde worlde. David and I often—' She checked herself. 'At least I hope it's still all right. It's a long time since I've been there.'

To Brenda's relief, the pub hadn't changed. They sat at a table for two in the nearly deserted, low-beamed dining room by a lead-latticed window that looked on to a well-kept garden. To one side was a large converted barn that served as a function room. Their waitress was a slow, elderly lady.

'There used to be several waiters, even at lunchtime,' said Brenda when the waitress had served their vegetable soup and shuffled off. 'But they've all gone.'

'They will be coming home soon. Four of my men were taken off yesterday.'

'I know. My record cards, remember.'

'Of course.'

'Not all of them will be coming home, Otto.'

The door opened and four young naval officers entered the dining room, laughing and joking. They sat at a table at the far end of the dining room so that their risqué jokes wouldn't be overheard. Brenda watched them in silence.

With quiet passion she suddenly said, 'What was it like, Otto? When you saw a ship through your periscope and gave the order to fire? What were your feelings?'

The question and the suppressed intensity in her voice unsettled Kruger but it was honestly asked and warranted an honest reply. He was silent for a moment as he marshalled his thoughts, uncomfortably aware of the young woman's lovely eyes on him.

'Well, for a start, I hardly ever looked through a periscope. I was always on the bridge – the conning tower. It had a torpedo-aimer and we always attacked on the surface at night. Always closing in with the wind behind us so that the lookouts on ships would be half-blinded by spray. And I would be, too. Looking for the black shapes of ships. Yelling orders through the hatch to the helmsman just below me. Firing torpedoes from the bridge when the target was in the right position. As for my feelings during those moments...' He hesitated, toying nervously with his bread roll. 'It was always fear. Raw fear. Real stomach-churning fear. Fear that the convoy escorts might find us; fear that we'd have to dive and then there would be hours of being depth-charged – as happened to *U-112* several times. Fear that the pressure hull might suddenly implode and the last thing I would ever see would be a wall of green water; fear that my crew would see my fear.

'Then there was another type of fear. After a convoy action, if the escorts weren't around or were busy elsewhere, we'd try getting a closer look at ships we'd hit when they were burning. Identify their silhouette and compare them with the Lloyds register. Sometimes we'd have to finish a ship off with the main gun rather than waste torpedoes. Sometimes there would be survivors in the water – screaming for help – begging us to pick them up. But it was impossible and against orders. The fear then was that I would weaken. The fear was that my crew would see my sickness and know that I had weakened.

'And the greatest fear of all turned into a terrible reality when a destroyer seemed to come from nowhere out of the darkness and rammed us. The sound of steel plates crunching and ripping will always be with me.'

'How many of your crew survived?'

'Ten. Thirty-four went down with *U-112*. And now I live with the fear that I may have done something wrong that caused their deaths. That I made an error of judgement that I can't recall even though I've relived those moments time and time again. It's a fear that's been my constant companion since that night. Of all those fears, perhaps it's the worst because it never goes away. The fear of battle can be easily displaced by elation when the battle is over. My fear is always there, with me every day, because there's no one to tell me if I was right or wrong and even if my conscience could tell me, how would I know that I could trust it?'

There was a silence between the couple for a few moments until Brenda nodded understandingly. 'I hope you didn't mind me asking, Otto.'

Kruger covered her hand with his own. 'I'm glad you did. I've never told anyone else and telling you has made it easier. It has been something I've wanted to do and I could not have wished for a more wonderful person to tell it to.'

The compliment made Brenda tremble. 'You have had all those unhappy memories. All my memories of David are happy ones.'

'I'm glad.'

The party of naval officers suddenly burst out laughing. Kruger gave a half smile. 'Let's hope that those young men never have to live through what we've had to live through.'

'God – I hope so, Otto. I do so hope so.'

After lunch they went for a walk along a well-trodden hikers' footpath that wound up through the hills to a panoramic view of Morecambe Bay. Brenda stumbled on the uneven ground in her high-heeled shoes. Kruger put his arm around her waist to steady her and didn't take it away when the ground evened out.

They sat on a bench at the highest point. Kruger kept his arm around Brenda. They didn't speak for some minutes, enjoying the warmth of the sun sparkling on the distant sea, and the closeness of each other.

'What will happen to you?' Brenda asked.

'When my papers come through?'

'Yes.'

'I don't know. There were times when I ached to go home but that has passed, I think. Oberleutnant Karl Shriver and Leutnant Josef Hinkel have applied to stay in England and open an architects' practice.'

'Didn't they do most of the work on restoring the banqueting hall?'

'Yes.'

'But what about you, Otto? Isn't there a girl waiting patiently at home? A real "Alice"?'

Kruger laughed. 'No. There was ten years ago but she decided to marry a banker. I was never very good at making friends.'

'Ah. Otto the Silent. I haven't heard any POW call you that for a long time. So the aloofness was all an act? Underneath you were really the shy little boy?'

'Perhaps. I think I now have more friends in England than I have at home. A year ago I began thinking that it would be hard to leave here.' He looked at her. 'Even more so now, I think.'

They lapsed into silence again.

'What are you thinking?' Brenda asked.

'Oh ... Wishing.'

'Wishing what?'

'That I could make the earth stop spinning so that the sun would stop moving. Just to make these moments with you last longer.'

Brenda gave him a playful punch. 'A shy little boy doesn't say things like that to a girl.'

Kruger turned his head and kissed her forehead. It was a fleeting kiss, little more than his lips brushing against her.

'Or do things like that.' Brenda gave an involuntary giggle and adopted a severe tone. 'Commander Kruger – I shall have to punish you.'

'Oh? How?'

Brenda cocked her head on one side and regarded him mischievously. 'Well now. I could make you stand naked and shivering in the corridor outside my sickbay door.'

They both laughed. Brenda looked at her watch. 'Unfortunately, Otto, the sun hasn't stopped moving. I want to be home before Stephen, and you have to get to the post office before they shut. We must be making a move and find a taxi.' She stood and suddenly looked faintly surprised.

'What's the matter, Brenda?'

'I've just realized. "We must be making a move and find a taxi" – I once said exactly the same thing to David. The same words. Right here. On this very bench.'

'You've been up here with him?'

'Only the once. This is where he proposed to me. It was late one evening. Getting dark. Just before that we'd...' She broke off, looking embarrassed.

Kruger stood, puzzled. 'Just before we what?'

Brenda pointed down the slope to a gnarled old yew tree, its branches touching the ground. 'It was just over there. I remember looking up at the moon shining through the branches and thinking how happy I was.'

'It's brave of you to tell me these things,' said Kruger. 'Coming back to the place where one has known great happiness can be a mistake. Sometimes it is better to leave the memories alone and not allow reality to intrude.'

She took his hand. 'Well, I'm glad I did let reality intrude. It wasn't a mistake. Come on.'

They set off hand in hand down the hill. 'David was the only man I'd ever known until then,' said Brenda when they resumed their conversation. 'Or since. He was a wonderful man, Otto. Caring and gentle.'

'And he has left you a wonderful living memory. Stephen is a fine boy.'

'It's strange really. When you think about it, it's Stephen who has brought us— What I mean is, that if it wasn't for Stephen we wouldn't be walking together now. It must be some sort of omen.'

'A very good omen.'

They found a taxi, which dropped them outside Brenda's cottage with fifteen minutes to spare before Stephen arrived home from school. Brenda turned to Kruger as she pushed her front door open. 'Thank you for such a lovely time, Otto. I've enjoyed every minute of it. It's been so long since I enjoyed myself so much.' She kissed her fingertips and pressed them against his lips.

Kruger seized her hand and pressed it harder to his mouth. 'The four hours with you has made every minute of the four years as a prisoner worthwhile. Thank you for your wonderful company.'

Brenda smiled. That impish, mischievous smile that Kruger was learning to love. 'Considering that English is not your first language, Commander Kruger, you certainly know how to use it to woo a girl.'

'And I know the meaning of to tell a white lie, too, Nurse Hobson.'

She looked puzzled.

'I told you a white lie about that parcel. It's not for posting. There's no address on it. We're not supposed to post things anyway. It's your birthday present.' He wagged an admonishing finger. 'And you're not to open it until I'm gone.' With that he clicked his heels, bowed and kissed her hand before turning away and walking off with long strides without looking back.

Neighbouring net curtains twitched. Let them, thought Brenda, slamming the front door shut with her bottom as a demonstration of her dismissal of any disapproval. She was too happy to care about what her neighbours thought. She took the parcel into her front room, cut the string and tore off the brown paper. Inside was a box. She lifted the lid, pulled aside the tissue paper and gasped at what she saw. She snatched up the box, raced upstairs to her bedroom and threw off her outer clothes. The first garment in the box was a silk slip. It fell smoothly over her shoulders and settled in place about her body, the cunning cut of the beautifully stitched darts caused it to cling so evenly to her that she hardly felt she was wearing it. She saw herself in the full-length mirror and caught her breath in wonder. Never had she ever had a garment that was such a perfect fit. She studied herself in profile. No matter which way she turned, the slip was marvellously perfect, hanging evenly from her hips as if she had been pinned into the material by a skilled seamstress. She pulled it off carefully and marvelled at the delicate embroidery – patterns of tiny flowers that decorated the neckline and sleeve hems. As far she could make out, everything was made of the finest silk.

The next garment was full length and was as stunning as the first. It was slightly heavier with a fine modesty lining in important places. She couldn't decide whether it was a negligee or an evening dress. The hem was so precise that it was an even three inches from the floor all around. She gave an exuberant twirl before the mirror and watched the material settle sensually about her, hanging perfectly straight from her hips like the slip. It was a garment to be seen in. She decided that it was an evening dress. It could even be a wedding dress.

Brenda loved the dressing gown. It had fashionable three-quarter-length cuffed sleeves and was secured at the front with a single tie which appealed to her tiny streak of exhibitionism which she pretended didn't exist.

There were two pairs of quite wicked frilly French knickers which Follies cancan girls would have gone to war over. The brassiere was the most comfortable she had ever known. A perfect fit that provided decidedly figure-flattering lift and support. Even that was fringed with painstakingly intricate floral embroidery.

She spread all garments on the bed to admire them and found a note in the box:

> *For Brenda. These are offered in the pious hope that they can add perfection to that which is already perfect. O*

It was all too much for Brenda. She began to tremble and had to sit on the bed. A turmoil of emotions she could neither understand nor control welled up from the centre of her being and she surrendered to tears.

30

Reynolds eyed Fleming's Bentley tourer in some alarm as it burbled across the courtyard and stopped. He had been warned that the naval officer would be arriving with company but the number was unexpected. He sent Private Knox hurrying to the kitchen to tell the chef, Leutnant Walter Hilgard, to expect four guests for lunch and to do his best.

'Hallo, James,' said Fleming cheerfully, jumping out from the behind the monstrous car's wheel and helping Sally down from the cramped rear seat.

'So they've finally allowed you petrol for this thing? We've all been wondering why we haven't seen you for so long.'

'This is Sally, my secretary. She swears that she's going back to London by train tomorrow even if she has to pay the fare out of her own pocket.'

Johnny Benyon shook hands with Reynolds as they were introduced and commented that women didn't appreciate the joys of travelling in fine cars.

'Actually,' said Fleming, 'I quite liked her hairstyle before she straightened it out at the hotel.' He introduced the fourth member of the party. A mild-looking, sallow-complexioned young man. 'And this is Rupert Driver. He's a lawyer, so he's used to not being spoken to.'

'A civil servant lawyer at that, to make matters even worse,' said Driver, smiling as he shook Reynolds's hand.

'We can poison him with Sergent Finch's coffee,' said Fleming as they entered Reynolds's office. 'Although I think we'd all rather he used this.' He presented Reynolds with a tin of Nescafé instant coffee.

'Hell, Ian, where did you get this?'

'Overseas posting, old boy.'

Sergeant Finch ordered Private Knox to make them all coffee. Then he and the soldier sat in the outer office, drinking some coffee they had made for themselves using the Nescafé, while wondering what the visit was in aid of.

'Christ knows,' Sergeant Finch muttered, sipping his mug. 'Who cares if they bring us stuff like this?'

'My mother's written to me from Italy,' said Private Knox. 'She said that you can get virtually anything there.'

'Bloody marvellous,' growled the NCO. '*We* win the bloody war and *we* get the bloody rationing.'

Private Knox nodded glumly. 'You wouldn't believe what I had to pay for a birthday card for Nurse Hobson.'

'I would if you bought it through that fat little thieving, lying Jerry.'

Private Knox's intercom buzzed. 'You'll have to decamp from that office until tomorrow afternoon,' advised Reynolds. 'It's needed. And would one of you please fetch General Dornberger.'

Ten minutes later Dornberger, looking relaxed and comfortable, was facing Fleming, Benyon and Driver across a table in the outer office. Another questioning from yet more typical chinless-wonder English aristocrats, he thought.

Fleming introduced himself and Johnny Benyon and Rupert Driver. 'And Sally will take shorthand notes,' he added. 'Johnny Benyon's technical German is far better than mine. Rupert – perhaps you'd open the batting for England.'

'General Dornberger,' Driver began. 'This is merely a preliminary investigation—'

'They've all been "preliminary investigations",' snapped Dornberger, glowering at Fleming. 'First in Germany, then in that

Island Camp Farm in Wales. A procession of lily-livered Englishmen like yourselves telling me about their pathetic investigations.'

'This is not quite like the other questioning,' said Driver, unperturbed. 'Firstly I'm from the office of the Official Solicitor. I'm not representing you as such, but later you will be allowed access to a lawyer—'

'If your conscience decides that you need one,' said Fleming dryly.

'But I am here to see that the questioning is fair should a future court require a report.'

'And to see that I don't use a rubber truncheon,' Fleming added.

Despite the flippant remark, Dornberger saw the steel in Fleming's hard gaze and wondered if he had misjudged the man. He prided himself on being a good judge of character and a good organizer with the ability to select the right man for the right job. But that was with his own countrymen who were open and honest in their tone and expression. But he had never got the measure of the English. They said one thing but their eyes could say something else. Perfidious Albion, Napoleon had called them.

'General Dornberger,' said Driver. 'If you wish for this interview to be conducted in German, we will do so. But English would be helpful for the shorthand transcript.'

'I sure my English is better than your German. Let it be in English if that's what makes you happy.'

Driver made a note observing that Dornberger managed to inject offensiveness into answers to even the most innocuous questions.

'Before you start, gentlemen,' said Dornberger determinedly, 'I have a simple statement to make. I have no wish to make my talents available to the British in the design and construction of long-range missiles. My ambitions lie beyond that. While I have every respect for the technical abilities of the British, I do not believe they have the money, facilities, energy or will to meet my exacting criteria for co-operation. Only the United States meets my standards. I will give you accurate answers where I can but do not expect or anticipate access to my expertise.' General Dornberger sat back in his chair and smiled. 'If the Americans ask me and my colleagues for the moon, we will be the ones to give it to them.'

'So you've made clear on several previous occasions, General,' Fleming observed coldly. 'You overlook the fact that it may not be your expertise that we're after. Shall we begin?'

The German officer shrugged.

Fleming's opening questions put Dornberger more at ease, as they were intended to do. They dealt with his early years as a ballistics student at Charlottenberg Institute of Technology. His degree and how he first met Wernher von Braun, as a fellow member of the German Society for Space Travel. He spoke freely about the early liquid-fuel rockets that Johannes Winkler and von Braun had built and launched and how, on a memorable day, one had reached an estimated height of half a kilometre.

'That marked the turning point,' said Dornberger. 'I realized then that Oberth was right. It would be possible for men to journey to the moon and that the only way to do it would be with a rocket.'

Driver thought the passion in the German's voice when he talked about manned space travel was genuine.

The questions turned to when Dornberger was commissioned into the army and how he convinced high-ranking officers that the rocket was a weapon that the German army ought to look at.

'They didn't need that much convincing. Rockets and their development were not prohibited by the Treaty of Versailles.'

Fleming's questioning changed tack. He asked Dornberger about his setting up of the army's rocket research facility in 1937 near the village of Peenemunde on the Baltic coast.

'We had an A4 engine working on the test bed by early 1940,' said Dornberger proudly.

'Thrust?'

'Without the test reports, I cannot say.'

Fleming raised an eyebrow. 'Surely you know?'

'The results of the first test ran into several dozen sheets of detailed data!' Dornberger snapped. 'Do you expect me to carry such a mass of information in my head?'

'Johnny?' Fleming queried.

'Yet the thrust would be the most important piece of data of the lot,' Benyon observed. 'It would be right at the top of the report.'

'About ten tonnes. That's not a precise answer. I prefer to provide precise answers to gratify the pedantic English and their craving for nit-picking accuracy. However ... it seems that you're not interested in my giving accurate answers – a fact that ought to be recorded in the minutes.'

Neat, thought Driver, making a note.

'Ten tonnes,' mused Fleming. 'How did you see the V2, General? What sort of weapon?'

'Artillery, of course. For use against military targets. How else could it be seen?'

'Used by armies facing each other across battlefields? With ten tonnes of thrust at your disposal, you'd be able to fire London double-decker buses at the enemy.'

'That is a singularly stupid comment, Commander. Most of a rocket's thrust is used to lift its own weight. The A4's payload was a fraction of its launch weight.'

'You used to test fire eastwards into Poland. How big was your target area? Within two or three hundred metres either way will suffice if you've forgotten the precise figure.'

'It had a diameter of approximately twenty kilometres. Farmland with few inhabitants whom we evacuated and resettled elsewhere.'

'About three hundred square kilometres.'

'The accuracy was improving.'

'That,' said Fleming mildly, 'is as far from

the truth as your V2s from their targets. They were hopelessly inaccurate when you told Albert Speer that production could go ahead.'

'We carried on development work on the guidance systems! Production of the main rocket did not depend on the guidance system development being completed.'

'And yet you went on with production after the first V2s were fired at London.'

Dornberger started to get angry when he saw the direction in which the questions were leading. 'The A4 was planned for attacks against military targets. Big targets. Airforce bases, naval bases, army camps. As I've made clear time and time again, target selection was an SS responsibility.'

Fleming smiled. 'We have an account from Wernher von Braun about the accuracy of V2s. In 1943 you were having problems with the rockets breaking up on re-entry into the atmosphere. It was decided to carry out test firings on clear days when it would be possible to film re-entries using cameras with special high-power lenses. When asked the safest place to site the cameras, von Braun said right in the centre of the target area because that was the one place that they never hit.'

'One hundred per cent accuracy is impossible,' said Dornberger frostily. 'There are many variations to be considered. Your bombing could hardly ever be described as accurate, yet it didn't stop the RAF from dropping bombs.'

'The difference between the RAF raids and your firings of V2s is that the RAF were trying to hit military targets.'

'Like Dresden?'

Fleming was unperturbed. 'When your V2s were actually hitting London, we put out reports on the BBC saying that they were falling a long way north of London. Guess what? The V2s then started falling short of London. There were too many instances of that happening to be a coincidence. Enough to convince us that the entire city was being treated as a target.'

'The RAF bombs didn't fall short of civilian targets when they raided Peenemunde,' said Dornberger. 'One wave of bombers attacked the technical complex, another deliberately attacked the residential area. Hundreds of civilians – men, women and children – were killed.'

Fleming removed a stapled sheaf of typewritten documents from his briefcase and tossed it on the desk in front of Dornberger. 'A complete list of V2 hits together with numbers of those killed and maimed. Thousands of men, women and children. In Antwerp I attended a memorial service to commemorate those killed when a V2 hit a crowded cinema. Nearly six hundred dead. In retrospect, that made Peenemunde a legitimate military target as far as we were concerned, General.'

Dornberger shrugged. 'As I've said before, I was not in charge of target selection.

SS-General Dr Hans Friedrich Karl Franz Kammler was put charge of the A4 programme. I had to play second fiddle to him. He was also made responsible for the construction of all the production facilities. We all objected to the SS having full control but we were overruled. It's all on record – some documents must've survived and will emerge – but we've already established that you're not interested in accurate answers.'

'What happened to the those records, General?'

'Kammler had them destroyed. He was thorough. His thugs went through all our offices, emptying filing cabinets. Demanding minutes of meetings – everything. Why aren't you questioning him?'

'He's disappeared without trace,' said Fleming.

'He's sure to turn up. He won't have gone east – not him. Like all SS, he hated the Soviets.'

Fleming looked down at some other documents he had removed from his briefcase. 'You claimed during your first interview with military intelligence officers after your capture that there was a meeting at Nordhausen shortly after D-Day in which Kammler said that the SS would select targets once the V2 offensive started. I take it that those minutes were included in Kammler's document round-up?'

'I said "everything". Perhaps you'd prefer it if this continued in German as you seem to be having trouble understanding English?'

Fleming smiled lazily. 'You refused to say who was at the meeting at the time.'

'I didn't have a list. I couldn't remember everyone. I try to give accurate answers.'

'Perhaps you've now had time to think?'

Dornberger thought for a moment and nodded. 'What I remember is that they were nearly all SS – Kammler's toadies. I'll give you their names first and any more later when I remember them.' He paused and recited names. Sally queried some spellings.

'That's all the SS personnel I can remember,' said Dornberger when he had finished. 'Not that it'll do you any good. I heard that they were all transferred to the defence of Berlin. If they're not dead, the Russians will have them.'

'And your people at the meeting?'

Dornberger started recalling names. Fleming requested them one at a time so that he could check each one in turn against a typewritten list. 'Either dead or missing, General, or fallen into Soviet hands. None of them are held by the Americans. Wasn't Wernher von Braun at the meeting?'

Dornberger shook his head. He opened his mouth to speak when something seemed to occur to him and promptly shut it again.

Fleming looked at him enquiringly. 'You were about to say, General?'

'Dr Eric Hoffmann was there.'

'Ah yes. Your regenerative cooling man. He seems to have disappeared, too.'

Dornberger made no reply.

Fleming sat back and steepled his fingers. 'Tell me about your plan to launch V2s from U-boats.'

The question stung Dornberger. 'That was Kammler's crazy idea!' he snapped. 'It was typical of the man. Senseless! Stupid!'

'So tell me what was senseless and stupid about it.'

'The problems of carrying an A4 in a watertight caisson on the deck of a U-boat would be insuperable, even on a Type XXI U-boat, to say nothing of the problems of fuelling and launching the weapon at sea. All I heard was that his crackpot idea never got beyond testing a prototype caisson. It was madness from the beginning and I said so.'

'What other problems would there be other than keeping the container watertight and launching the V2 at sea?'

Dornberger gave a crooked smile. 'Aren't they enough?'

'Of course,' said Fleming, smiling icily at Dornberger. 'Accuracy wouldn't be a problem because the targets would be seaboard cities. New York; Los Angeles; Cape Town.'

Dornberger realized that he had blundered and remained silent for some moments. 'Listen,' he said harshly at length. 'Find Kammler. He was a bully and a coward. He'll talk if he thinks it will save his neck.'

'We not talking about necks, General,' Fleming observed mildly, lighting a cigarette. 'At least – not yet.'

31

'Ian! How good to see you!' Kruger exclaimed, smiling in genuine pleasure when Willi showed Fleming into his office. The two men shook hands. The German officer's handshake was firm, his smile genuine. 'I saw your car in the courtyard.'

'Hallo, Otto. How have the months been treating you?'

'So-so. Just whiling away the days until my repatriation papers come through. They're all going home, one by one. Thank you for the cigars. They were very welcome.'

'Sorry I've neglected you. Wartime shortages and all that.'

'I'm sure I can persuade Willi to help out with any shortages you may be suffering. You name it, Willi is certain to have it.'

Fleming laughed. 'You've changed, Otto.'

'In what way?'

'The old Otto has been demolished and a human being has been erected in his place.'

'Really?'

'The old Otto would've frozen me with a look at that joke. You're still smiling.'

Kruger produced a bottle of sherry and two glasses.

'I hate to be rude, old boy, but I'm pushed for time. I need to talk to you and wonder if we could take a stroll around the grounds.'

'Yes – of course.' Kruger put on his cap. 'That's one thing I haven't changed. I'm never seen around the camp without my cap.'

The two men left the building via the courtyard where a table tennis tournament between the Luftwaffe and the Kriegsmarine was in progress. 'Good Lord,' said Fleming. 'Who's the incredibly lovely blonde nurse?'

Kruger glanced at Nurse Hobson, who was heading towards the gatehouse. 'You're getting forgetful, Ian. Nurse Hobson has been here longer than me.'

'I don't remember her looking like that. She was positively dowdy. What's changed her?'

'Perhaps it's you who has changed and not us?'

'She really is something,' said Fleming, watching Brenda enter the gatehouse.

'And how is Mrs Cathy Standish? Your merry widow?'

Fleming grimaced. 'Don't remind me, old boy. I owe her a visit but I can't because I simply don't have the time. By the way, how is Leutnant Mark Schiller getting on? That young man gave us a few problems. Nothing serious and not his fault.'

'He's fine. He's already had one operation on his eyes and they're not hurting anymore. He can get around the hall by himself with little trouble now. He has a remarkable spacial memory and the camp cat follows him everywhere. I've brought in rules that no rubbish is to be left in corridors or on the stairs and Willi has found him some Braille books. So long as he has Leutnant Dieter Muller around and Hermann – that's the cat – he seems reasonably happy here.'

The two men rounded the building and crossed the lawn, following the perimeter wire.

'Strange,' Kruger commented. 'We can now leave the camp but I still prefer to take my daily walks around the grounds. What did you want to talk to me about?'

'Have you made any plans about what you want to do now?'

Kruger shook his head. 'The Kriegsmarine is no more. My thought has been to get home, and take it from there.'

'In other words, you've no idea?'

'None at all,' Kruger admitted.

'Well, I've got an idea that might appeal to you.'

The two men walked around the perimeter twice, deep in conversation. At the end Fleming looked at his watch. 'Must fly. So you'll give it some thought, old boy?'

'I promise to give it very careful thought, Ian,' Kruger replied. 'But I do need more details.'

Fleming promised to return as soon as possible with more information. The two men shook hands.

Willi was waiting for Kruger when he returned to the hall to tell him that Nurse

Hobson wished to see him in her sickbay and that she hadn't said what it was about.

Kruger rapped on her sickbay door and entered when she called out. She greeted him with that warm, mischievous smile.

'Lock the door, Otto.'

The room darkened as he did so. When he turned she had closed the blind and was re-positioning the screen.

'Who's the boss in here, Otto?'

Kruger smiled, wondering what she was planning. 'You are, Nurse Hobson.'

'Good.' She pointed. 'You will sit in that chair and you will not move until I say you can move. Sit!'

Greatly intrigued, Kruger sat. Brenda disappeared behind the screen. It sounded as she was busy doing something but he could not be sure what.

'OK, you will now close your eyes.'

Kruger closed his eyes.

There was the sound of the screen being moved.

'You may now open them.'

He opened his eyes and gasped.

'Da-da!' Having provided her own musical sting, Brenda gave a little pirouette. She was wearing the silk evening dress. The light shining through the blind's narrow slats behind her provided perfect illumination, outlining the loveliness of her slim body. She gave a swaying gyration of her hips, dancing sensually to inaudible music while holding her arms up like a flamenco dancer, turning slowly, keeping her eyes fixed on Kruger to gauge the effect she was having on him.

He sat transfixed.

She smiled. 'There's more. Don't go away.'

'I wasn't planning to.' His voice was hoarse.

She laughed, disappeared behind the screen and emerged wearing the dressing gown, loosely fastened at the waist so that he could see that she was wearing the French knickers and the brassiere underneath. This time she stood immediately before him so that he could've reached out and touched as she went through the little Salome dance routine again.

'Wearing this brings out the slut in me, Otto.'

'There's no slut in you, Brenda.'

She laughed and swirled the dressing gown provocatively across his cheek, giving him a glimpse of her legs. 'Don't you believe it, kind sir! Don't you believe that for one moment.'

With that she sat astride his knees, pulled him close and kissed him, nervously and uncertainly at first and then with a sudden surge of passion that surprised her and most certainly surprised Kruger.

32

Dornberger swept into the room without knocking.

'The British want to hang me,' he announced.

Eric was stretched out on his bed. He closed his book, thinking that if that were the case, then he might be prepared to lend a hand.

'Why do you say that, General?'

'I've been subjected to two days grilling. Their questioning left no doubt in my mind that they think I'm responsible for selecting the targets during the A4 offensive.'

'Do they have evidence that you did?'

'I don't have evidence that I didn't! Eric – you've got to help me. You were at that meeting. You always kept a diary of everything. I remember you always writing in it.'

'What evidence is a handwritten diary, General?'

'The entry will be against the date – in the midst of all the other entries. Impossible to forge or alter afterwards. You'll have to say who you really are and tell the British where to find your cache. It's my only hope.'

'I've sworn to myself that I won't do that until Mark no longer needs me.'

'That could be the rest of his life!' Dornberger snapped.

'I hope not. There's a possibility that his eyes are treatable. We'll have a better idea tomorrow after his hospital visit.' Eric shot a worried glance at Dornberger. 'You wouldn't betray me, would you, General?'

The question annoyed him. 'To these British? Never. Nor to anyone else.'

It was the answer Eric expected. Dornberger was an exasperatingly arrogant man but he had the high principles of the old Prussian officer cadre and stuck to them.

'So what the hell am I going to do? OK – so I haven't been arrested yet, but I'm certain that it's only a matter of days. You didn't see the faces of those bastards that grilled me. Dear God – if only I hadn't blundered into the British army.'

Eric was thoughtful. 'Have you read the US newspapers, General? There are a few in the library.'

'I don't read *any* British or American papers. All they print is lies.'

'A *New York Tribune* came in a couple of days ago. It has an article about John J. McCloy, President Truman's Assistant Secretary of War. McCloy is the driving force behind the Americans' Operation Paperclip to get as many A4 technicians on to US soil, give them US citizenship and get them working fast on long-range liquid-fuel missiles. He actually said that wherever the Soviets plan to go, it was his avowed aim that America would be there first. I think you should write to him, set out your case. My guess is that he'll put pressure on the British to release you into US custody. The paper reports that McCloy even favours letting Alfred Krupp off the hook.'

'Easier said than done. Firstly I'm not allowed to set foot outside the camp, we've all given our parole about mailing letters, and I wouldn't want to ask any officer to do so for me anyway. Furthermore, I don't imagine for a moment that the British are susceptible to political pressure from the Americans.'

Eric grinned. 'US political pressure on the British is exactly why I'm here with Mark, General. As for asking an officer to break his parole by posting a letter for you, Willi Hartmann would do it for a small payment. Correction, knowing Willi, more likely a large payment.'

'That man is a liar and a cheap crook,' Dornberger fumed. 'He's a disgrace to the Wehrmacht uniform.'

'A useful disgrace if he'll post a letter for you, General.'

'He'd open and read it.'

'Of course he would. But not if I gave it to him to post outside a post office and paid him to post it there and then.'

Dornberger stared at Eric. 'You know – I think that might be a good idea.' He beamed. 'In fact it's a brilliant idea.'

Eric looked doleful. 'Nothing has changed, General. You were always congratulating me on my brilliant ideas when you had a problem.'

'Who should I address it to?'

'Simple. John J. McCloy, Assistant Secretary for War, care of the United States Embassy, London. Put it in an inner envelope marked "Operation Paperclip" and it's sure to get to someone high up in double-quick time. Perhaps it would be better if the letter is posted from a town such as Ulverstone. Such an address on a letter in the village post office is certain to attract unwelcome attention.'

Dornberger thanked Eric and turned to leave. 'I'll make an immediate start. What was that American newspaper?'

'The *Tribune*, General.'

Dornberger returned two hours later.

'It's all there,' he said, handing Eric a bulky envelope. 'I did as you suggested. There's an inner envelope marked "Operation Paperclip".'

'I'm sure it'll do the trick, General,' said Eric, taking the envelope and slipping it into an inside pocket in his jacket.

Dornberger counted out three one-pound notes into Eric's hand. 'That's sure to be more than enough for your fares and so forth. Don't give that little crook more than ten shillings – not for just posting a letter.'

'I'll account for every penny spent when I give you the change,' Eric promised.

'See that you do.'

As it happened Eric never did have to give General Dornberger his change. An hour later a black police Wolseley turned up at

Grizedale Hall. Two grim-faced plainclothes officers entered Reynolds's office.

Dornberger was sent for. Word spread through the camp in minutes and all the POWs gathered in the courtyard in time to see Dornberger, his wrists handcuffed, leave the office flanked by the two policemen, and get into the back of the car. The Wolseley swept out of the courtyard.

That evening at dinner Kruger rose to announce that General Dornberger had been arrested on a charge of participation and execution of aggressive warfare with the possibility of more charges to follow. He added, his expression inscrutable, that this was the same charge that his old flag officer, Grand Admiral Karl Doenitz, was facing.

After dinner Eric sought out Willi.

'I'm taking Mark to Barrow-in-Furness tomorrow for his hospital appointment, Willi, and wondered if you would like to accompany us – all expenses paid.'

Willi was suspicious. 'Why?'

'We thought we'd like your company, Willi,' said Eric cheerfully, clapping him on the back. 'You go around with such a hunted expression. You need to get out. Who knows? There might be a chance of your making a few shillings.'

The plump Bavarian was immediately interested but saw a problem. 'It is difficult for me to leave the camp.'

'Why? You're not on movement restriction.'

'Carol Bunce is always waiting for me outside. In here I am safe from her.'

Eric was sympathetic. 'I'll get Private Knox to send for a taxi to take us to the station.'

33

Ian Davison didn't need his ophthalmoscope to see the extraordinary improvement that had taken place in Mark's eyes in the week since he and Harold Ridley had operated. Some ninety per cent of the minor lesions of the epitheliums of both corneas were healing well, and the remaining ten per cent were improving markedly. By holding his ophthalmoscope at an angle he could see some flare from scarring of the Bowman's layers below the epitheliums but they were away from the pupil and would most likely not cause any problems. Quite a lot of minor housekeeping surgery would be needed once the healing of the corneas was complete but what was called for was routine repair work.

'Wonderful,' he said to Mark. 'Your corneas are healing fast. Far better than I thought possible a week ago.'

Mark was elated. 'I knew something had to be getting better because the pain started easing off after the operation and was gone by two days ago. Will it be possible to do something, Doctor? Will it?'

'We need to leave it another week, Mark. The healing isn't complete but we're getting there.'

Mark was impatient during the week that followed, counting the days and even going to bed early to make the time pass a little quicker. He was almost trembling in anticipation a week later as Davison removed the dressings from his eyes, but he forced himself to calm down and did his best not to follow the tantalizing point of light from Davison's ophthalmoscope – that wonderful spark of hope that told him that his retinas and optic nerves were fine.

'Marvellous,' said Davison when the nurse had replaced the patient's dressings. 'We're well out the woods now. Your corneas have healed so well that the danger of infection is pretty well passed. It means we can start thinking ahead.'

'You mean I'll be able to see, Doctor? Really see?'

Davison laughed good-naturedly. 'You're not going to pin me down just yet, Mark. Let's say that there are grounds for cautious optimism and leave it at that for the time being. But you've still got several lesions that are going to need sutures. What I call some housekeeping work. General tidying up. All routine and nothing to worry about. I want to book you in for about five nights next week if we can find a bed. That will enable me to have a good look at you a few days afterwards. OK?'

'OK?' Mark exclaimed delightedly. 'It's more than OK! It's marvellous. Only thing is, poor Dieter might get fed up trailing back and forth.'

'"Get"?' Eric echoed, giving Mark's hand an affectionate squeeze. 'What do you mean "get"? I already am fed up to my back teeth lugging you back and forth but I daresay I'll cope a little longer.'

As Davison put his ophthalmoscope back in its case and snapped the lid shut, he reflected that in future, when the talk among his colleagues turned to vitriolic condemnation of Dr Harold Ridley and his ideas, he was going risk ridicule by being a dissenting voice for the defence.

34

A strong breeze suddenly got up, sweeping up the steep fell, so that the kite Berg had made for Stephen no longer needed Kruger's valiant running efforts to keep it aloft. He handed the stick wound with string to the boy, crossed to the picnic rug and sprawled on his back, exhausted. Brenda propped herself on an elbow and looked down at him, smiling mischievously.

'No stamina, these old men today,' she observed.

Kruger's answer was to grab hold of Brenda's hair and pull her head down for a kiss. He had learned that she wasn't wholly adverse to a little rough treatment, but not too rough. Finding out about her was proving to be more fun than he imagined possible.

Brenda lay beside him and they watched Stephen's kite swooping back and forth. 'It was kind of Berg to make that,' she said. 'And all the other things. I did think of putting on a little "thank you" show for him, like the one I put on for you, but I didn't think you'd have approved.'

'I don't own you, Nurse Hobson.'

'Ah – but I wouldn't mind being owned by you.'

'Like a dog, do you mean? Your nose isn't wet enough and you never fetch sticks.'

Brenda laughed and twisted around to rest her head on his hip, happy and relaxed, as she always was in Kruger's company. This was their second picnic together with Stephen. He now adored Kruger and had dubbed him Uncle OK. 'You still haven't told me what Ian Fleming wanted.'

'A tentative sounding out of my feelings about a job.'

'What sort of job?'

'Being part of the building of a new Germany. Specifically, a new navy. Right from scratch. It'll have a new name. Federal Navy – Bundesmarine. Something like that.'

Brenda groaned. 'Oh no, Otto. We're not starting all over again, are we?'

'It'll be a peacetime navy.'

'They always are until some lunatic comes along and makes them unpeaceful.'

'That won't happen again. There'll be a new constitution with many built-in safeguards.'

Brenda rolled on to her stomach and looked at him, her eyes large and serious. 'Have you accepted?'

'It's all far in future. Long term. I wanted to talk it over with you first. I can't imagine doing anything with my life unless you're a part of it.'

'Is that a proposal, Otto Kruger?'

'Would you like it to be?'

'Because if it is, not only would I say yes, but the wicked slut in me might even say yes please.'

Kruger could think of nothing to say, so he kissed her.

Stephen's string broke. He rescued the crashed kite, knotted the string, and had the kite airborne again in no time.

'There are too many problems, my darling,' said Kruger quietly.

'List them. My mother says that problems listed one by one can be solved one by one.'

'I'd have to live in Germany.' He was suddenly talking fast. 'But Germany isn't like those newsreels of Berlin. It's a huge country, much of it untouched. I was brought up in a little village near the Danish border. Overlooking the sea. A farming community. It's a beautiful place. I've always wanted to buy a place and live there.'

'So that's one problem solved. Where to live.'

'Brenda – you have to think about it seriously. It's an awesome step to take which—'

'Which I want to take,' Brenda interrupted sharply.

'But, Stephen—'

'Is going to boarding school. David's old school. It's what he wanted. It's what I want. It was planned a long time ago. We could always keep my cottage and I could fly home for holidays and half-terms.'

Kruger sat up and stared across the valley with troubled eyes. 'That would be expensive. Brenda – I have to be honest. My pay will be good but perhaps not good enough. There might be some back pay for the time I've been a prisoner, but it's not certain. Every penny I have will be yours but I'm not rich—'

'That's not a problem either,' said Brenda shortly. She saw Kruger's look of surprise. 'David left me all his money from his father's estate and his father's share of the family business. It's a lot of money. I don't know exactly how much, but it's a lot. David came into it after we'd bought the cottage. We were half-thinking of selling it, but then there was the war and then he was ... He was killed. There – I've said it. I wanted to sell up there and then because it had so many memories but my mother said that I shouldn't add to the stress I was going through. That I should stick to my daily routine ... My job ...

Looking after Stephen ... Doing that would help me get through the whole wretched business. She said that having a routine removed the stress of having to make decisions at a time when I was in no state to cope with decision-making. She was right.'

'She sounds like a wise woman,' said Kruger quietly.

'She is. Practical and down to earth. You'll meet her next week. I know you'll like her, and she'll like you despite ... Well – you know.'

'I don't know what to say,' said Kruger. 'I'm overwhelmed with happiness.'

'Well, I know what to say. The answer's yes.'

'Yes to what?'

'That I'll marry you, you idiot!'

Kruger cradled her face in his hands. 'Brenda – you know so little about me.'

'I don't want to know a lot about you all at once. That's the fun of marriage. Each day I want to open another little door into that dark, inscrutable soul. A disgraceful secret lust revealed to me each day. You have got disgraceful secret lusts?'

'Lots,' Kruger replied, matching her impish mood.

'That's good. So have I. Let's hope that some of them overlap.'

They fell back on the picnic blanket, helpless with laughter.

'And I can think of yet another problem that's been solved,' said Brenda, wiping her eyes.

'Oh? And what's that?'

'Thanks to Berg and Krantz, I've already made a good start on my trousseau.' Brenda grimaced. 'Unless these stupid clothing coupons are scrapped, my garter's going to be a matter of Hobson's Choice.'

'I'd like to see it before you buy it.'

'Never! You've already had your little treat. You'll have to wait, sir.'

'My impatience will be a problem,' Kruger admitted, tracing the outline of her chin with his finger.

'So what will you be in this new navy?' Brenda demanded.

'An admiral.'

'An admiral! Good grief. Looks like I'm condemned to being a naval wife. What's admiral in German?'

'Admiral.'

'You see?' said Brenda in triumph. 'My mother was right. Problems solved one by one. There won't be a language problem.'

35

Eric wandered uncertainly along the busy ward, looking for Mark. The nurse he had spoken to had been quite sure he was in this ward. She seemed sorry that he had come to take Mark away.

A voice behind him said, 'I'd know the smell of that disgusting shaving soap you bought in Antwerp anywhere.'

Eric wheeled around and gaped at the fully dressed young man sitting beside a made bed. He had intense blue eyes that seemed to be looking straight at him.

'Mark?'

'Hallo, Dieter. Have you missed me?'

'Missed you? With General Dornberger gone, and a week without your snoring? Life has been bliss.'

Mark grinned and rose. The two men embraced.

'Look – no dressings. What do you think?'

'It's the first time I've seen you properly without them. I had no idea you were so ugly.' Eric held Mark by the shoulders and took a good look at his eyes. There were a number of bloodshot spots, one quite large, but otherwise they looked healthy. They were disturbingly blue.

'What can you see, Mark?'

'I can tell where windows are. People are big blotches. I can just about tell the difference between doctors and nurses. But the nurses cheat – they're lovely girls – all starch and sexy rustling of skirts.'

'I wanted to visit you,' said Eric, 'but you were so adamant that I shouldn't.'

'I wanted this to be a surprise.'

'It's that all right. What happens now?'

Mark groped for a small suitcase on the floor and found it. 'I've said all my goodbyes, but Mr Davison wants to see both of us before we go.'

Mark took Eric's offered forearm with their long-practised smoothness, and they made their way to the door. Some patients called out to Mark, wishing him well. One said, 'Pity all Jerries aren't like you, old son.'

'You've made some friends,' said Eric.

'There's one who refused to speak to me but they were mostly very kind. There's a nurse who fell in love with me, so I got her to read *Tristram Shandy* to me when she was off duty, and she got quite embarrassed by some bits.'

'Wicked swine.'

In response to an orderly's directions, Eric followed the signs to the ophthalmic department, where another orderly registered Mark's name and told them to wait. Thirty minutes later they were shown into a consulting room. Ian Davison rose and shook them both warmly by the hand. He had Mark's notes spread out on the desk.

'I wanted to see you both together because I've a few things to show you, and Dieter will be able to explain everything afterwards to you, Mark, that you may miss. Firstly, we're all delighted with your progress. As you can see, Mr Muller, his eyes are healing nicely. There's hardly any danger of infection now, so he doesn't need bandages. More importantly, we can now look ahead and see what more can be done.'

He opened the desk drawer and placed a powerful magnifying glass in Mark's hand. He slid a folded newspaper across the desk. 'Tell me if you can read anything.'

Mark held the magnifying glass close to his eye and bent over the newspaper so that it was almost touching his nose. To his great excitement, he discovered that he could read some of the large print sub-headlines. He read them aloud and looked up in wonder.

'And the small print?'

'Just a blur. But surely that I can see something is important?'

'It certainly is,' said Davison. He took down a large model of the human eye off a shelf and guided Mark's fingers over the cornea.

'It's a model about four times life size. Can you feel its curve?'

'Yes.'

'The cornea is more than just a protective covering over the eye. It also acts as an external lens that directs light and images through the pupil and through the lenses itself, which finally focuses images of everything we see on to the retina – the screen at the back of your eye. Your lenses were damaged and had to be removed by the surgeons in Antwerp. Your corneas have now healed nicely with an excellent profile and are still doing their job, but without your real lenses, the images are not being focused. Are you with me?'

Mark nodded, listening intently.

'As you saw with this big magnifying glass, it is possible for you to see something – all grotesquely enlarged. That's because even when you were holding it close, it's not close enough and the lens is too big – much of the image is scattered and lost – it doesn't pass through the eye. But if we can get a lens right against the centre of your cornea, smack against the eye, it's a very different story. Such a lens will do the job of your lost lens. And that's exactly what can be done with these.'

He opened a box and took out a clear plastic item that resembled an egg cup without a stem. He placed it in Mark's fingers. 'That's a contact lens. It fits over the eye and under the eyelids. Can you feel the raised bit in the centre? That's the lens. That's what will do all the work. It sends focused light images directly on the retina to give you near normal vision.'

The magic words had Mark trembling with excitement but Eric was more cautious. He took the contact lens from Mark and looked at it critically. 'It's huge, Doctor.'

Davison nodded. 'It fits right over the sclera – the white of the eye, and goes under the eyelids. And yet you can hardly see them. You'd never know that someone was wearing them unless you looked closely from the side.'

Eric had doubts. 'Surely to have such a thing in contact with the cornea is going to be agony for the wearer?'

'You'd think so,' said Davison smoothly. 'The trick is to make the inside of the contact lens a perfect match with the eye so that a film of water forms a cushion that prevents the contact lens coming into contact with the epithelium – the cornea's sensitive outer layer. Contact lens is a bit of misnomer.'

Eric's doubts were still not allayed. 'So how do you ensure that the contact is a perfect fit short of making a mould of the eye?'

Davison grinned. 'That's exactly what we do thanks to Joseph Dallos – a Hungarian optician now working in London and training contact lens technicians. Over ten years ago he developed a technique for making moulds of the human eye. From them we can make a reversed mould that is used to buff and polish a contact lens to a perfect fit.'

He assembled Mark's notes into their file, which he handed to Eric. 'We started a small contact lens department a year ago. So far we've fitted over twenty people with contact lens and almost all have been a success. Take this file and Mark along to see Mrs Runfold in the contact lens department and she'll take charge. She won't make a start right away – in about four weeks. I want Mark's corneas to be as tough as old boots before she starts work.'

They all stood. 'Is this the last time you'll being seeing me, Doctor?' Mark asked.

'Well, I hope so.'

Mark held out his hand. 'I don't know how to thank you. I really don't.'

'I had a letter from your father,' said Davison. 'He said much the same. I told him that you've been a pleasure to have as a patient. I've heard that some of the nurses think so, too.'

'Yes – he told me he had written. He's coming to see me as soon as he can get permission to travel.'

'There is one last thing I'd like to see you about, Mark,' said Davison. 'When Mrs Runfold has fixed you up, I shall expect a game of darts with you in the hospital's social club.'

36

The month at Grizedale Hall passed with agonizing slowness for Mark. Several prisoners left, so the number of POWs dwindled to forty. Those that remained came from homes under Soviet control. They had no close ties and had expressed an unwillingness to return. The rehabilitation committee had been to the camp several times and were working on finding the men jobs in the West. They were talented men with good qualifications and such people were often offered key civil service posts by the three Western occupation powers.

Eric received a letter, written in General Dornberger's familiar handwriting. It bore a London post mark and had been opened and resealed with a War Office censors' label. He ripped it open, worried in case Dornberger had said anything about his secret identity. Some words had been obliterated by the censor's pen.

Dear Dieter,

Maybe that POW, Hauptmann Willi Hartmann, isn't such an unspeakable rogue after all. I'm no longer in custody.

They dropped all the charges and have let me go. I'm now the guest of the [word inked over] who have put me up in this hotel, all expenses paid. Each day I take a taxi to the [two words inked over] where I'm debriefed by a [several words inked over] and his staff.

It looks as if I'm going to be offered an important job soon with some old colleagues. Do you remember my talking with great affection about an old colleague of mine, [words inked over]? Such a shame that he seems to have disappeared because everyone is interested in him.

Please give him my very warmest regards if he does turn up as a POW and tell him that I know for certain that there's an exciting job awaiting him with my hosts. Please don't forget. Best you paperclip this letter to your bedroom wall as a reminder.

I hope you'll be repatriated soon.

Best wishes

Walter Dornberger

So the old devil has landed on his feet? thought Eric. His Paperclip letter to the Americans that Willi had posted worked. Well – it was good of him to write and pass on so much news. It set Eric thinking about his own future but, as always, he postponed the matter because Mark still depended on him.

He took the letter down to Berg in his

workshop.

'Any chance of finding out what's written under all that crossing out, Dietrich?'

Berg used a magnifying glass to study the letter. 'Things are getting lax,' he observed. 'There was a time when they actually took scissors to letters and cut out bits they didn't like. Still – I suppose it's all a bit academic now. Well, let's see ... Ah, yes – it's the same with most letters now – they just delete most of the names without bothering with context. Pointless really. I'll try diluted methylated spirit first.'

Berg wrapped a clean piece of cotton wool around a matchstick and dipped it in a bottle of what looked like blue-tinted water. He then carefully tested the solution on a censor's flourish. The pen stroke spread. He next tried a quick wipe across the first deletion and soaked up the fluid with blotting paper. He bent over the letter to study the result as the censor's pen work spread. '"Americans",' he announced.

Eric had guessed that much but said nothing.

'And the second deletion is "American Embassy".'

'The last deletion at the end of the first paragraph is important,' said Eric. 'I think it's a name. Please be careful.'

Berg prepared a fresh cotton-wool swab and repeated the treatment. '"Captain George Halliday" or "Holliday"...' He peered closer. 'It's "Halliday" – that's definitely an *a*.'

Eric was tempted to kiss his helpful POW comrade. 'I think the last deletion is "Eric Hoffmann",' he said. 'Dornberger often talked about him. But it's not so important.'

'Eric Hoffmann it is,' Berg confirmed a moment later. 'General Dornberger had a knack of getting under my skin, but I'm glad all is turning out well for him.'

'He had a knack of getting under everyone's skin,' said Eric. 'And he snored like a pig, but he wasn't so bad. Just his unfortunate manner.'

Berg nodded. 'What an odd thing to say about paperclipping his letter to the wall,' he commented.

'Weird,' Eric agreed.

Mark was waiting impatiently in their room when Eric returned. Hermann was on his lap. 'It's a letter from my father, Dieter,' he said holding out an envelope. 'I know it is.'

'It is,' said Eric, glancing at the handwriting. 'Thicker than his usual letters.' He ripped open the somewhat bulky envelope. The letter was wrapped around a number of press cuttings. Eric read the letter to Mark.

'My Dear Mark, Thank you for your letter and please give my thanks to your friend Dieter for writing it. He is a true friend. The news about your being fitted with contact lenses is very exciting although I must say that I can't believe that it's possible to go around with such things in your eyes.

'I'm still hoping to come to England to see you, and take you home but that can't be until you've had your contact lenses fitted, so I'm delaying things here. An American airmen's charity fund has very kindly paid me all my expenses, so money isn't a problem.

'You mentioned a London doctor who did the first operation on your eyes in England – Dr Harold Ridley. I've got some friends in Bonn to keep an eye open for information about him. I've enclosed some newspaper cuttings. He sounds like a bit of a lunatic, so it's a good job you only saw him once. I'm keeping my fingers crossed for you.

'Your loving father ... And he's enclosed some English money.' Eric counted the one-pound notes. 'Forty pounds.'

'Forty pounds! Were did he get such an amount?'

'From the Americans, I suppose.'

'He shouldn't accept their charity.'

'Mark – we have just emerged from over five years in a world that's been torn apart by hate. Let's not condemn those that want to give.'

'I suppose ... So what does the press say about Dr Ridley?'

Eric looked through the cuttings. 'The most lurid is: "EYE EXPERTS SLAM BRITISH DOCTOR. Yesterday top eye doctors were universal in their criticism of British eye specialist Harold Ridley, who claims that it might be possible to implant artificial plastic lenses in the human eye to replace lenses diseased by cataracts or where the lenses have been lost through injury. A leading eye specialist even went as far as to call Harold Ridley a crackpot of the first order."'

Eric skimmed through the rest of the cuttings. 'They all say much the same thing. There's an article here from a professional journal. It's like the others although their language is more restrained.'

'It seems unfair,' said Mark when Eric finished reading the condemnation, 'when you consider what he did for me.'

'He didn't try to shove lumps of plastic in your eyes. He took lumps of plastic out.'

'They weren't lumps – they were tiny specks which he said my eyes didn't react to but that they did inhibit healing.'

'Whatever,' said Eric indifferently. 'Commonsense tells me that the idea of putting foreign objects inside the eyes after all you've been through is a singularly stupid notion. At least contact lenses, bizarre as they are, are a proven option.'

37

Dr Helen Runfold was a kindly woman who was not only the contact lens department's chief clinician, but also its technician and general administrator. Her only help was a surly, but extraordinarily pretty girl called Sandra who acted as receptionist and tea maker. She was 15 and this was her first job. Her surliness disappeared when she met Mark for the first time and encountered his impossibly blue eyes.

'Now then, Mark,' said Helen when she had seated her patient in a dentist's chair and conducted a preliminary examination with an ophthalmoscope. 'Mr Davison would've told you what we're going to do. The first thing is to make a mould of your eyes.' She showed a cup-like device to Eric and put Mark's fingers around it. 'I'm going to clip your eyelids back, stick that thing over each eye in turn, and squirt in some quick-setting compound.'

'Supposing I move my eyes while it's setting, Doctor?'

'You won't. I hope you've done as you were told and eaten nothing since before eight this morning?'

'A slice of toast at seven,' Eric reported.

'Good. Good. Sandra, go and find that anaesthetist. He should've been here by now.'

Helen was still busy at her little workbench when the effects of the anaesthetic wore off and Mark was able to take an interest in what was going on.

'Good. Good. We have two excellent moulds, Mark, and will be able to make a start.' She sat in a chair opposite her patient and took his hand. 'Now listen, Mark. This is going to be long process. You'll probably have to come here at least ten times. Buffing and polishing your contact lenses to make them a perfect fit is a tedious, uncomfortable business. It will mean putting in and taking out your contact lenses several times during each visit.'

'I don't mind, Doctor, really I don't.'

'You say that now. However, just to give you an idea of what to expect, we're going to do a little test.'

She switched on a light that illuminated the Snellen chart on the wall and held a card over Mark's left eye.

'Can you read the top letter?'

'All I can see is a bright blob,' said Mark miserably.

She switched the card to his right eye.

'Just the same, Doctor.'

'Only to be expected, of course. Right. I'm going to pop a contact lens in your eye, Mark. Its lens won't be exactly right but it'll be a useful starting reference, and it'll be very uncomfortable because it's a dummy. But it won't be in for long and it'll give you an idea of what to expect.'

She went to her workbench and selected a contact lens from a display box. She turned to Mark. 'You're going to get used to hearing me saying this: I want you to look straight ahead and keep your head still.'

She filled the contact lens with fluid, opened Mark's eyelids and slipped the lens under his lower eyelid and then under the upper eyelid, all accomplished with one swift movement. When she took her hand away and when Mark blinked automatically to clear the surplus fluid, he gave an exclamation of delight and astonishment. The bright Snellen chart seemed to leap from the wall, hurling its bold, black dagger-sharp capital letters straight at him.

'I can see!' he cried, thumping the arm of the chair in delight. 'I can really see! It's fantastic!'

Helen carried out some tests when he had calmed down. It wasn't easy because her patient was so overcome with excitement and joy. She tried four different lenses in each eye, each one an improvement on the previous one, and with the last one Mark could even read some of the letters in the bottom row of the Snellen chart. Her final tests were with Mark wearing two contact lenses. There was no evidence of double vision, which she had been a little worried about because the rectus muscles that controlled the movements of the eye and their co-ordination could become lazy over a long period of not being used.

Before she removed them, Mark insisted on getting up and looking around. His tears passed unnoticed because the trial lenses hurt abominably, causing his eyes to water profusely. When he saw Sandra standing in the doorway, he exclaimed that she was beautiful.

He turned to Helen. 'So are you, Doctor. So beautiful. Everything is beautiful.' He saw a chance to settle an old score with Eric and declared that there were exceptions. But he was thrilled to actually see the man who had been his companion and friend for so many months and he hugged him joyously. He also hugged a not-unwilling Sandra and would've accorded Helen the same treatment had she not ordered him back into the chair. It was such moments that made her job worthwhile and this young German was a delightful patient who was never afraid to show his emotions.

'Same time tomorrow then,' she said when she had removed the contact lenses.

'Sandra,' said Mark as they moved into the outer office.

'Yes?' she answered.

Her voice gave Mark the bearings he needed. He seized the girl and gave her a long, passionate kiss, squeezing her buttocks hard with both hands. She disentangled herself, laughing in a mixture of embarrassment and delight.

'Sandra – when I've got my contact lenses,

will you go to the pictures with me?'

'Yes – of course. I'd love to!'

Eric had to drag him into the street before he renewed the assault.

'You're a disgrace,' Eric scolded Mark as they walked to the station. 'The way you held that girl.'

'You're only jealous,' said Mark cheerfully. 'I've kissed two girls since I was captured and you've had none.'

'Two! When was the first?'

'At the hospital in Antwerp before you arrived. A nurse heard me crying to myself late one night. All the patients were asleep so she put the screens around my bed and gave me a little cuddle. Actually we both got carried away and it was quite a big cuddle.'

'One of the nuns?'

'No. An army nurse. Nuns rustle too much.'

38

The next six days consisted of daily one-hour visits to Dr Runfold during which time she repeatedly fitted Mark's contact lenses, giving him brief moments of normal sight while she examined them using her ophthalmoscope and went back for endless buffing and polishing while Eric read a book in the outer office. One the eighth day she suddenly announced that they were finished.

'You mean I can leave with them?' Mark exclaimed.

'When you've learned how to put them in and take them out, and look after them.'

She put one lens in his eye so that he could watch as she showed him the little channels on the inside of the contact lenses for draining away surplus fluid, and the tiny raised dots on the outside of the lenses where they would be hidden by the lower eyelid. One dot for the left eye, and two dots for the right eye.

'You'll know if you've got one in the wrong way around because it'll hurt. Don't panic. Just take it out. OK?'

Next she demonstrated putting them in on herself by bending over a clean towel, filling the contact lenses with fluid from a dropper and using a little rubber sucker to grip it on the outside.

'Bubbles,' was her cryptic response to Mark's nervous first attempt. 'Now take it out and try again.'

It took an hour before Mark was able to take the lenses in and out to her satisfaction. He put the lenses in and she presented him with a little storage box like a jeweller's presentation box for earrings with the rubber sucker sitting in its own recess. There was a bottle of cleaning fluid and fluid for filling the lenses before wearing them.

'Right,' she said smiling. 'Everything's in the instructions. You can now read, remember: wear them for three hours for today, then four hours each day until Friday. After that wear them for as long as you're comfortable with them. You can wear them alternately if you wish but I shall expect your tolerance to have built up to at least five hours a day when I see you next week. Get some cheap dark glasses if you find everything a bit bright for a while at first. Sandra will make an appointment. God bless, and mind how you go.'

Mark's biggest thrill was to walk out the room unaided and melt Sandra's heart with the blueness of his eyes. 'No one would ever know you were wearing them. You can't see them at all,' she said, and offered Mark a mirror.

'They're a bit sore.'

'You'll soon get used to them.' She gave him

a little appointment card and a big kiss. 'Come back in a week, Mark, and we'll decide what film we're going to see.'

All three laughed when Eric automatically offered his arm and realized that it was no longer needed.

39

'I can't get over it, Dieter,' Mark kept saying on the train when they were returning to Grizedale Hall. It was his favourite expression, and keeping his nose pressed against the window to marvel at the passing scenery was his favourite position. 'But they do hurt. They hurt so very much.'

'That's only to be expected. You were warned that they'd be uncomfortable at first.'

'This isn't uncomfortable, Dieter. This is pain.'

They reported back to Reynolds on their return and Private Knox ensured that word spread through the camp that Mark Schiller now had his eyes. The welcoming party that gathered rapidly in the courtyard consisted of the entire camp with everyone wanting to shake his hand and congratulate him, even Sergeant Finch joined the eager throng despite the fact that Mark was one of 'them bloody Jerries'.

'Quite amazing, Commander,' said Nurse Hobson, finding herself beside Kruger. They had taken great care to ensure that no one suspected anything about their affair – even Private Knox still came in for some gentle flirting and playing along from Brenda – and her neighbours had been fed a story that Kruger was a financial advisor from Bowness. 'I've heard of contact lenses, but never actually seen them. Not that you can see them.'

'It's worrying that his eyes are watering so much, though.'

'You'll be worried by some of the tricks I know that'll make your eyes water,' said Brenda softly, having made sure that no one was within earshot. She took a perversely wicked pleasure in trying to rattle Kruger's sangfroid.

'And you might be equally worried by my spanking abilities, Nurse Hobson.'

'Promises ... Promises...' But the usual impishness was missing from her voice because Mark had drawn near, laughing and shaking hands, and she could see that his eyes were troubling him. 'Do you think I ought to look at him? They look awfully bloodshot.'

Once the welcome was over, Mark went straight up to his room; such was the pain that he was hardly able to comprehend that he was seeing his home and surroundings of several weeks for the first time. Hermann followed him. He prepared an area on his bedside table and took the contact lenses out using the little rubber sucker. The relief from the pain was immediate. He cleaned and dried them and put them in their case. Eric entered the room and found him stretched out on his back on the bed, a wet flannel across his eyes, Hermann on his stomach.

'Not only was there the pain, but a fog and a bright rainbow around lights,' said Mark miserably. 'I think the fog is still there but I don't know.'

Eric squeezed his friend's arm. 'It'll be better tomorrow. You'll see.'

But it wasn't better, it was worse. Mark managed to read his father's letters and the press cuttings about Harold Ridley. It was a joy to be able to read his father's letters without having to depend on anyone else, but by midday his vision was so fogged and the pain so intense that he was forced to remove the contact lenses. He tried again in the evening with one lens. The fogging had cleared but it returned quickly and the pain proved to be too much after an hour.

The rest of the week continued like that with Mark doing his best to heed Eric's exhortations to 'stick at it' and always having to give up. By the time it was the day to visit the hospital again he was in state of deep depression and even Eric began to suspect that something was wrong. Nevertheless he persuaded Mark to put the contact lenses in early that morning so that Dr Runfold would be able to see the bad effect that they were having.

During the wait in the waiting room, Eric had to visit the lavatory. When he returned Sandra was sitting beside Mark, holding his hand, trying to comfort him. When Dr Runfold got to see Mark, her welcoming smile faded when she saw his badly reddened, bloodshot eyes and the handkerchief he had to hold to his face all the time to staunch the flow of tears. She listened in mounting concern as Mark told her about the pain he was in, how his vision fogged badly and vivid rainbow halos appeared around lights.

She removed the lenses and subjected Mark's eyes to a close examination, turning his head from left to right, before studying his contact lenses under a small microscope. With a muttered 'excuse me' she left the room.

'What do you think, Dieter?'

'She's not as chatty as usual,' Eric replied.

Helen Runfold returned with Ian Davison.

'Sorry you're having problems, Mark,' said the registrar. 'Right – let's take a look at you.'

His examination took even longer. He asked Mark about the longest period that he'd been able to tolerate the contact lenses while making notes. He went into the outer office for a conference with Helen Runfold, closing the door so that not even Mark could make out what they were saying.

Their faces were solemn when they returned and sat opposite Mark. Davison drummed his fingers on Helen's little workbench. 'I don't have the exact figures, Mark, but there are failures with contact lenses in which the wearers cannot develop any tolerance. It's about three per cent and unhappily, it seems that you're one of that three in a hundred figure. We could suggest you try for another week, but from what we've seen, we've decided that there is no point in subjecting you to further pain.'

'So I won't be able to wear them? I won't be able to have my eyesight back?' said Mark despairingly.

Davison wondered if he ought to tell the young man about the work of Kevin Tuohy, a New York optician who had designed what he called corneal lenses. These lenses were manufactured from a hard plastic material and covered only the central area of the eye, but Tuohy's work was still in its infancy and there was no certainty that even his tiny lenses would work in Mark's case. If they proved successful, well and good, but Davison saw little point in building up his patient's hopes yet again only to have them dashed.

'I'm sorry, Mark – but there's nothing we can do. Things might be different in a few years ... There's a huge amount of research work going on. But there's nothing we can do at the moment.'

'Couldn't I take painkillers or something?'

Davison shook his head. 'That would be futile and dangerous and it wouldn't cure the basic problem.'

'What *is* the basic problem?'

'As always, it's with your epitheliums – the outer layer of your corneas. They're water permeable – they absorb water. They have to be because one of the functions of the epithelium is to absorb nutrients from tears and pass them to the inner layers of the cornea. In your case your epitheliums are absorbing too much water which causes them to swell and distort. They wrinkle, just like the wrinkling on the skin of your fingertips from water absorption if you've been in the bath or swimming for a long time. Those hundreds of tiny wrinkles on your cornea act as prisms. They break up the light, causing the fogging of your vision and the rainbow haloing effect that you're getting around lights.'

'So it's the wrinkling that's causing all the pain?'

Davison shook his head. 'Not directly. What we think the wrinkling does is break down the film of water that prevents the contact lens coming into contact with the sensitive epithelium.

'It happens with all contact-lens wearers, and it governs how long they can wear contact lenses for. It can be anything up to ten hours. In your case, it's only about an hour to two hours, and the reaction of your corneas is the worst we've seen although they've certainly healed nicely thanks to Dr Ridley.'

'So I'm back to being blind again?'

'Take your contact lenses, Mark. They're

tailor-made for you, so you might as well have them. At least you can put one in if there's something you need to read or see. That's better than nothing.'

Sandra watched Eric and Mark moving down the corridor, the younger man holding dejectedly on to his companion's arm. Such was his misery that he hadn't even tried to kiss her goodbye. She flipped open the card index on her desk and copied Mark's full name and address into her pocket diary.

40

Fleming looked around the empty courtyard in surprise as he shook hands with Reynolds. 'Looks like you've had a mass breakout, James old boy.'

'Only thirty-eight POWs left now, Ian. Most of those left come from the Soviet zone. The repat committee are doing what they can for them. A surprising number are being accepted into fairly high admin posts.'

'A lot of politically colourless talent in this place,' Fleming observed. 'You'll be losing another one today.'

'Who's that?'

Reynolds whistled when Fleming told him.

'We'll celebrate getting rid of him with a

drink,' said Fleming cheerfully. 'Have you still got some of that Canadian rot-gut stuff you like?'

'Canadian bourbon is the best in the world,' said Reynolds, and sent Private Knox on an errand.

Ten minutes later Kruger knocked and entered. Fleming was surprised to see that all the Kriegsmarine insignia had been removed from his uniform.

'What the hell happened to your uniform?' Fleming asked as the three sipped their drinks.

Kruger shrugged. 'The Kriegsmarine does not exist anymore. I've ordered officers of the Wehrmacht and the Luftwaffe to do the same. I understand that that's an occupying power regulation at home.'

Fleming grinned. 'Always the stickler for protocol, eh, Otto?'

'I refuse to believe you've come all the way here to sample Major Reynolds's dreadful whiskey, Ian,' was Kruger's dry answer.

Fleming opened his briefcase and handed Kruger an envelope. He gave a smaller envelope to Reynolds.

Kruger slit his envelope open and tipped the assorted documents on to the desk.

'All present and correct,' said Fleming cheerfully. 'Sally made doubly sure. Your repatriation papers, old boy. Certificate of release as a prisoner of war, travel warrants, ID cards. Everything. And that's a new issue of your old Kiel bank account and a new bank book. Strings have been pulled with the finance appropriations committee of the occupying powers. That's the British, French and US zones only. The Soviets insist on doing things their way and aren't having much to do with us. You've been credited with one third of your back pay and you may get more.'

Reynolds raised his glass. 'Congratulations, Commander.'

Kruger looked up from the documents and eyed him frostily. 'I'm *Mr* Kruger now, Major. But, in view of our long association, you may call me Otto.' And then he was unexpectedly smiling. 'In fact, I'd like you to.'

Fleming laughed. 'He'll never change, James.'

'Do I have to leave the country right away, Ian?' There was an anxious note in Kruger's voice.

'No. You can stay. If you do, you'll have to register with the nearest police station and report once a week. There's a screed amongst all that bumpf that gives you all the dos and don'ts. I daresay you could even stay on here if James can be persuaded to put up with you a day longer than is necessary. So what do you plan to do?'

Kruger thought for a moment. 'What are *you* planning to do up here, Ian?'

'What now? I've got a month's well-earned leave. I'm staying up here a couple of nights – looking up some old friends. Then I'm off to Jamaica. I'm having a house built there.'

'Would you consider staying here a few more days?'

Fleming was puzzled. 'Well – I don't know. Why?'

'I hope you can, Ian. You ask me what I'm planning to do.' Then Kruger was smiling. 'I'm planning to get married and I'd like you to be my best man.'

41

'The sly old dog,' said Eric to Mark, entering their room and sprawling on the bed. Hermann glowered at him. 'The rumpus downstairs is because Kruger's papers have come through.'

'I'll miss him,' said Mark absently. He was holding a handkerchief to his cheek because he was wearing a contact lens and reading.

'It's not only that. He's marrying our Nurse Brenda Hobson, would you believe? The lucky devil. They're down in the main hall now. A bit of an impromptu party. Coming down?'

'You go, Dieter. Give them my best wishes.'

'What are you reading?'

Mark rose from his bed and bent over his table to remove the contact lens. Eric saw his father's letters and the press cuttings about

Harold Ridley scattered on his bed.

'The only times you put a lens in is to read that. Put it back and come down to admire the lovely Nurse Hobson for a few minutes. They don't come much lovelier.'

'I'm not in the mood!'

Eric shrugged. 'Sorry I spoke.'

'Dieter,' said Mark with sudden intensity. 'I've got to see Dr Ridley. He's the only man in the world who can help me!'

'He's the last person in the world you should see. For God's sake put your eye back in and read those cuttings again. The man's a lunatic. All the world's experts say so.'

'But I know he's right! There's only two ways of giving me back my eyesight. That's with a lens in front of the cornea or behind the cornea. In front has proved impossible. That leaves only one option.'

'Actually in the eye!' Eric snapped, his patience wearing thin because they had had this argument before. 'A foreign body actually right inside the eye? Doesn't your commonsense alone tell you just how stupid that is?

'I've got to go to London to see him,' said Mark dully.

'So write to him. Give Willi five shillings and he'll post a letter for you so that the censors don't get shirty. You've got plenty of money.'

'And my papers might come through before he replies, and my father will come for me to take me back to Germany, and I'll never have the chance to see Dr Ridley again. *Please*, Dieter. I *must* go to London.'

Eric snatched up the cuttings. 'Listen,' he grated. 'When one eye expert says Ridley is mad, you listen politely; when two experts say he's mad, you listen more attentively. When experts all over the whole bloody world say he's mad, don't you think it would be sensible, just a little bit sensible, to accept that what they say might possibly be right and that you and this Ridley are wrong?'

'Please, Dieter. I must see him.'

'Why? Corneal lenses is a new science. I know for a fact that once men have their teeth into a new science, the rate of progress is phenomenal! It's worth waiting for. Christ, you're only eighteen! In ten years who knows what will be possible?'

'It's not new!' Mark almost shouted. 'That's just it! They've got a long history already!' He groped for and caught hold of Eric's arm, and recovered the sheaf of press cuttings from Eric's hand. 'These cuttings, Dieter. Read the new one again my father sent me a couple of days ago! It's about the history of contact lenses. They were invented in 1887 by an Adolf Eugen Fick. Nearly sixty years ago! So maybe they weren't very good, but the point is that over a half a century of development has resulted in contact lenses that cause me agony! How long before I have to wait for contact lenses that I can wear for even a few hours without pain? Twenty years? Thirty years? When I'm an old man having gone through my life blind?'

Eric shook his head and touched Mark on the arm. The younger man seized his hand and held it tightly.

'I have to see Harold Ridley, Dieter,' he repeated. 'I can't get to London by myself.'

'We could never get to London and back in a day. If you want to abscond to London, pay Willi to go with you.'

Mark bowed his head. 'You're the only person in the world I trust, Dieter.'

'Well, I don't want the police hunting for me. The answer is no. No. No. No. Understood?'

42

'Willi Hartmann?' Brenda queried when she looked at Kruger's provisional guest list.

'Brenda, my angel. I can't leave out poor Willi,' said Kruger. 'He's been running errands for me every day for nearly five years.'

'You should've made him do some running around the grounds every day for five years. Well – at least it'll be in a register office, so there won't be a collection plate for him to steal. But I'll be worried about the Star's silverware during the dinner, though.'

'I'm worried about the cost of this sit-down dinner.'

Their wedding planning meeting was being held at the dining table in Brenda's front room. The magical way sunlight shone through her hair kept overwhelming Kruger, leading to frequent suspensions of business and at one point had nearly led to the agenda being abandoned all together. The bottle of Brenda's home-made wine they'd been working through hadn't helped.

Brenda looked quizzically at Kruger. 'Why?'

'All these people, Brenda. It'll be the entire camp at this rate.'

'They're all my admirers.'

'It all seems so expensive.'

Brenda sat on his knee and nuzzled his chin. 'It's my money and I'll spend it how I damn well like, and I've no intention of pandering to your Calvinist, frugal streak. Besides, I want as many people as possible to witness our marriage so that you can't wriggle out of anything.'

'Right now it's *your* wriggling that's worrying me.'

Brenda laughed, kissed him, and they returned to the task in hand that was threatening to take all day.

'Right,' she said, resuming her seat and becoming businesslike. She was a good organizer when not distracted. 'Add Willi Hartmann. And if we have Willi, then we have to include the light of his life – Miss Carol Bunce. Oh, God, Otto, do you remember that gala Christmas dinner you and the POWs laid on a couple of years ago? That pink dress she wore when she dragged Willi around the dance floor? I nearly died. Do you think she's still got it?'

'It's possible. I don't think she's the sort of girl to worry much about spending time and money on her wardrobe.'

'Then she definitely goes on the list,' said Brenda, pouring herself another glass of wine. 'Just to see them dancing again with Willi's head buried between those awful breasts.'

'Hauptmann Hertzog is of the opinion that she has beautiful breasts.'

'So have I!' Brenda declared.

'I've only got your word for that.'

'Down, boy. You'll just have to wait.' She eyed Kruger mischievously over her glass. 'God – I'm tempted, though. It's wonderful that I don't have to throw you on the street before it gets dark.'

'It's ironic,' mused Kruger. 'The day after I get my freedom and Reynolds scraps the roll-call. Prisoners leaving the camp merely have to sign out at the gatehouse.'

'And half of them don't bother,' Brenda remarked. 'And they're sometimes not around for their check-ups. Discipline's gone to pot since you left. Anyway, you'll need all your energy keeping me in order.'

They continued their enjoyable work, with Brenda frequently having to tell Kruger to stop worrying about the mounting cost.

'I keep telling you that the cost is not a problem,' she scolded. 'But the next item is a problem with this bloody rationing. The cake. I want a proper three-tier cake. Not one of those ghastly cardboard model horrors that confectioners hire out with a sponge cake inside. Yuck.'

'That's something that Leutnant Walter Hilgard mentioned to me. He would very much like to make the cake.'

'That great, hairy brute!'

'You liked the birthday cake he made for Andy Todt. Hilgard may be a bull of a man, but put an icing bag in his hand and he's a Picasso.'

'Picasso would love to draw Hilgard's balls. You wouldn't believe the size of them. I need two hands to—'

'Brenda!'

Brenda giggled and hiccuped. 'Sorry, Commander.'

'Are we agreed that Hilgard makes the cake?'

'Yes, of course. But where would he get the sugar? A big cake will need pounds of the stuff and it's like gold dust.'

'I'm sure Walter Hilgard will find a way around the problem.'

43

The pounding on his door stilled Willi's heart. Discipline was so lax now that yesterday Carol Bunce had wandered into the camp and found her way to his room. But this wasn't her pounding. Only one man in the camp pounded on his door like that.

'Coming!' he yelled.

He quickly gathered up the money he had been counting and crammed it into the cavity behind the length of detachable skirting board. The pounding was renewed as he pushed the skirting board into place and wedged it home.

He darted to the door before it was broken down, but was too late. One shove was all it took for the door to fly open and for bits of deadlock, chains, woodscrews, and all the miscellaneous components of Willi's security measures to shower on to the floor. The huge frame of Walter Hilgard filled the doorway. Behind him, filling the corridor, were his kitchen henchmen, Kurt and Gunter. The three mighty bears entered the room and regarded the indignant Goldilocks.

'You've no right to come barging in here like this!'

'But the door wasn't locked, Willi.' Hilgard saw the screws and other bits on the floor. 'Oh – perhaps it was. Sorry, Willi. Kurt and Gunter will tidy up.' He looked around the room for somewhere to sit. 'Your bed's broken, Willi.' He sat in a chair and picked up some letters.

'What the hell do you gorillas want? And put those letters down. They're private.'

'We have a problem, Willi.'

'Well, take it away. I'm not interested.' Willi watched Kurt and Gunter picking wood-screws off the floor.

'We want to make Commander Kruger and Nurse Hobson a wedding cake,' Hilgard murmured. 'For this we need sugar.'

'I can get you sugar – at a price.'

'We're hoping for a donation, Willi. Knowing of your generous nature, we're sure you'll want to do everything possible for the happy couple.'

A screw fell between a gap in the floor-boards. Kurt used his penknife to try and prise it out.

Gunter was after a screw that was worryingly near Willi's cash cache. He gave a cry of triumph and held up a ten-shilling note.

'That's mine!' said Willi in alarm.

'Of course it's yours, Willi,' said Hilgard taking the banknote and pocketing it. 'And very good of you it is, too, to make such a generous contribution to the camp's wedding present fund.'

Willi looked close to tears. He didn't mind Hilgard reading private papers, or even taking them, but the money was of great sentimental value.

'There's a loose floorboard here,' said Kurt. He pulled up a board to reveal about two dozen one-pound bags of granulated sugar arranged in neat rows between the joists.

Hilgard regarded the treasure trove sorrowfully. 'Hoarding, Willi? The British have such strict laws against it. Lucky you have us on hand, otherwise you could go to prison.'

44

Mark shot Hermann on to the floor and sat up when Eric entered their room. 'I hope you didn't mind, Dieter, but I put ten shillings from both of us in the wedding present collection.'

'You shouldn't spend your money on me,' Eric replied irritably, settling on his bed with a book.

'But I want to, Dieter. Dieter, listen. Have you seen your wedding invitation?'

The question made a change from the young man's usual opening gambit about going to London. 'Yes. What of it?'

'Kruger and Nurse Hobson are getting

married in Ulverstone a week today. Friday. It says that Major Reynolds has granted a special late-night exemption for all guests to be back in at one in the morning on that night. A coach is being hired.'

'So?'

Mark became animated. 'You've got a parole waiver on distance you're allowed to travel if you're taking me to receive medical attention. Right?

'So?'

'So if we went to London that day, got the first train, we could go to Moorfields Eye Hospital to see Mr Ridley—'

'No!'

'You haven't heard what I was going to say.'

'I know what you're going to say. The answer's no. How many languages do I have to spell it out in before it finally sinks into your thick head that we're *not* going to London!'

'As you keep making clear,' said Mark, suppressing his anger. 'I'm going to pay Willi to be my guide.'

'If he sees how much money you've got, he'll rob you blind.'

'That's not funny.'

'Willi robbing you won't be funny.'

'I don't care! So long as he gets me to Moorfields! Don't you realize just how important this is to me? Anyway, I've got it all worked out. We could be in London by about 1300, take a taxi from Euston to Moorfields, see Dr Ridley, and get a train back in time to get a taxi that will get us to the reception by about 2300. There'll be so many guests – everyone in the camp will be there – and they'll be too drunk to notice that we weren't around.'

'And supposing you're a long time seeing this Harold Ridley? Supposing you miss your return train?'

'Does it really matter if we're late back? Who checks the gatehouse book now? Yesterday we went to the pub and forgot to sign out because there wasn't a guard on duty.'

True enough, thought Eric, and started reading.

'I had a letter from my father.'

'Well at least you can read them for yourself now.'

'They're going to send a copy of my papers to him. He thinks they'll be through in three weeks. He'll come to England to take me home.'

Eric continued reading.

'At least I have a family that cares about me.'

'That girl Sandra at the hospital seems to care about you. Do you reply to her letters? No.'

'How come you've never had a single letter in all the time I've known you? Why is that you never talk about your background? Where you come from. I know nothing about you. And I don't suppose for a moment that you'll give me an address before I leave.'

Mark's words set off a train of thought.

'When did you say he'll come for you?'
'In about three weeks.'
And then you'll no longer need me, thought Eric. He realized that the time had come when he should start thinking about his own future. London ... He could do much in London. He had an idea. He put his book down and took Mark's hand – the signal that he had something important to say.
'I've been unfair with you, Mark. I can't possibly let that rogue, Willi Hartmann, rob you. So OK – we'll go to London on Kruger's wedding day and find Dr Ridley.'
Mark's sudden yell of joy frightened Hermann.

45

The start of their London trip was uneventful. The taxi Eric had booked to take them to Windermere station called for them at 6:00 a.m. They signed out – the gatehouse was unlocked and deserted – and just over an hour later they were on a London fast train, travelling first class because Mark insisted.
'Are you still writing your letter, Dieter?'
'Yes,' said Eric noncommittally, starting on the sixth page. He would have to rewrite it because he kept having afterthoughts and crossing passages out. There were so many

details to remember and the scientist in him demanded that the facts were arranged with logical precision.

'It seems like a long letter.'

'It is.'

'I've never known you to write a letter.'

'That's why it's a long letter.'

After that Mark remained silent until he heard his companion give a sigh of relief, fold the letter into an envelope and seal it.

There were no delays. The train pulled into Euston on time. They found the taxi rank. Eric held the door open for Mark and doubled around the vehicle to talk quietly to the driver. 'First stop the American Embassy and then the Moorfields Royal Eye Hospital.'

'Why the American Embassy,' asked Mark as Eric got in and the taxi moved off.

Eric cursed the young man's exceptional hearing. 'I want to pick up some leaflets on living and working in America.'

The taxi drew up outside the American Embassy. Eric approached the marine on duty outside the main entrance and stated his business.

'There's a letterbox for mail, sir,' said the marine.

'No – I have to deliver this letter in person.'

'If it's correctly addressed, it'll find him, sir.'

Eric had no intention of violating his parole conditions by posting a letter, not even through an internal mail letterbox. 'My instructions are to deliver it in person. It's a very important letter for Captain George

Halliday.'

The marine glanced at the address on the envelope and decided to allow him through. A woman behind the front desk took the envelope and assured Eric that Captain George Halliday would receive the letter if there was such a person.

'If he's not available, would you please ensure that it goes to John J. McCloy, Assistant Secretary of War,' said Eric, pointing to a note he had written under the address. He was determined that a letter upon which his whole future hinged would find an important reader.

Half an hour later the taxi deposited them outside the front entrance of the forbidding granite edifice of Moorfields Royal Eye Hospital. They entered the building.

'Have you got your contact lenses with you?' Eric demanded when he saw the men's toilets.

'Yes, of course.'

Eric steered him into the toilets and guided his hands to a ledge. 'OK. Put them in.'

'What for? You're not going to leave me, are you, Dieter?'

'Don't be stupid. Just do as I say!'

Whenever Mark put in the lenses and was rewarded with glorious, wonderful vision, there was always that little spark of hope that the pain would not come. But the red-hot needles of impending agony had already started their work as Eric sat him at a table in the hospital's cafeteria and fetched him a cup of coffee.

'Why aren't we going to the outpatients department, Dieter?'

'Because both of us need a breather and a coffee.'

'But my eyes will be hurting like hell in a few minutes.'

'Exactly.'

'I don't want them so inflamed that it won't be possible for Dr Ridley to examine them.'

'Just stop fussing and relax for a few minutes.'

The harshness in his companion's tone discouraged further questions, so Mark sipped his coffee in silence and tried not to think about the steadily increasing torment.

After a few minutes wandering up and down the labyrinth of corridors, Mark spotted a distant sign that led them to an outpatients waiting room crowded with servicemen with bandaged eyes or eye patches. Dr Ridley's name was one of three names on the duty board.

'Let me do the talking,' Eric warned.

They approached the receptionist, who eyed Mark with a mixture of concern and interest.

'Excuse me, miss,' said Eric. 'This is Mark Schiller.' He spelt the name. 'Mark is a patient of Dr Ridley's.' He added quickly when the girl went to open a desk card index, 'I don't think you find his name in there. Dr Ridley operated on Mark at Barrow-in-Furness some weeks ago. Perhaps something has gone wrong because he's in such terrible pain now. We've all been so concerned about him that I insisted on bringing him here to see Mr Ridley if it's at all possible, please. It's very urgent.'

The girl looked worried and had a quiet word with a senior nurse, who came from behind the desk for a closer look at Mark's eyes.

'Would you take a seat, please,' she said briskly. 'I'll be back in a moment.' Her heels clip-clopped down the corridor and clip-clopped back again five minutes later. 'If you would come with me, please, Mr Schiller.' When they both rose, she requested Eric to remain seated and said that Mr Ridley would see Mark right away.

She and Mark disappeared down the corridor. Eric filled out a hospital card for Mark, feeling that at least this would lock him into their system. He found a pile of *Picture Post* magazines and leafed through them, while keeping an eye on his watch.

Mark was no longer wearing his contact lenses when he returned forty-five minutes later, guided by the nurse. His step was jaunty and he was smiling.

'Now you remember what Mr Ridley said, Mr Schiller,' said the nurse, handing him over to Eric. 'If you change your address, you must let us know immediately.'

'So you saw him?' Eric quizzed, hurrying along the corridor, pushing Mark by his elbow.

'Yes – he was very kind. He said—'

'Save it for the taxi. If we get a move on, we'll get the early train.'

Luckily Mark spotted and hailed a taxi as they were leaving the hospital. The promise of an extra two shillings prompted the taxi driver to keep his speed up and dodge traffic expertly.

'So what happened?'

'He was wonderful, Dieter. He said that he had heard from Barrow that my eyes had healed well. He said that his views that the eye doesn't react to Perspex are now becoming accepted among colleagues who work with him and they're spreading the word but ita slow process. But he hopes the way will be clear for him to perform an intraocular lens implant in two to three years. Once he's established the technique, he promised to send for me because my case would be ideal for treatment – nothing is lost if it doesn't work and the artificial lenses have to removed. But he's confident that that won't happen. Just think, Dieter – he's the only man in the world considering such an operation and thanks to you, I got to see him. Another two patients and he would've gone off duty. I would never have thought of your little ruse.'

'I was always good at coming up with solutions.'

One of those solutions was the speed at which the taxi driver got them to Euston station with five minutes to spare. Eric looked at his watch as their train pulled out of the station. He had never expected that they would be able to catch such an early return. They had been in London a little over two hours.

'With luck, we won't miss too much of Commander Kruger's wedding party after all.'

46

'Sounds like quite a party,' the Ulverstone taxi driver commented when he dropped Eric and Mark outside the Star.

They followed the sound of a live band giving a passable rendition of Glenn Miller's 'American Patrol'. It led them to the converted barn function room where it all seemed to be happening.

'Dieter! Mark!' Berg shouted above the music, clapping them on the back as they pushed through the thong, Mark holding on to Eric's forearm. 'We wondered what had happened to you.'

'I had to take Mark to the eye clinic.'

'There's still some cake left, so dig in. The buffet's over there somewhere if you can work your way around the dance floor.'

'Bloody hell!' Eric exclaimed when he saw Brenda in Kruger's arms as they swept around the dance floor, everyone's eyes on them. Her wonderful, dangerously low-cut evening dress was a white wraith that clung bewitchingly to her body as though it were afraid of losing her.

'Like Fred Astaire and Ginger Rogers,' said Berg proudly. 'We made that dress in the camp workshop.'

'She's much lovelier than Ginger Rogers,' said Eric – like every male in the room he was hypnotized by the vision. 'Mark, if you want me to describe Nurse Hobson, forget it. I don't have the words, either in German or English. I suppose it *is* our Nurse Hobson?'

'It's her all right.' The comment came from Private Knox, looking desolate.

Eric trailed Mark around the edge of the room to the buffet were they stuffed themselves on sausage rolls and fat, fruity crumbs from the devastated remains of Hilgard's wedding cake. More couples were encouraged on to the dance floor when the band changed tempo to a waltz, playing 'Moonlight Serenade'.

'Oh Christ,' said Eric suddenly when he saw Willi firmly imprisoned in Carol Bunce's embrace. 'Mark – you've got to put your eyes in to see this, even it's only for a few minutes.'

They found the toilets and Mark emerged a few minutes later, blinking. His gaze fastened hungrily on Brenda, and then he saw Willi and Carol. He and Eric shared snorts and guffaws with other guests. Carol was spilling out of a tight, pink dress. She was holding her beloved Willi close, his head almost hidden between her breasts.

'Escape is impossible,' said Reynolds, grinning broadly, parodying his own welcoming spiel that he gave to all new arrivals at Grizedale Hall. He had a point. Willi's head was firmly embedded. It couldn't go any further forward, left or right movement was out of the question, and a rear retreat was prevented by a broad, work-calloused hand clamped to the back of his neck. Carol's eyes were closed as she danced; what Willi's eyes were doing was anyone's guess.

The master of ceremonies tapped the rostrum microphone and announced that it was now a ladies' and gentlemen's excuse me free for all.

Suitors scrambled for Brenda as she relinquished Kruger but she singled out Hauptmann Anton Hertzog. 'I've learned that you did all the drawings of me so that Berg could make this wonderful dress,' said Brenda, scooping a wine glass off a table and finishing off its contents. 'I can't thank you enough, Anton.'

'It's nothing,' said Anton absently. He was about to turn his head to look for Carol but Brenda pulled him close and gave him kiss of such warmth that Anton decided that although Nurse Hobson fell into his 'bag of bones' category of womanhood, she was quite an acceptable bag of bones.

'How is it, my dear Brenda,' said Fleming smoothly when he seized a chance to dance with the bride, 'that you decided not to marry a fine, upstanding Englishman such as myself?'

'Well, now, let me see,' said Brenda, neatly returning an empty wine glass to a table as Fleming spun her around. 'Have you ever read Jane Austen's *Pride and Prejudice*?'

'But of course. A long time ago.'

'Can you remember the tall, brooding hero?'

'Er ... Mr Darcy?'

'Good. And the villain?'

Fleming's forehead creased. 'Er...'

'Like you, he was an officer.'

'Ah, yes. Mr Wickham. Wicked Wickham – always seducing impressionable young girls.'

'Well, Ian. It could be that Otto reminds me of Mr Darcy, and you remind me of Mr Wickham.'

Brenda spotted Mark and gave a cry of delight. She cut Fleming adrift, and hauled the young man on to the dance floor. 'Mark! You weren't at the wedding! I was desolate. Where were those wonderful blue eyes when I needed them?'

Mark quickly explained what had happened.

'London? You've been to London?'

'Mr Ridley thinks he might be able to operate on my eyes.'

'They certainly look sore now.'

'I don't care. I think you're the most beautiful woman in the world and I wish you every happiness.'

'And you're suffering agonies just so that

you can see me,' said Brenda softly as they danced. 'That deserves a reward.' Kruger had been kidnapped by Brenda's mother, so he didn't see his wife's bare arms go around Mark's neck and draw him very close for a sensuous circuit of the dance floor. Brenda stepped back when the music stopped and wagged a finger at her partner. 'Mark. Naughty.'

'I'm sorry, nurse. I couldn't—'

A kiss silenced his stammered apology. Her eyes twinkled. 'I shall have to report your behaviour to Sandra Clarkson.'

'Sandra?'

'The girl in the contact lens outpatients at Barrow of course. I'm based at the hospital, remember. She sought me out and told me how you'd stolen her heart and hadn't answered her letters.'

'Oh.' Mark wasn't sure what to say, so he blurted out the first thing that came into his head. 'I won't able to see her again. If you see her, will you please tell her that I'm always thinking about her?'

'Of course, I will, Mark. Please answer Sandra's letters. She's really concerned for you and I'll pray that all goes well for you. You're a lovely boy and I envy any girl that gets you. Now you promise to see me when your Mr Ridley has given you your new eyes.'

Mark promised. Brenda was claimed by a succession of suitors but she managed to spend more moments sitting on male laps and finishing off their drinks than Kruger considered good for her ... Or him.

When staff began moving surreptitiously around the room to make a start on clearing up, he moved in.

'I think you've had enough, darling.'

'I want to make a speech.'

'We've had all the speeches, Brenda.'

'But I never made one!'

'I really don't think—'

'I want to make a speech to all these lovely people,' Brenda insisted. 'You can't stop me, Commander. You're not my hus— Oops!' She clapped her hand to her mouth and giggled as she realized her mistake. The guests applauded and cheered the passionate kiss she gave Kruger. 'Now you're not going to deny me the right to make a little speech to my guests, are you? All my big, hunky POWs?' she wheedled, ruffling his hair.

He had little option but to relent.

'And that rostrum isn't high enough. I want everyone to see me!' She threw out her arms, nearly flooring a guest.

Kruger could refuse her nothing. Two tables were pushed together and a chair positioned as a step. She took Kruger's hand as she climbed on to the tables. The master of ceremonies turned a spotlight on her.

Brenda clapping her hands and calling for quiet wasn't necessary because everyone fell silent apart from a few who couldn't resist appreciative cheers and wolf whistles. Brenda acknowledged them with dazzling smiles. 'Why thank you, kind sirs. Thank you.' She swayed a little and her speech was slightly slurred.

'Oh Jesus, she's lovely,' Mark whispered to Eric.

'I've got a little speech to make. I spent ages writing it. I've no idea where it is now but I can remember it, so pay attention.'

Kruger was sufficiently concerned by her swaying to stay close to her makeshift dais.

'I want to thank you all for coming and for making this the happiest day of my life. There are so many to thank, I hardly know where to start. But how can I ever thank Dietrich Berg and his wonderful team enough for making this wonderful dress? Isn't it something?'

The tables wobbled as Brenda hitched up the hem and twirled around. The brief glimpse of her legs provoked a chorus of 'More! More!' cries.

'More?' cried Brenda. 'There isn't any more! This dress is all I'm wearing! Well – almost. But I can show you something that my mother made.' She hitched the dress right up to reveal a lacy garter high around her thigh. The two-second glimpse resulted in an explosion of joyous acclaim from the roomful of bewitched males.

'Down, boys, down.' Brenda was revelling in being the centre of attention and had Kruger wondering what he had let himself in for. He decided that whatever it was, it was marvellous.

'Now listen,' said Brenda, her voice becoming serious. 'Back to my speech. I want you all to remember tonight, not because we're celebrating my marriage to a wonderful man, but because we've all come through a cruelly stupid, futile war which has achieved nothing and taken many of our loved ones from us, and caused so much needless suffering such as young Mark, over there – still in his teens and blinded, although there is reason to hope that his sight may be restored one day. Tonight we are many from both sides who've shown that we can all enjoy being together and enjoy the wondrous gift of life that God has given us.

'After tonight we will all be going our separate ways. Most of you young men here will be returning to your homeland to begin rebuilding lives that you hardly had a chance to begin building in the first place. At times it will seem a hopeless task, which is why, when your spirits are low, I ask you all to remember the happiness and love of this night. That must be our goal – the creation of peace and harmony on a continent that has known little else but war in its long history.' She paused and wagged a finger at her enthralled audience. 'And to make sure that you all do just that, I'm going to hold a progress meeting. A reunion. Maybe not for two or three years. I don't know when. But I will hold that reunion. I give you my solemn promise on that. And remember – I have all your names and home addresses on my record cards, so there's no chance of escape.'

Brenda had to make a real effort not to

sway. She was too high for comfort above the sea of faces looking up at her.

'And most important of all ... Most important of all. Never has a bride, facing nearly fifty young men on her wedding day, been able to say in all honesty that she's had most of them by the balls at one time or another.'

With that Brenda passed out and fell into her husband's arms.

47

Few of prisoners felt like facing breakfast the following morning but by lunchtime most of them managed to make it to the dining hall.

'Just seeing that Carol Bunce carrying Willi to the coach like a baby her arms made it worth leaving my eyes in for a little longer,' Mark confided in Eric.

He laughed at the recollection and looked around. 'I wonder where he is now?'

The wedding was the only subject of conversation that ebbed and flowed at their table.

'So what happened to Reinhold and that bridesmaid? They were never seen again after the wedding at the register office.'

'Anton did the drawings.'

'Rubbish – he would've drawn her too fat for the dress to fit.'

'Amazing what Berg can turn his hand to.'

'I tell you she was! I was nearer the table she was standing on than you were.'

'Do you reckon she woke up when Kruger got her upstairs?'

'Of course. He would've ordered her to her feet.'

'Or knees.'

The laughter was silenced instantly when the double doors burst open and Sergeant Finch marched in flanked by two guards, their rifles held across their chests.

'Leutnant Dieter Muller!' the NCO bellowed. 'You will accompany me! Everyone else is to remain seated.'

This is finally it, thought Eric as he rose.

'What's happening, Eric?' Mark stood as well, frightened.

Sergeant Finch's voice roared across the hall. 'I said everyone else is to remain seated! Are you deaf as well as blind?'

The guards fell in behind Eric. He turned at the door and looked back at Mark. It was to be the last time he would see his young friend for nearly eight years.

Eric was marched to Reynolds's office between the two guards. He guessed that the black Wolseley parked outside was the same car that had taken General Dornberger away. Sergeant Finch's stentorian voice herded him into the office.

'Left! Right! Left! Right! Atten–*SHUN*! Prisoner of war 1-4289 Muller, Dieter, Leutnant, *SAAR*!'

There were two plainclothes men standing

by the door that led to the outer office. Reynolds stared at Eric with his lone eye.

'Remain at attention. Do not move unless I say. Understood?'

'Yes, sir.'

Reynolds crossed to the outer door and opened it. He spoke in his slow German. 'Fraulein Muller. Would you come in, please.'

A small woman about Eric's age entered the office. She locked eyes with Eric. 'Fraulein Muller,' said Reynolds, taking her arm and positioning her in front of Eric. 'Will you please tell us if this man is your brother. Please take your time.'

'No!' the answer was spat out without hesitation. There was hatred in her eyes. 'I've never seen him before in my life.' She threw herself at Eric, clawing at his face. 'You swine!' she screamed shrilly. 'You killed him and stole everything! You shot him in the head and stripped him of everything and left him dead!' The two guards dragged her off.

48

Eric's nineteenth day in Wandsworth Prison started the same as the eighteen preceding days. At 11:00 a.m. he heard the warders outside his cell come to collect him for his daily interrogation. They were always on time and always the same two warders. But the interrogators changed. Sometimes one, usually two, and in the early days there had been three. Their questioning was clever, often the same questions but worded differently, sometimes switching unexpectedly to cover events on a different day. Always their intention was to trip him up, but there was nothing for him to trip over because he had told the truth throughout with one exception: he had not told them about the buried Kilner jar containing all his documents. It would've been a simple lie to stick to had they gone back to it repeatedly like everything else but they didn't; they had accepted his story first time round that he had burned everything and had never referred back to it.

The only thing that had caused Eric concern since he had been taken to London, was not the three-minute appearance in a magistrates' court to enter pleas of 'not guilty' in response to the charges of murder and planning to wage aggressive war, but that a dentist had carefully examined his teeth to ensure that he wasn't harbouring a cyanide capsule. More than anything else, that suggested that the British were treating him as a war crimes suspect. They had kept saying that there could be more charges.

The cell door swung open. The same two Monday to Saturday warders beckoned him out and walked down the same short corridor, and tapped on the same door.

From that moment the daily routine changed abruptly because one of the men waiting for him was Fleming. His eyes were hard and unfriendly as Eric took his customary seat at the table. The warders posted themselves either side of the door.

'Dr Hoffmann, I presume?' said Fleming without a trace of humour.

'Good morning, Commander Fleming,' said Eric, not betraying his surprise. 'I trust you are well?'

'This is Rupert Driver,' said Fleming, indicating his companion. 'He's a government lawyer and has something to say you.'

'Good morning, Mr Driver. General Dornberger mentioned you to me. You questioned him at Grizedale Hall. Why wasn't I accorded that honour?'

'Possibly because he wasn't facing a murder charge,' said Fleming harshly. 'I'm here because I wanted to take a look at the only German who managed to make me look a damned fool. That doesn't endear you to me.'

'I have no objection to your taking a long, hard look at me, Commander.'

Fleming nodded to his colleague.

'Dr Hoffmann,' Driver began. 'His Majesty's government have decided to drop the charge against you relating to planning to wage aggressive war.'

Eric shrugged. 'Just as you dropped them against General Dornberger. May I ask why?'

'Indeed you may,' Driver replied. 'But you would be wasting your breath. With reference to the charge of the murder of Feldgendarmerie officer Leutnant Dieter Muller, that, too is being dropped – at least by the His Majesty's government.'

Eric smiled thinly at Fleming.

Driver continued, 'The place where the alleged offence took place is in the US controlled zone. The American authorities wish to conduct their own investigation therefore we are transferring you to their custody.'

'One can only wonder how our American colleagues found out about the alleged murder,' Fleming observed.

'Maybe their intelligence snooping is better than you think?' said Eric. 'If you're fishing, commander, I give you my word, under oath if you wish, that I have not discussed these affairs with any Americans, nor have I mailed them any correspondence.'

Fleming shrugged and lit a cigarette. 'It's all academic now.' He smiled faintly. 'You've done well, Dr Hoffmann, and have earned my extremely grudging admiration.'

49

Eric's US military police escort who had driven him by jeep from Wandsworth, released his handcuffs once he was inside the nondescript mansion in, as far as he had been able to work out, a quiet residential street in west London.

He was required to fill out a long form before he was shown into a small office on the second floor. It was not the palatial office that Eric had thought of as being that of an important American officer. There was a stars and stripes propped against the wall beside a picture of President Truman. A small desk, two chairs, and that was all. The man sitting behind the desk was Captain George Halliday. That much Eric knew because the name was inscribed on a wooden block.

His grip was firm when he rose and shook hands with Eric and invited him to sit. He was about 40, a broad, impassive face, his hair cropped short, his uniform immaculate.

'If you are, indeed, Dr Eric Hoffmann,' he began, speaking in a slow drawl, 'you will be flattered to learn about the man hours we've spent looking for you.'

'Is there any doubt about my identity, Captain?' Eric noticed that one of the documents before the officer was a photographed copy of his long letter. It was a mass of official stamps and coloured markers.

Halliday's answer was to reach down and place a Kilner jar crammed full of documents on his desk. Eric's eyes widened in surprise. 'My jar!' he exclaimed. 'You found it!'

'The directions given by whoever wrote this letter were very precise.'

'I wrote the letter, Captain.'

Halliday picked up a paper. 'Then perhaps you can describe the jar's contents.'

Eric recounted from memory all the papers that he crammed into the jar in that ruined farmhouse. 'There may one or two others that have slipped my mind,' he finished. 'But those are the important ones.'

'Which would you say were the two most important?'

Eric thought for a moment. 'My diary is the most important to me, personally. In connection with the safety of my neck, I'd say the minutes of the meeting in which the SS said that they would be responsible for the selection of A4 targets.'

Halliday gave a faint smile at the answer. He unscrewed the Kilner jar's lid and fished out Eric's diary. He opened it and asked a few questions which Eric answered promptly and to the US officer's apparent satisfaction. He compared the diary with the letter. 'There's a slight difference in handwriting.'

'As I explained in the first paragraph. I wrote the letter on a train, Captain.'

Halliday glanced at the first page of Eric's letter. 'So you did.'

'So you accept that my story is genuine, Captain?'

'Perhaps.'

'I didn't murder that Feldgendarmerie officer.'

'Now that we know to be true. His body was found when the farmer returned to his farm. An SS POW was the driver for the two officers who did kill him. He provided a full eye-witness account of what happened.'

'It was a brutal murder,' said Eric with passion. 'I hope you find those SS animals.'

Halliday nodded. 'One more question to satisfy me,' he said, fishing another document out of the jar and unfolding it. 'This appears to be a report of some sort.'

'If it's what I think it is, I included it as a sample. In itself the information is of no great value now.'

Halliday tipped his chair back, holding the paper before him. 'So tell me about this information that's of no great value now.'

'In April 1942 we were having test firing problems with burn through around the rim of the thrust chamber where the liquid oxygen wasn't circulating properly as a coolant. At best it would create asymmetric thrust that would cause the A4 to veer off course. At worst it would lead to catastrophic failure and the A4 blew up. We filmed every test launch so some spectacular footage ought to be coming to light.'

Halliday made no comment.

'I redesigned the rim inlets, and added baffles to ensure more even distribution of the liquid oxygen and—'

Eric was interrupted by the phone ringing. Halliday listened for a few moments, thanked the caller and hung up. 'Our calligraphy people confirm that the person who filled in that form just now and the writer of these documents is the same person. I have to say, Dr Hoffmann that we're very pleased that you wrote that letter. We didn't altogether believe General Dornberger when he said that you were a prisoner of war of the British under a different name. He wrote that letter to you with our permission. I worded it.'

Eric relaxed. Everything was going well. 'So what happens now, Captain?'

'I have a question to put to you. Would you be prepared to work for the United States government in the development of long-range, liquid-fuelled rockets?'

'For use as missiles? Yes.'

'I have to ask why.'

'Because it's the only way of getting to the moon.'

Captain Halliday laughed. 'Not for the money or anything else? Yes – you share the same views as Dornberger and von Braun. They were right about you, but I don't think my government is interested in going to the moon, Doctor.'

'But you will be.'

'Maybe. OK. Here's the deal. We give you

temporary US citizenship – I stress temporary – and accommodate you in a London hotel. Once you've signed a few forms, you'll be on the payroll and you'll receive a month's pay in advance plus a grant and coupons so you can buy yourself clothes and other essentials. We'll collect you from time to time for questioning by some technical people. This may take several months but the Secretary for War is anxious to get you guys back home and working as soon as possible. In the meantime, you must not contact anyone without my permission.' He rose and stretched out a hand. 'Is that all understood, Doctor?'

'Perfectly,' said Eric, elated as he returned the warm handshake.

'Good to have you aboard, Doctor.'

50

London. May 1953.

It was ten days before the coronation of Queen Elizabeth II and the tourists were beginning to converge on the city.

Mark and his father arrived on a flight from Bonn. On the taxi journey to their hotel, Max Schiller described the activity to his son as teams of workmen were busy erecting spectator stands along the procession route.

'Looks like it's going to be the greatest show on earth, son.'

Mark didn't answer. Now that he was actually in London, he was nervous, unable to relax. Max gave his son's arm an affectionate squeeze. 'It'll all go off fine, son, you'll see.'

That night Mark was unable to sleep and was irritable and snappy the following morning as he and his father waited outside the entrance to Moorfields Royal Eye Hospital. He kept opening his watch and feeling the time.

'What's keeping him? He promised he'd be on time.'

'There's still another fifteen minutes. Did he ever let you down?'

'No – never.'

'Well then.'

A taxi drew up. Eric, wearing an expensive lightweight suit jumped out and paid the driver.

'Hey! Dieter!' Max called.

Eric looked around, saw the father and son, and joined them. 'It's been a long time since anyone has called me that.'

'Sorry – I forgot.'

But his apology went unheard because Mark and Eric were embracing and both talking at once. 'I can't tell how wonderful it is to hear your voice again, Diet— I mean Eric.'

'I'm surprised you still recognize it after ... What is it? Nearly eight years?'

'It's something I'll never forget,' said Mark

earnestly.

'You look suntanned,' said Max.

'New Mexico sun,' Eric replied. 'White Sands. Firing V2s into the desert. We've nearly run out of them.'

'Right,' said Max, picking up his son's overnight bag. 'Do we go in? We mustn't keep Dr Ridley waiting.'

'Just for old times' sake, Eric,' said Mark.

'Old times' sake,' Eric agreed, taking Mark's hand and placing it on his forearm. The group moved to the steps and paused as Eric studied them. 'Five up. Fifteen-fifteen.'

51

London. June 1st, 1953. Eve of the coronation.

'This,' said Fleming, tanned by life in Jamaica, looking around the Cumberland Hotel's huge function room and admiring the view of Marble Arch, 'must've cost a fortune.'

'It did,' said Brenda, grabbing five-year-old Astrid as she charged past with her older brother, William, in hot pursuit. She took hold of both them and dragged them clear of the hotel staff who were preparing a long banqueting table for the reunion dinner planned for that evening. Fifty place settings were being laid and yet the table looked lost in the palatial room. 'Stephen! Will you please look after these two and use death threats to keep them in order!'

Stephen, now a gangling teenager, took his half-sister and brother to the corner where a Monopoly game was spread out on the rich carpet. It was a dispute over rent that had led to the all-out war between the two younger children. Much to his wife's annoyance, Kruger avoided being involved in looking after his children by sitting in an armchair and hiding behind the *Times*.

Brenda suddenly took a dislike to the flower arrangements that a West End florist was setting out on the table. She and the florist got into an argument over the best positions for the huge displays.

'Otto – you think the lilies would look better at the ends, don't you?'

The *Times* didn't so much as rustle.

'Otto!'

The *Times* was lowered. 'Yes, darling?'

'The flowers!'

'They smell a bit but they look fine.'

'Honestly,' said Brenda to Fleming. 'What would you do with him?'

'Just leave me out of this, angel.'

Kruger folded his newspaper. 'You told me, my precious, that in doing this, you would have no problems. That everything would be taken care of and that you would be able to relax. But you've been fretting and fussing for an hour now.'

Brenda stood over him. 'Don't you want the

table to look nice?'

'Just so long as there's not enough room for you to dance or give speeches on it.'

Fleming collapsed into a chair laughing and Brenda pounced on her husband like an angry cat and reduced him to tears by tickling him.

'What he forgets, Ian, is that organizing this is a lot more than just writing out an obscene cheque. I've been writing bullying letters non-stop for the past two months. It's been a big worry but I've enjoyed every minute of it. Even the moaning from old misery guts here.'

'Well, the worry hasn't changed you, Brenda. You look even lovelier now than you did at your wedding.'

'Why, thank you, Mr Wickham! I never get such lovely compliments from this one, do I?' She gave Kruger a dig in the ribs and followed it with a kiss.

'Who's Mr Wickham?' Kruger wanted to know.

52

Four hours later Brenda was alone in her hotel suite, making final adjustments to her hair when a phone call from the function room set off her butterflies. It was the maître d'hôtel to say that most of her guests had arrived and had been supplied with drinks.

'Who are we short of, Charles?' Brenda queried.

'Numbers 15, 16 and 17 on the list, madam. Their names are—'

'There should be note to say that they're not due until eight and that the reception are to detain them if they're early.'

'Ah, yes – indeed there is, madam. My apologies. I will remind Reception.'

'Thank you, Charles. I'm coming down now.'

'Very good, madam. And may I say on behalf of the hotel and all the staff that we hope it will be a memorable, enjoyable and successful evening for you, and that we'll do our utmost to ensure that you and your guests enjoy tomorrow.'

Brenda thanked him, replaced the telephone, and mentally upped the £100 staff tip she had in mind. She went into the main bedroom and studied her reflection in the many mirrors that the hotel provided. She did a little pirouette and watched the wonderful dress settle about her slim figure.

The maître d' entered the function room, now crowded with guests, laughing and chatting, renewing old friendships. 'Ladies and gentlemen!' he called out in a loud voice that stilled the chatter and turned all faces to the entrance. 'Your hostess for this evening and tomorrow, Mrs Otto Kruger!'

The double doors were thrown open and Brenda made her grand entrance. There was a sudden silence. Berg was the first to start clapping and then the applause rose steadily with puzzled wives and those who hadn't met Brenda before joining in last.

'Brenda!' Berg exclaimed going forward. 'You're wearing the dress! And you look fantastic!'

'Of course I'm wearing it,' said Brenda happily as her admirers gathered around. 'How could I not do so?' She spun around. 'Eight years and two kids later. What do you think?'

'Sensational. I'm so proud!'

'Well I would have never recognized you in a suit. Or any of you men!'

Brenda circulated among her guests, exchanging kisses, gossip and laughter. She spied Sandra, looking alone and a little overawed.

'What's the matter, Sandra?'

'Is he coming?'

'Of course he's coming. He told you in his last letter, didn't he?'

'I always feel so guilty when I get a letter from him. He has to put a lens in to write them.'

'Well, you can say sorry at dinner. Have you seen the place settings? Your name is next to his.'

'Gosh. You must've had so much to remember.'

'Tell that to my husband.'

'Is he all right? I mean—'

'You'll have plenty of time to find out during dinner.'

Stephen slipped through the press around Brenda to give his mother a clipboard holding a sheaf of letters. Brenda thanked him and signalled the maître d', who called for silence for their hostess.

'Table!' someone shouted.

'Not this time,' Brenda declared firmly. 'Otto would kill me.'

All the male guests took up a chant.

'Table! Table! Table!'

One was found and quickly set up. Brenda looked across at Kruger, who was trying to frown her to death. 'It's all right, darling. I've had nothing to drink.' With that she hopped on to the table and stood, clutching her clipboard.

'Firstly, thank you all so much for coming and for answering my nagging letters. We're all going to have a wonderful evening and enjoy a marvellous spectacle tomorrow. The procession will pass virtually right under our windows.'

She glanced at her watch. She had five minutes. 'Sadly not everyone could come. Major Reynolds is in some remote place in Canada catching fish, several are in Australia, and in other scattered parts of the world. But all send their very best wishes and hope that everything goes well.'

'Where's Willi?' a voice demanded.

'Yes! Where's Willi?'

There was danger of another chant starting, so Brenda abandoned her agenda.

'Willi can't be with us. His wife's expecting another baby any minute. Their fourth. For all those who don't know, Willi married the light of life, Carol Bunce.'

The news was greeted with howls of laughter.

'Willi had to get married. Carol thought it a good idea, and so did her brothers and her father – all bigger and stronger than her, and Willi wasn't that keen on going home. You'll be pleased to know that Willi is still in Grizedale Hall. It's now a hostel and a campsite. Willi is the warden, so he's now busy fleecing fell walkers and campers.'

Brenda glanced at her watch during the laughter and decided to work quickly through the rest of the letters. 'I'll leave them out for you all to read later,' she said when she finished them. 'Finally, everyone, I want to say what a pleasure it's been learning how well most of you have been doing. For example,

Berg owns a thriving factory in his home town making women's underwear. Ian Fleming has built a house in Jamaica. It's wonderful hearing how you've all landed on your feet.'

'Which is more than what you landed on when I last saw you standing on a table!'

The comment provoked a storm of laughter.

The maître d' was peering into the corridor. Brenda saw his signal. 'And now, everyone. I want you all to welcome our very special three last guests!'

The double doors opened. Eric Hoffmann, Max Schiller and his son entered the function room. All three stared in surprise at the Brenda on the table and the gathering around her.

'Dr Harold Ridley operated on Mark's left eye at Moorfields ten days ago,' said Brenda. 'They've kept a close watch on him and the operation has been declared a success. Mr Ridley will operate on Mark's right eye in three weeks. Ladies and gentlemen! Mark can now see and I know that if I give him a dazzling smile, he'll help me down off this table.'

The storm of applause that greeted Mark was loud and prolonged. Everyone gathered around him, shaking his hand, clapping him on the back, offering heartfelt congratulations. Somehow he managed to fight his way to Brenda and held out his hand for her.

'You have absolutely no idea what those

lovely blue eyes do to me, Mark,' Brenda scolded as she regained the floor and kissed him warmly. 'However,' she said, pushing him away. 'I'm a respectable married woman. But the girl right behind you isn't.' She laughed. 'Isn't married, I mean.'

Mark turned around. His face lit up with a smile and his eyes shone in delight.

'Hallo, Mark,' said Sandra.

After dinner, Mark and Sandra left the room and found a window that opened on to a small balcony. They stood together, not speaking, their arms around each other as they watched crowds settling down in sleeping bags on the pavements for the night to be certain of a good place for the procession the next day.

'The forecast is rain,' said Sandra. 'I hope they won't be cold.'

A test firework was fired from Hyde Park. Mark watched it climbing into the sky. It exploded as a huge, expanding bubble consisting of thousands of brilliant lights, every one sharp and clear as they fell slowly to earth, their glowing colours vivid and captivating.

At that moment Mark felt that he had to be the happiest man alive.